# ON THE WINGS OF EAGLES

# ON THE WINGS OF EAGLES

## DAN VERNER

eLectio Publishing
Little Elm, TX
www.eLectioPublishing.com

*Enjoy! Thanks!
Dan
June, 2014*

*On the Wings of Eagles*
By Dan Verner

Copyright 2014 by Dan Verner
Cover Design by eLectio Publishing, LLC

ISBN-13: 978-1-63213-024-2
Published by eLectio Publishing, LLC
Little Elm, Texas
http://www.eLectioPublishing.com

Printed in the United States of America

Without limiting the rights under copyright reserved above, no part of this publication may be reproduced, stored in or introduced into a retrieval system, or transmitted, in any form, or by any means (electronic, mechanical, photocopying, recording, or otherwise), without the prior written permission of both the copyright owner and the above publisher of this book.

If you purchased this book without a cover, you should be aware that this book is stolen property. It was reported as "unsold and destroyed" to the publisher and neither the author nor the publisher has received any payment for the "stripped book."

The scanning, uploading, and distribution of this book via the Internet or via any other means without the permission of the publisher is illegal and punishable by law. Please purchase only authorized electronic editions, and do not participate in or encourage electronic piracy of copyrighted materials. Your support of the author's rights is appreciated.

**Publisher's Note**
This is a work of fiction. Names, characters, places, and incidents either are the product of the author's imagination or are used fictitiously, and any resemblance to actual persons, living or dead, business establishments, events, or locales is entirely coincidental.

The publisher does not have any control over and does not assume any responsibility for author or third-party websites or their content.

# CONTENTS

Chapter 1 Flight 224 May 1946 .................................................................. 1
Chapter 2 Back Home June 1946 ............................................................... 7
Chapter 3 Flight Lessons August 1946 .................................................... 15
Chapter 4 The Santa Claus Express December 1946 ............................ 21
Chapter 5 An Announcement March 1947 ............................................. 25
Chapter 6 The Bells Are Ringing June 1947 ........................................... 27
Chapter 7 Day of Labor, Days of Toil February 1948 .......................... 35
Chapter 8 Hard Times December 1948 .................................................. 43
Chapter 9 Aftermath December 1948 ..................................................... 57
Chapter 10 Back Home Again March 1949 ............................................ 59
Chapter 11 Offutt Air Force Base April 1949 ........................................ 63
Chapter 12 On the Flight Line April 1949 ............................................. 67
Chapter 13 Building Time May 1949 ...................................................... 71
Chapter 14 Going Home June 1949 ........................................................ 75
Chapter 15 A Week in the Life June 1949 .............................................. 79
Chapter 16 Back on the Flight Line June 1949 ...................................... 83
Chapter 17 A Letter to Mata August 1949 ............................................. 87
Chapter 18 Back Home in Pioneer Lake August 1949 ......................... 95
Chapter 19 A World-Wide Reach April 1950 ........................................ 97
Chapter 20 California or Bust April 1950 ............................................ 101
Chapter 21 The Long Reach April 1950 ............................................... 105
Chapter 22 The Layover April 1950 ...................................................... 111
Chapter 23 Twelve O'Clock High April 1950 ...................................... 115
Chapter 24 Winging Eastward April 1950 ........................................... 125
Chapter 25 The Return April 1950 ........................................................ 129
Chapter 26 All's Come Undone June 1950 .......................................... 135
Chapter 27 Call of Duty July 1950 ........................................................ 141
Chapter 28 Strangers in Paradise July 1950 ........................................ 147

Chapter 29 Once More into the Breach August 1950 .................................. 155
Chapter 30 Home Matters August 1950 ...................................................... 159
Chapter 31 Gathering In September 1950 .................................................. 165
Chapter 32 Air Power October 1950 ........................................................... 173
Chapter 33 Changes January–March 1951 ................................................. 177
Chapter 34 Things Fall Apart April 1951 .................................................... 181
Chapter 35 Night Riders May 1951 ............................................................. 191
Chapter 36 Going Home July 1950 ............................................................. 197
Chapter 37 A Wisconsin Idyll August 1951 ................................................ 199
Chapter 38 Fields of Gold August 1952 ...................................................... 205
Chapter 39 Progress November 1952 .......................................................... 209
Chapter 40 Generations November 1952 ................................................... 213
Chapter 41 Things Present and Matters Past March 1953 ........................ 217
Chapter 42 Days Like These April 1954 ..................................................... 223
Chapter 43 The Flying Circus July 1953 .................................................... 229
Chapter 44 A New Day May 1954 ............................................................... 233
Chapter 45 The Show Goes On July 1954 .................................................. 237
Chapter 46 What Is Past Is Prologue September 1954 ............................. 241
Chapter 47 Seems Like Old Times September 1954 ................................ 243
Chapter 48 The Long Good-Bye September 1954 .................................... 255
Chapter 49 Take Me Out to the Ball Game September 1954 ................... 261
Chapter 50 You Belong to Me October 1954 ............................................. 265

# Chapter 1
# Flight 224
# May 1946

Otto was flying.

Sitting in the pilot's seat of M & M Airlines Flight 224 from Pioneer Lake, Minnesota, to Minneapolis Airport, he turned the silver and white Beechcraft onto the final approach leg, pulling the throttles back as the ship lined up on the runway, which seemed to slide toward them.

"Flaps twenty!" he called to Jimmy, his co-pilot, who pulled the flaps lever down. Otto cut the throttles a bit more to compensate for increased lift. Jimmy was a good flier and a good man, Otto thought. He guided the Beech down as if it were on rails, touching the runway smoothly, main gear first, and then letting the aircraft settle gently onto its tail wheel. Much easier than a big, heavy bomber, he thought, even if that bomber was empty of bombs and low on fuel.

Flying still brought back quick mental flashes of his crash landing a year and a half earlier. That seemed so long ago and far away now. He had endured recovery in the burn unit, rehab in the hospital after a hard ocean crossing, the long, slow train trip home, and the reunion with his sister, Mata, and later with Betty. Dear Betty. He was glad all the flights for M & M were turnarounds and he didn't have to spend nights away from her. She had pulled him out of the pit his injuries and disfigurement had put him in.

M & M Flight 224 rolled out to the first taxiway on the runway. Otto applied the left brake and the aircraft obediently turned. They proceeded at a walking pace to the terminal, where Otto cut the engines. He could see a Northwest ground crewman hustle to chock his wheels as another rolled a portable set of stairs up to the door. He and Jimmy got up and went to stand by the door to greet the deplaning passengers. Otto nodded to each person, saying, "Thank you for flying with us today."

Most of the people half smiled and looked away quickly. One young mother, holding the hand of a girl about eight years old, met his gaze and said, "Thank you for a nice flight, Captain." As they walked down the steps, Otto heard the child ask, "What is wrong with that man, Mommy?" He couldn't hear the mother's answer. He supposed he should be used to reactions like that from children after all this time, but they still made him feel bad. The last passenger, a man about forty years old, came up the aisle. Otto recognized him from other flights. His name was Waters and he ran an insurance company with offices in Pioneer Lake and Minneapolis.

"Excellent landing, Captain," he boomed, extending his hand.

Otto shook it and answered, "Thank you, Mr. Waters. Always a pleasure to have you fly with us."

"Well, you have a good service at a good price, Captain! That's the name of the game in business and you have it figured out! It's a pleasure to fly with *you*! Believe me, I know something about flying. I was on a lot of aircraft during the war and *they* never made smooth landings. It was bounce, bounce, bounce all the way down the field. And hard—they landed so hard it's a wonder they didn't snap the landing gear off!"

"Well, sir, I'm sure they were doing the best job they could under the circumstances," Otto replied, trying not to look at Jimmy, who was rolling his eyes.

Waters clapped Otto on the shoulder. "Sometimes someone's best is not good enough. I think you understand that, Captain! See you next week!" He strode off into the terminal.

Jimmy watched him disappear through the double glass doors. "Guess he never tried to land an aircraft under combat conditions," he remarked.

"Maybe so," Otto said mildly, "but he's a good customer and entitled to his opinions."

"He sure likes you, Otto. Or should I call you 'Captain?'"

At least he takes me for who I am, Otto thought. He waved his hand. "'Otto' will do. C'mon, let's get something to eat. I'm starving." Flight 224 left Pioneer Lake at noon and got into Minneapolis about 1:30 PM. Neither Otto nor Jimmy had eaten lunch.

They pushed through the same set of double doors that Waters had gone through a few seconds earlier. The terminal was bustling with travelers free from wartime restrictions and shortages. They were all going somewhere, and they were all in a hurry.

The two men pushed through the crowds to a small stand-up hamburger stand. A harried young man in a white uniform with a white hat looked at them. "What'll it be, fellas?" he asked as his eyes flickered across Otto's face. It was as if people had been trained to do that. It was a natural reaction to someone who had scar tissue instead of skin on his face, Otto thought. Still, it was tough to take. He let Jimmy order first.

"I'll have a hamburger, well done, with everything on it, fries, and a Coke to drink." The young fellow nodded and looked at Otto as if he expected him not to be able to speak.

"I'll have a cheeseburger, loaded, with fries and a Coke, please," Otto said. The young man looked at him about a beat too long and then wrote down his order. He turned to the fry cook at the grill behind him to give him the slip of paper, saying, "You got it, gents!" as he did so. He turned back and called to the next customer in line, "What'll it be, Mac?" Otto and Jimmy stepped back from the counter and looked for a seat at one of the red-topped tables scattered in front of the hamburger stand. Almost every seat was taken. *I'm glad people can afford to travel*, Otto thought. There were a few uniforms among the crowd, but everyone had pretty well demobilized—"de-mobbed" in military parlance—in the nine months since the war had ended.

Jimmy strode over and claimed a couple of seats by putting a hand on each of them. Otto joined him and sat down, and they studied the crowd in silence. "Lots of people goin' places," Jimmy offered.

"Yes," Otto said. "Good for business, too."

A young woman in a white uniform pushed through the crowd carrying their meals and drinks aloft on a tray. Otto marveled at her sense of balance as she did not spill the load although she was jostled several times on her way to them. She set the tray down in front of them. "There you go, guys," she smiled. "Enjoy." She winked at Otto and turned away.

*Why do women have less trouble than men with my appearance?* Otto thought. Then he shrugged and picked up his burger.

"Look at that," Jimmy said, looking over toward the counter. Otto turned and saw a young man about his age. He was looking for a seat and carried his duffel bag hooked over one arm. Both arms ended halfway down the forearms. His efforts to find seating went unnoticed, except by Otto, who jumped up and made his way over to him.

"Hey, fella, you want to sit with us?"

The young man smiled. "I'd be grateful." He did not flinch at Otto's appearance. With half his arms missing, he probably got plenty of stares as well. He followed Otto over to the table, and Jimmy pushed the remains of their lunch aside to give him room. He sat quickly in a chair. "My name is Jones. Jay Jones," he said, extending his right stump. Jimmy took it without hesitation in his right hand. Otto did the same. "Are you fellas pilots? I don't recognize the uniforms."

Otto nodded. "We're with M & M Airlines out of Pioneer Lake."

"I'm not familiar with that one. I'm just passing through on my way to Chicago to visit family." Just then his food arrived. He picked up a knife with his stumps and skillfully used it to cut a piece off his burger. Then he put down the knife and picked up a fork, speared a chunk and put it in his mouth. "These burgers are pretty good, don't you think?"

"Yeah," Jimmy said. "We usually grab a quick meal before we fly back to Pioneer Lake."

Jay nodded. "You're probably wondering what happened to my arms. Most people do, even the ones who don't stare at me."

Otto nodded. "I know what you mean."

"I was aboard the *Indianapolis* when she was torpedoed and went down. I spent two days in the water. Sharks kept attacking us the whole time. Some guys were eaten. I kept fighting but they got my hands and wrists. The medics had to amputate further up to save my life. So here I am."

Jimmy responded, "I flew B-29s off Tinian. You guys delivered the A-bomb to Tibbets and his crew."

Jay nodded. "Yep, we did. And then we went through hell."

The three men sat silently for a second. Then Otto said, "After all you've been through, I owe you an explanation about my appearance."

Jones waved his hand. "You don't owe me anything. It's nice to find strangers who will talk to me."

"Nonetheless," Otto said, "I crash-landed a B-17 and it caught fire. This"—he gestured toward his face—"is the result."

Jay nodded. "Looks like you've done well since then," he offered.

"Yes," Otto returned. "It was a struggle, as I'm sure you know."

Jones looked lost in thought for a moment. "I spent six months in a VA hospital. When I was released, my girlfriend broke up with me. She couldn't stand the thought of life with a cripple, she said."

Otto flashed back to Alice. "About the same thing happened to me. But then a wonderful woman married me."

"Good for you," Jay told him. He finished his meal. "I'd better go catch my flight. Thanks for your kindness." He stood, and they shook all around again. He lifted his duffel and made his way through the crowd to his gate.

Otto and Jimmy watched him go. "There goes one brave guy," Jimmy murmured.

"You bet," Otto said. They stood and went back out onto the tarmac, where the ground crew had finished servicing the aircraft. Otto did a quick walk-around of the airplane after he signed off on the crew chief's report. All was in order, so he slid into the left seat of the cockpit, where Jimmy had started the preflight checklist.

"You know, these Beeches have been great to start with, but we're carrying enough passengers I wonder if we ought to upgrade to DC-3s. There are plenty of surplus C-47s out there."

Jimmy shrugged. "You're the boss. You buy 'em, I'll fly 'em."

They both laughed. "I'll have Mata run the figures when we get back. She'll know if we can swing it."

The flight attendant stuck her head through the cockpit door. "Are we ready to board, Captain?" Mata had hired several young women after they graduated from Pioneer Lake High School and trained them as flight attendants.

Otto flipped a switch. "OK, Polly," he smiled. She moved out into the cabin and went down the stairs. Otto could feel the aircraft shaking as the passengers came aboard. He heard Polly close and latch the door.

"OK, let's get this show on the road," he told Jimmy.

"You got it, boss," Jimmy answered. "Number one TURNING!"

"Number one TURNING!" Otto responded. They rapidly ran through the startup sequence and taxied out to the active runway. "You do the takeoff," he said to Jimmy.

After clearance from the tower, Jimmy turned the twin engine onto the runway, held on the painted numbers, and ran up the engines. Otto keyed the intercom that his ground crew had installed on all the Beeches. "Good afternoon, folks, this is Captain Kerchner speaking. Welcome aboard Flight two twenty-five, direct service to Pioneer Lake. We'll be taking off in just a few seconds. The weather is good all the way to our destination, and our flight time should be just under an hour and a half. So sit back, enjoy the view, and as always, we thank you for flying M & M."

Jimmy released the brakes. Flight 225 sped down the runway and lifted off into the bright sunshine.

# Chapter 2
# Back Home
# June 1946

Otto guided Flight 225 on the final approach to Pioneer Lake Airport. Mata had arranged for the runways to be paved and marked in May. She said that a professional airline deserved a professional airfield. Lights had been installed the previous year, so, although they did not have a control tower, they used a UNICOM and were able to operate twenty-four hours a day. M & M Airlines ran four flights a day from Pioneer Lake to Minneapolis, with return flights. Otto was bringing the noon flight back, landing at 3:30. He would take the aircraft back at 5:00 PM, and then return to Pioneer Lake about 7:30. By the end of the day and the fourth round trip, he and Jimmy were ready to call it a day.

The Beechcraft touched down smoothly and taxied to the small terminal building. A full load of passengers deplaned as Otto and Jimmy greeted them and welcomed them to Pioneer Lake. The crew, led by Polly Peters, the flight attendant, went down the stairs to the tarmac. All three of them headed for the ops shack next to the terminal.

Pete and Mata were bent over some papers in the ready room off the office where they ran the airline operations. Pete had his hand on Mata's back as Otto, Jimmy, and Polly came in.

"None of that at work," Otto teased them. Pete and Mata straightened up as if they had been caught doing something wrong.

"We were just going over the figures for last month," Mata said.

"Looks like you were going over each other as well," Jimmy offered. Mata stuck her tongue out at him.

"Jimmy's jealous because he doesn't have a girlfriend," Polly said as she flopped down on the sofa and put her feet up on a table.

"That's not what I hear," Mata said.

Otto turned to Jimmy. "Have you been holding out on me?"

Jimmy blushed. "Well, I have been seeing Anne Peterson from time to time."

"Pete's sister? Isn't she a little too young for you?" Otto ventured.

"Let's ask her brother," Jimmy replied, nodding toward Pete.

Pete shrugged. "She was old enough to practically run the farm after I went to work out here, so I guess she's old enough for Jimmy."

Jimmy smiled at Otto, who shook his head. "Can't get over you children dating seriously."

"With all due respect, Boss," Jimmy answered, "I'm just a year younger than you."

"And Anne is what—twenty?"

"Twenty-one."

"Well, OK." Otto sat down and changed the subject. "We need more pilots. This four-a-day is getting to me."

"That's because you're such an old man," Jimmy told him.

Otto snorted. "Still, wouldn't it be nice to have a day off every once in a while?"

Jimmy nodded and took a soft drink from the cooler. "Anyone else want one?" They all shook their heads. Otto got up and got a cup of coffee from the urn on the counter.

"That reminds me," Pete said. "I was thinking I would love to learn to fly and become one of our pilots."

"We need you to run the airport," Otto said.

"Anyone can do that," Pete returned. Mata punched him. He laughed and said, "I mean, I can train someone to take my place. I think I'd be of more use at this point as a pilot."

Otto sat up straight. "I can get my instructor's ticket updated fairly easily and teach you. You can build time taking the Beeches out on maintenance tests."

Mata chimed in, "Yes, the first couple of DC-3s will be here next month, so we'll be transitioning from the Beeches over the next six months." She had gotten a great deal on a couple of war-surplus C-47s. They were being overhauled and painted in the blue and white M & M livery.

Otto stood up. "It's settled, then. We start lessons next week, Pete. My update should take about a month, but I can instruct you in the meantime." He went over and shook Pete's hand.

Pete grinned hugely. "Thanks, Otto. I'll make a good pilot. I'll have a great instructor."

"And so the sucking up begins," Jimmy whispered. Mata threw a rolled-up chart at him. He ducked, laughing. "Hey, careful with company property. Those charts cost a bit!"

"I know what they cost," Mata told him. "I do the books, remember?"

"Before you two go fifteen rounds, is Betty here?" Otto asked.

"She was, but she went back to the house to fold some laundry."

"I'll just pop over to see her and be back for the five o'clock." The house they had built after they married was right at the edge of the airport.

Otto strode out into the bright sunshine and walked along a gravel path to a wooden fence. He opened a small gate and came shortly to their house, a Cape Cod, comfortable but not ostentatious. It was a considerable comedown from the houses Betty had grown up in, but it was comfortable and had plenty of room for the new couple, with two extra bedrooms for children who might come. Betty and Otto both wanted children and were trying their best to have them, with no results so far. Betty's parents had offered to build them a bigger house, but they did not want to accept money from them. So what they had built they had paid for. The GI Bill provided an incredibly low mortgage rate on their loan, so they were fine with what they had.

Otto pushed the front door open, calling for Betty as he did so. He heard her from the direction of the bedroom. "I'm in here."

With rapid steps he went down the hall and found her just finishing folding clothes. "There you are! I'm so glad to see you!" He caught her in his arms and they kissed long and hard.

She pushed him away, laughing. "Let me get these clothes in the drawers and then we'll talk."

"Here, let me help you." They quickly put all the clothes away.

"How was the flight?"

"Routine," Otto said. "We like routine flights." He grabbed her again and they fell onto the bed. He began unbuttoning her dress, but she reached up and stopped him.

"Don't you have a flight to pilot?"

He kissed her neck. "Yes, but I don't have to be there for an hour."

She laughed and pushed him off her. "Slow down, big boy! There'll be plenty of time for that later."

"But we want to have children," he told her.

"I know, but it'll wait a few hours. We're no longer newlyweds, although you wouldn't know it by the way you act."

"Making babies is an ancient and honorable occupation. A baby is one of the few things that can be made at home using unskilled labor."

"Well, speaking of labor, I promised I would go over and help Mata transfer some figures. So let's go, Captain America."

Otto stood up and pulled her up by the hands. "All right, ma'am, but only if you keep your promise to me."

She kissed him lightly. "You know I will, cowboy."

He swatted her lightly on the rear as they walked into the hallway. She wiggled her behind as they went through the entryway and stepped out into the sunshine. She took his hand and they walked over to the ops shack.

"Well, I wondered when you two would get here," Mata told them. "I thought maybe you had gone on to an activity other than folding laundry."

"I wanted to," Otto said, "But Mrs. K. wouldn't cooperate."

Polly plugged her ears and sang loudly, "La la la la la la!"

"There are children present," Mata scolded him, smiling.

Polly took her fingers out of her ears. "I'm too young for such talk."

Jimmy started to answer and then thought better of it. He and Pete were playing poker at the table. "Want us to deal you in, Otto?"

"Thanks, I never cared for card games. I always lose."

"It's a friendly match, just for pennies."

"Thanks just the same."

Otto sat down across from Mata, who was going through a pile of papers.

"Pete wants to learn to fly to take some of the load off the elderly aviators," Otto told Betty.

She looked at him quizzically. "I thought Sparky died a long time ago."

"No, not Sparky, Jimmy. And me."

"I wouldn't regard you as elderly," Betty reflected. "Not at twenty-six."

"You're heard of old married men? Being married has made me old," Otto started, and ducked as Betty threw a paper clip at him.

"All kinds of flying objects in here today," Polly said. "I'm *so* glad I'm around my mature elders all the time."

"What other flying objects have there been?" Betty asked.

"Mata threw a chart at Jimmy."

"Shoulda been a brick," Mata mumbled.

Betty laughed. "And I thought this was a friendly family workplace."

"If it got any friendlier or more family I don't think any of us could stand it," Pete said.

"Easy there, buster," Mata told him. "You're not family."

Otto saw a quick look pass between Mata and Betty and then between Mata and Pete. Hmmm, he thought, something's up. He went over to the couch, stretched out, and closed his eyes. He felt content and happy, even as tired as he was, and quickly drifted off to sleep.

***

Otto was flying again, but not in one of the M & M Beechcraft. He was back at the controls of the *Mata Maria*, winging his way through a sunlit, cloudless sky. He did not recognize the landscape far below. It could have been France; it could have been Germany or England or Wisconsin. It could have been anywhere in the world, for all he knew.

He hadn't thought about flying the old Fort since his injury. The engines thundered around him, and, just to check, he keyed the intercom. "Stations, report."

There was silence in his headphones. "All stations, this is the pilot. Report, please."

Still no response. He engaged the autopilot and went back through the bomber. The rest of the ship was empty. There was a full load of bombs in the bay, but no crew members anywhere. He made his way back, suddenly realizing that the ship was at 33,000 feet but he didn't need bottled oxygen. He could breathe perfectly well. He pulled himself up onto the flight deck and saw a figure in the co-pilot's seat. Well, at least Donovan was present.

"Hey, Bob," he started to say as he settled into the left seat. "Where's—" He stopped short.

It wasn't Donovan in the right seat; instead, it was the pale form and likeness of his father, dressed in a flowing white robe, looking much as Otto had seen him in his—dream, vision, journey to heaven?—right after he crashed. He had never told anyone about that experience, including Betty. He wasn't sure what to say about it, and the subject never seemed to come up.

Once again his father looked at him with a wise and kindly countenance. And once again Otto sensed his words in his head rather than hearing them. He looked quizzically at his father.

Hans' words came slowly. "You are doing well, my son. Do not, for all your activity, neglect your purpose in life."

"And what is my purpose, Father?"

"I cannot tell you," Hans said softly. "Only you can find that out for yourself. But find it you must." He slowly faded to transparency and his words seemed to echo Otto's mind. "You must . . . you must . . . you must . . . "

Otto was alone again in the giant bomber boring its way through the skies. He advanced the throttles and climbed, reaching through thirty-five thousand to forty thousand feet. The earth seemed a distant blue presence far below him. He continued climbing until he could see the curvature of the globe. The sky slowly blackened and the stars came out, their small flickering lights a warm blue against the velvet black of the sky. Then, gradually, as if the heavens were being washed out, the canopy of sky faded from black to dark gray to light gray and then to a dull white, which became a brilliant and almost blinding white. Otto put on his dark goggles, holding his hand up to block the glare. He felt warm and contented and wondered what this almost palpable presence of light was. The aircraft he was in faded away and he was somehow standing miles above the earth.

He felt a warmth unlike any he had ever experienced, and he somehow understood that his role was to care for his family and those he loved, and beyond that, everyone he met. If he had been a conventionally religious person, he would have said he was in the presence of God. Maybe he was. Maybe this was the revelation of the purpose he had been created for. He closed his eyes.

***

He sensed a white light beyond his eyelids and opened them to the glare of the overhead light. He had fallen asleep on the sofa. Pete was over helping Mata and Betty, while Jimmy nodded in his chair. Otto glanced at the clock. 4:15. Time to preflight the aircraft.

He got off the couch and shook Jimmy awake. "C'mon, Sleeping Beauty! Time to go flying."

Jimmy sprang to his feet. Evidently he had learned in the service to sleep lightly and awaken quickly. He walked toward the door. Otto went around to

Betty and gave her a long kiss. Mata smiled. "I'll be seeing you," he sang, "in all the old familiar places . . . "

Betty smiled. "Hurry back, Boogie Woogie Bugle Boy!"

Polly rolled her eyes. "Could you two be any more out of date with your music? Honestly!"

Betty let Otto go. "So what are the young folk listening to these days, Miss Polly? Pray tell!"

Polly didn't hesitate. "Perry Como and Frank Sinatra. They're the dreamiest."

"Well, let's go do some dreaming while we're flying," Jimmy told her.

Otto smiled slightly. Apparently he had already been dreaming. Or had he? He walked through the door and out to the waiting Beechcraft.

# Chapter 3
# Flight Lessons
# August 1946

Otto watched Pete closely as the Beechcraft let down toward runway thirty at Pioneer Lake Airport. Pete had been an apt pupil over the past several months. Otto was pleased that he had learned so quickly, particularly considering that they had to have lessons only as time permitted. It was midmorning on a sunny Saturday, and with only a morning and afternoon flight to Minneapolis, they were able to get in several hours of flight time. Otto had just about decided that Pete was ready to take the ship by himself.

Pete brought the ship in on a tight, smooth line to the runway, pulling back on the wheel just before they touched and kissing the tarmac with the landing gear. He pulled the power to idle and touched the brakes to slow the airplane. Otto nodded his approval. Another picture-perfect landing. Pete was ready to take it.

He taxied to the end of the runway and held there. "Want to go around again, Boss?" he asked. Otto started unfastening his harness.

"Yep. And why don't we call it your check ride. You're ready to fly this thing on your own." He slapped Pete on the shoulder. "You fly; I'll ride!"

Pete grinned. "Will do, Captain!"

Otto turned to the next page on his clipboard and filled out the top lines on the check-ride form. Pete rotated the Beechcraft and lined up on the centerline of the runway they had just landed on. He advanced the throttles and the twin radials responded with a smooth roar. The blue and white Beech rolled smoothly down the dotted white line and lifted into the hot August air.

"Let's fly out about ten miles and then come back and land," he told Pete. Pete nodded.

Pete took the Beech out and brought it back. There was no traffic, so he brought it straight in. The white and blue aircraft bored in on a gentle slope toward the runway, executing another flawless landing. Pete ran the Beech to the taxiway and pulled up to the operations office. "Congratulations!" exclaimed Otto. "You've passed your check ride."

Pete grinned widely. "Thanks, Boss! Look, there's Mata!"

Mata came out of the ops building and stood, applauding. Pete opened the pilot's window and gave her a thumbs-up. He cut the engines and soon appeared at the door. Mata ran over and hugged him.

"I am so proud of you!" she exclaimed.

"How'd you know I was qualifying?"

"A little bird told me," she smiled.

"Soon we'll have another pilot," Otto told them both. "I have a feeling you'll qualify very quickly."

"It'll be nice to help out with the family business."

"Especially when it doesn't involve milking cows," Otto told him. The three friends laughed and walked toward the office.

They pushed through the door and Mata went back to her work at the table.

"I'm starving," Pete told them. "Anyone want anything from the snack bar?"

Mata shook her head. "I'll just get some coffee here," Otto said. Pete went back out.

"So Pete's ready to fly by himself."

"Yeah, after he builds a little time I'll have him co-pilot for me and Jimmy. That will give us a break. Jimmy's ready to command anyhow. And then maybe we can hire someone else and have two crews."

Otto thought that there had not been a surge of interest in flying after the war as some had predicted. He understood that veterans were eager to get back to their normal lives and put the war behind them, but not many of them seemed eager to return to the skies. He didn't understand this since even with all that had happened to him he still loved to fly. He dismissed the thought, got his cup of coffee, and sat down at the table with Mata.

"So, how are you and Pete getting along?"

"Wonderfully. He's so good to me. I just wish we had more time to do things away from the airport."

"I know," Otto told her. "I'm trying to add to our staff so we all don't have to work so hard. That's what it takes to build a business, I guess."

"Well, we're certainly prospering. I wanted to talk to you about selling the dairy business."

Otto had not thought much about the family dairy business. Mata ran that, as well, with the help of a manager. He did know that there were several large companies in the area that were buying up smaller concerns to meet the demand for dairy products with the baby boom that was beginning to make itself evident.

"Have we had any offers?"

"Several, actually. And they're good ones."

Otto thought for a moment. "In a way, I hate to let it go since Mama and Papa worked so hard to make it. But maybe we're at a crossroads and need to choose."

"Maybe we do," Mata said quietly. "Can we talk about it this evening?"

"Sure. Why don't you and Pete come over for dinner? We can eat and talk."

"Great! I'll see what Betty wants me to bring." The two couples frequently had meals together on the spur of the moment.

"All right," Otto said. "I'd better go out to see Pete land."

"I'll go with you," Mata said. She stood up and went through the door with Otto.

\*\*\*

"So, how long do you think I will need to get my commercial ticket?" Pete asked, taking a drink from his Coke.

"Oh, about twenty hours, more or less," Otto told him. "I think less in your case. That'll get you qualified. Then you'll have to fly fifteen hundred hours as a co-pilot. Don't worry; that won't take long. Each trip to Minneapolis is about an hour and a half, two hundred miles, so if you run all four flights, that'll give you seventy-two hours a week. At that rate you'll have your ticket in about five months."

"And Jimmy heard of another vet who might be interested in flying with us," Mata offered.

"Oh, which theater?" Otto wanted to know.

"I didn't ask. If he's qualified, it shouldn't matter."

"It doesn't. I'm just curious to meet other fellows who served where I did." Otto had not run into anyone who had been in the European Theatre in the bomber corps. Of course, he hadn't been much of anywhere to meet people, just the runs to Minneapolis and back. Even then, he didn't tarry at the airport. Northwest handled the ticketing, boarding, baggage handling, and servicing of the aircraft, so they didn't really know anyone there. From repetitious layovers Otto recognized most of the workers there, but he didn't know names or backgrounds. He supposed with his appearance that people were not in a hurry to rush up and greet him.

At that point the door opened and Jimmy walked in with Polly. He generally gave her a ride to the airport. Otto wasn't sure that Polly knew how to drive. They would have to remedy that. If they could do flight instruction, they could teach one of their flight attendants how to drive. "Hey, crew!" he called to them.

"Hey, Captain!" they answered, more or less in unison.

"We have a newly qualified pilot today," Otto stated, nodding toward Pete. Jimmy came over and shook Pete's hand. "Congratulations, old fellow! Welcome to the club!" Polly was right behind him and enveloped him in a huge hug.

"Hey there, young miss," cautioned Mata with a smile. "Not so fast with my man."

"*Can't help lovin' that man of mine*," Polly sang in a clear alto voice as she stepped back from Pete. He blushed and looked at the floor.

"I thought you didn't like old fogey music," Otto remarked to Polly.

"I don't, but I *love* musicals. That's from *Porgy and Bess*, by George Gershwin. He writes amazing songs."

Mata and Otto looked at each other. "We know," Mata said. "We love Gershwin, too."

Polly looked somewhat amazed. "I love musicals like *Oklahoma!* and *Show Boat*. And I hear there's a new one on Broadway called *Annie Get Your Gun*. I'd love to see it someday."

Mata clapped her hands. "Maybe we can all take a vacation to New York City and see some musicals on Broadway! Wouldn't that be exciting?"

Otto said, "That would be nice, but right now we need to take a certain DC-3 to Minneapolis with some of *our* ticket holders. Pete, we'll need all the Beeches taken to the shop there for maintenance. Soon as we get your paperwork, you can run one a day over. After the first one, deadhead back on the two o'clock flight. Then you can take the others over and bring the others back one at a time. It'll take you five days, but you'll be on the crew payroll. Congratulations."

"I know I'll never be the kind of the pilot you and Jimmy are," Pete told them. "But I'll work hard and build my time."

"Well, you won't have anyone shooting at you, and I'm glad for that," Jimmy said.

"Amen," Otto echoed. "It's a hell of a way to build time."

"Well, I'm grateful for the hard job all you fellows did."

"And that's done, so let's do some flying, OK?" Otto offered.

"OK, Captain OK!" everyone chorused. Otto grinned. He had told them about his nickname in the air corps and was pleased that they remembered. He led the way out the door to the glistening silver, blue, and white M & M DC-3, hosting Flight 226 to Minneapolis.

# Chapter 4
# The Santa Claus Express
# December 1946

Otto pulled back the throttles and set up his approach to Pioneer Lake. Pete sat in the right seat, peering around for traffic, although they didn't expect much. Still, they had to keep alert for anything out of order. The bird settled toward the runway, and they heard the chirp of the tires as they touched. Pete changed the pitch of the props to help slow them. They reached the taxiway and turned toward the terminal. Flight 1225 had arrived.

The flight from Minneapolis had a special number because it was a special flight. Pete hauled himself out of his seat and opened the cockpit door. The seats were filled with orphans from Minneapolis. Mata had read about the orphanage in a newspaper article and had broached the idea of a flight to the "North Pole" with Otto. She contacted the nuns who ran the facility, and they were delighted with the idea. It grew from there. Mata and Betty came up with the idea of costuming the crew, although Otto steadfastly refused to wear an elf costume. He did agree to an old-time aviator's outfit. With a leather coat, goggles, and white silk scarf, he looked much as he did when he was taking lessons in the fleet from Sparky. Mata teased him that he did look like Sparky, except for the whiskey bottle.

Pete was similarly outfitted, and Polly jumped at the chance to dress as an elf. She and Mata and Betty worked for weeks sewing costumes, including the outfits for Jimmy and Betty to wear as Mr. and Mrs. Claus. Mata ran up an elf costume for herself as well. Otto told her she was the world's biggest elf.

On a bright Sunday in mid-December, Pete and Otto decorated one of the DC-3s for the occasion with holly and red ribbons and the words *North Pole Express* over the door. The ground crew at Pioneer Lake got into the spirit by doing the decorations and asking for elf costumes as well. Mata lined up the *Pioneer Lake Press* to cover the event with a photographer and reporter.

As they landed and rolled up to the terminal, Otto and Pete could see a war-surplus army bus waiting beside the doors. Otto thought idly that it looked like the ones he had ridden on in the service. The nuns obviously operated the orphanage on a shoestring. The gleaming aircraft came to a stop and Otto cut the engines. He and Pete went back in the cabin, where Polly had the door down. "You make a wonderful elf," Pete told her.

"I'm so excited about this. I love children! I hope we can make them happy."

"Well, brace yourself for a whole lot of excitement from this crew," Otto offered. "You're going to be one busy elf." They had arranged to serve the children hot chocolate and cookies on the flight.

The three crew members went down the stairs and over to the bus. The door opened and a short nun in a black habit met them. She beamed. "I'm Sister Angela," she said, "and this is Sister Lucia Thank you so much for doing this. I want you to meet the children before we take off."

Otto saw small faces pressed against the windows of the bus. The sister went over to the door and climbed aboard. She quickly returned, herding her small charges down the steps. The air crew was stunned at how small and poorly dressed they were. Their clothes were patched and either too large or too small for them.

"Boys and girls, here are the people who are going to take us all to the North Pole. I'll let them introduce themselves to you."

"Hi," Otto said. "I'm Captain Kringle and I'll be flying the airplane today with my co-pilot, First Officer Nicholas. You'll be helped in the cabin by Pixie the elf." He saw Polly wince at the name he had just made up for her. She waved gamely at the children.

"Before we board, does anyone have any questions?"

A small boy with a runny nose raised his hand. "Yes, young man?"

"Do you know Santa Claus?"

"Yes, I do. In fact, he's my brother-in-law. I married his sister."

"Will he be there today?"

"I hope he'll get out to see you. He's busy getting ready for his trip Christmas Eve. He does have a lot of help from elves like Pixie." Polly shot him a look that would have killed had he been closer.

Another boy raised his hand. "Yes, young fellow?"

"What happened to your face?"

"Francis, that is a rude question. You apologize to Captain Kringle." Sister Lucia's expression was severe.

"No, it's OK," Otto told her. "I was burned in a fire. You have to be careful around flames and never, ever play with matches. Does that make sense?" The boy nodded seriously. "Well, who wants to go to the North Pole?"

The twenty children clapped and cheered. "Me! Me!" they shouted.

"Let's get on board, then. We'll go first to get the airplane ready."

Otto and Pete climbed into the fuselage and made their way to the cockpit. As they passed Polly, she whispered, "I'll get you for this."

"Why, Pixie, is that any way for an elf to act?"

They settled in the seats and began their preflight. When the engines had started, Otto went back into the cabin. "Who is going on their first flight?"

Everyone in the cabin raised his or her hand, including the two sisters. Otto smiled at them. "I hope you'll enjoy the experience," he told them. "Just relax and we'll soon be heaven-bound."

"We're very familiar with that place, thank you," Sister Lucia told him.

"I'm sure you are," Otto said to her and then made his way back to the cockpit.

They made the flight in clear sunshine, with Otto narrating various "landmarks" along the way. Snow-covered terrain could very well be on the way to the North Pole, he thought. He enjoyed pointing out Santa's birthplace, the farm where the reindeer came from, and especially the land of elves where Pixie was born. In for a dime, in for a dollar, he thought.

Once landed, Pete opened the cockpit door to find a cabin filled with excited children. Polly had a forced smile on her face. "How's it going, Pixie?" Otto asked her.

"I love children but not this many and not in such an excited state," she replied without taking the smile off her face. "I thought we would have a riot when I served refreshments. These kids are so starved for something special they don't know what to do. Luckily the nuns helped me."

Otto held up his hand. "We'll be deplaning in a few minutes for Santa's workshop. Please allow us to get off first, and then follow Pixie to the room where there are some special surprises in store for you!" The kids cheered wildly, and Otto saw Sister Lucia roll her eyes at Sister Angela. Still, the two nuns looked about as excited as the children did.

Otto and Pete climbed down the steps and stood at the bottom. Polly led her small charges off the aircraft. They were also escorted by two of the ground workers in elf costumes. Otto thought they were the ugliest elves he had ever seen.

Once the kids had gotten well into the terminal, Otto and Pete followed. Mata and Betty had outdone themselves decorating the room to look like

Santa's North Pole workshop. Mata also wore an elf costume. Otto decided her name was Trixie. Betty was dressed as Mrs. Claus, although Otto thought she made a very young-looking Mrs. Claus. Jimmy had dressed as Santa, but he was in a back room waiting to make his entrance.

The kids saw the huge table piled with cookies, cakes, and drinks. Betty and Mata had gotten local merchants to donate it all, as they did with the toys that had been brightly wrapped and loaded onto another table. The orphans were awestruck into silence. Betty spoke. "Welcome to the North Pole, boys and girls! Santa is feeding his reindeer, but he'll be here soon with presents for good little boys and girls. Have you all been good?"

There was a murmured chorus of "Yes," but Otto thought some of the boys in particular didn't seem too certain. He remembered those days of being terrified that he would not measure up to Santa's standards and receive a lump of coal and a bundle of switches in his stocking.

Just then they heard a loud "Ho! Ho! Ho!" and Jimmy dressed as Santa burst into the room. The room was pandemonium. The kids cheered, screamed, and jumped. Jimmy went over to a big chair that had been set up as Santa's throne. He spread his arms wide and shouted "Ho! Ho! Ho! Merry Christmas!"

The room answered, "Merry Christmas!' Mata, Polly, and Betty corralled the youngsters into a line that led to Santa. Pete and Otto ferried presents from the table to Jimmy, who held each child on his lap, listening intently to them and then giving each one a present. The children then went to sit at the tables, where some of the airport elves served drinks and cookies and cakes.

Otto stood apart and looked around at the happy scene. This is what it's all about, he thought. Merry Christmas.

# Chapter 5
# An Announcement
# March 1947

Otto walked toward the operations room with Pete, glad it was Friday and they only had two flights to operate the next day. Pete had helped spell Jimmy, but Otto continued as pilot in command of all the flights. He thought it was about time to raise Jimmy to that role. He was supposed to interview a fellow who had been with the Eighth the next day, and that would give them two full crews. Polly's sister Susan had come on as a flight attendant in February, so that helped as well. They were all exhausted.

Otto put his paperwork for the flight in Mata's mailbox. She jumped up when they came in and hugged Pete. In a few seconds, Betty came through the door. "I'll have dinner ready in about a half an hour. Will you two be joining us?"

"We'd like that," Mata said. "But please have a seat. Pete and I have an announcement."

Betty and Otto sat in the conference table chairs with expectant looks on their faces. Looking at Betty, Otto wondered if she knew what the announcement was. She and Mata spent a lot of time talking and exchanging confidences.

Mata and Pete sat down next to each other. They took each other's hand. "We're getting married!" Mata exclaimed.

Betty jumped up and ran over to hug Mata first and then Pete. Otto followed to hug Mata and shake hands with Pete. They all talked at once.

"When will you get married?"

"Will it be at the church?"

"Whom shall we invite?"

"You can have the reception here!"

Mata laughed and waved her hands. "Wait, wait, Pete just asked me. We'll have to decide all that. There will be time for that."

"Well, I'm so pleased," Betty said, and Otto nodded. "You know we will do anything we can for you."

"I feel like this is my family more than my actual family," Pete told them. "You have been so good to me."

"We've feel the same way about you," Otto told him. "This just makes it official."

"Well, this will make tonight's dinner a celebration. We'll talk then." The four friends walked out the door. Otto was the last to leave, and he turned off the light before he closed the door.

***

Two months later, Otto switched Jimmy to pilot on two of the daily flights and had Pete continue as co-pilot. The airline had continued to prosper, and they had added Bob Rogers as a third pilot. This enabled them to add an early morning flight to Minneapolis. Some local businessmen needed to get to the city earlier in the day, and M & M Airlines was happy to oblige them. Otto, Jimmy, and Pete rotated co-pilot duties on the flights Bob commanded. He had thirty-two combat missions over Europe and a host of decorations. He had heard of Otto and seemed honored to meet him and fly for him.

The plans for Mata and Pete's wedding continued apace. They set the day for a Saturday late in June and reserved the Lutheran church where both families attended. The church had a new sanctuary, educational wing, and reception hall to accommodate growing numbers and growing families after the war.

Mata and Otto sold the dairy farm to a large milk cooperative run by some of their neighbors. They went over and walked around the home place. There were so many memories there, but it was time to move on. They couldn't run two growing businesses. They invested the profits from the sale in upgrades to the airport, including a larger terminal building. Otto began talking to the Civil Aeronautics Board about a control tower. While there was not as much sport flying as he would have liked, there was some, and with M & M running five flights a day, he felt they needed Bob Rogers at least part of the time. He and Mata sent the paperwork in and waited.

Late in May, Pete had accumulated enough hours to fly as pilot in command. Otto continued him as co-pilot for a couple of weeks and then had him pilot the morning flights, again with rotating co-pilots. He figured it would be prudent to have qualified pilots with Pete for a few weeks. That would give them time to hire a couple of co-pilots as well. The early summer passed uneventfully.

# Chapter 6
# The Bells Are Ringing
# June 1947

Mata stood in the vestibule of the church in her white satin wedding gown. One of the ladies in the church had sewed it from a Butterick pattern. She had made dresses for about half the women in the church. The result was professional and stunningly beautiful. Its simple lines lacked (and did not need) embellishment, and it had full sleeves and a modest train. Mata wore a veil and carried a large bouquet of mixed carnations and mums. Otto thought she might disappear into it, but no one had asked his opinion about the flowers.

Betty fussed with the train for a few seconds. Otto wore his air corps reserve captain's uniform, as he had recently arranged to join the reserve. It was easy since he had demonstrated beyond all doubt his ability to fly, although he hoped he would not have to do so for the military again. Now that he had a family and job responsibilities, it would not be as easy to go off and fight another war. He was willing to do so; he just hoped it wouldn't happen.

Mata had asked Betty to be her matron of honor, with Polly and Susan as bridesmaids. Her attendants wore matching light-blue sleeved dresses, modest and simple with scalloped necklines that echoed Mata's. They all carried bouquets similar to Mata's but slightly smaller. Otto pictured the wedding party at the front as looking somewhat like a small florist's shop.

Jimmy served as Pete's best man, while Pete's brothers Erik and Verner acted as ushers. Jimmy, Pete, and his brothers were dressed in dark suits with matching blue ties.

The church was just about filled with friends and neighbors, including several families of businessmen who dealt with the airport. Looking through the small windows in the narthex doors, Otto saw several people who flew with the airline frequently. It was great that so many of them could come.

Mata, Betty, and the bridesmaids had spent the previous evening decorating the new reception hall with white crepe streamers, red paper hearts, and enough white paper doilies to choke a horse, Otto thought. He had taken a cursory glance at it the evening before and thought as long as the women were pleased with it, he was pleased. The ladies of the church were providing food and drink for the reception, and one elderly lady who specialized in cakes make a beautiful white wedding cake with a little plastic bride and groom figure on the top. Otto knew that her cakes tasted even better than they looked, so he was hoping he could get a big piece. The ladies had known Mata since she was born, so they were overjoyed to provide their specialties for the reception. They had planned and baked and called back and forth all week to make sure their dishes were the best they could be. Church people are good people, Otto thought.

He and Betty had gone to the services ever since they were married. The Episcopal church Betty had attended for years was closer than the Lutheran church, but she said being there reminded her of her first husband. She liked the Lutheran service and the people in the church, who she said were not as snooty as the ones at her old church. Sometimes Betty's parents joined them for worship and they all went out to lunch at one of the best restaurants in Pioneer Lake. Mr. and Mrs. Ross were long-time members at Trinity Episcopal and had a lot of friends there, but they did not believe in interfering in Betty and Otto's lives. They were always there to help. About the only thing that Betty's mother did that bothered her a bit was hinting about grandchildren. Betty wanted to say, "Believe me, Mother, we are trying as hard as we know how!" but Mrs. Ross was of an older generation who did not want to know all the details. She just wanted a grandchild to hold, and Betty and Otto were attempting to oblige her. Someday, Otto thought.

Mr. and Mrs. Ross had been seated by one of the ushers, and the organist took that as her cue to crank up the bridesmaids' music, "Trumpet Voluntary," by Jeremiah Clarke, which Betty had used for her attendants. Each proceeded down the aisle as people in the congregation turned toward them, smiling widely without exception. Otto saw Pete standing with his groomsmen at the front beside the minister in his dark robe and white stole with a silver cross on it. Even from this distance, he thought Pete looked nervous. He remembered his wedding and also feeling just that way.

With the bridesmaids at the front, the organist ceased playing for a moment. Otto could hear the click of the stops and soft thud of the shutters on the organ. Mrs. Price adjusted her feet near the pedals, placed her hands carefully on the keys, looked at the music on the rack, and started Handel's "The Rejoicing" from *The Fireworks Music*. Mrs. Ross stood, and the congregation followed her example.

"Here we go," said Otto to Mata, who looked perfectly composed and perfectly beautiful. They stepped together down the aisle, Otto being careful to not trip, Mata smiling all the way. Otto was dimly aware of the people in the congregation smiling back at Mata. His appearance was accepted here at the church, and he knew they were not looking at him because, after all, he was not the center of attention.

After what seemed like an interminable walk down the aisle, they reached the front. Pete looked at Mata with shining eyes. Otto delivered her to his side and the three of them stood there.

"Dearly beloved..." the minister began, and Otto flashed back to his wedding not so long ago. He glanced sideways at Betty, who looked happy and serious at the same time. She did indeed look lovely.

He heard the minister say, "Let us pray," and bowed his head. The prayer was a short one, and then the minister made a speech about the purposes of marriage and asked if there was anyone who could show cause as to why Pete and Mata should not be married. There was silence, followed by a low chuckle of relief from the congregation. As if, Otto thought, anyone ever did object. That only happened in movies and novels. "You may be seated," the minister said to the congregation. Next he asked, "Who gives this woman to be married to this man?"

That was Otto's cue. "Our family gives her." He placed Mata's hand in Pete's, kissed his sister on the cheek to a quiet "aw" from the ladies in the sanctuary, and went back to sit on the bride's side. Betty smiled back at him from her place beside Mata. He pantomimed wiping sweat from his brow and smiled slightly. His part was done and he was glad.

Otto sat there thinking of all the years growing up with Mata. He was busy with manly chores on the farm and the airport and not around her that much. Their mother spent much more time with her, doing the traditional work of women: church, children, and cooking. Those were the duties of women according to Hans and Maria's generation. Well, Mata had broken that mold. She ran the farm after their parents couldn't and completely managed a growing dairy operation while Otto was away at war. She had the dairy in such extraordinary shape that when Otto returned he was able to devote himself to developing the airport after Wilson had willed it to him.

Then they started the airline and Mata did all the accounting and paperwork. All he and Jimmy had to do was fly. Now they had Pete and Bob and Polly and Susan to help them out. The future looked bright.

Otto couldn't help wishing that Hans and Maria could have been there to witness this day. Maria would have been so happy and Hans, well, Hans would have been Hans, pleased but trying hard not to show it. He thought very highly of the Peterson family and would have been glad that Mata was joining their neighbors' family.

Otto snapped out of his reverie as the minister spoke the words, "I now pronounce you man and wife! You may now kiss the bride!" Betty drew back Mata's veil and Pete planted a brief kiss on Mata's lips. Betty handed her the bouquet she had taken when the vows were exchanged, and Mata and Pete stood there for a second. Mrs. Price cranked up her own arrangement of "Now Thank We All Our God" as the couple walked rapidly down the aisle to waves and smiles from those assembled. Otto had to smile at Mrs. Price's playing. She had been organist for forty years and was a dear soul, but she played the same pieces enough that Otto thought he could play them after a while. He came back to the moment at hand and went over to escort Betty out, followed by Jimmy with Polly and Erik with Susan. Verner trailed down the aisle alone after eliciting laughter from the congregation by shrugging his shoulders at having no one to escort. He grinned widely as he went to the narthex.

The wedding party congratulated each other, hugging and kissing all around. They went into a small parlor not far from the sanctuary to allow the crowd to proceed to the social hall. This enabled them to come back into the sanctuary for pictures. Betty led the way down the aisle this time to where the minister and Mrs. Price stood waiting. They smiled at the wedding party, and the photographer, who ran a portrait studio in town, quickly posed them and took what seemed like hundreds of shots of all possible combinations of the members of the wedding party. Otto saw spots in front of his eyes.

At last the picture taking was over, and the wedding party walked back down the aisle and over to the social hall. A roar went up from the people, and Mr. and Mrs. Ross started a receiving line. They had agreed to stand in for Mata's parents. Mata and Pete were next, then Pete's parents, and the groomsmen and bridal attendants in a random order. Otto went over to the punch bowl and got a couple of glasses for Mata and Pete. They took them and drank them gratefully.

The ladies of the church had outdone themselves with the refreshments. Otto wasn't sure he recognized some of the little sandwiches and hors d'oeuvres; they were quite different from the usual covered-dish suppers at the church. No tuna hot dish this time. And the cake was beautiful, standing fully three feet high and looking like a confectioner's dream in white. Mrs. Crocker had outdone herself this time.

Otto got two more glasses of punch for himself and Betty, took them over to her, and stood beside her as they drank. "Lovely wedding," he told her. "I hope they'll be very happy." Betty nudged him.

"I can't take you anywhere," she whispered. "Now, behave!"

The time in the receiving line passed in a blur as they greeted their guests. Otto found his legs stiffening up from standing and pulled up two chairs after the guests had passed through and had made a beeline for the food. He sat there for a minute, taking the scene in, and then got up, filled a couple of plates with food, and took them back to their seats.

"Thank you, sir," Betty smiled. "I'm starving!"

"I thought everything went very well," Otto told her.

She nodded. "I did, too. Mata looks so pretty." They looked over at her and Pete, who were busy greeting their guests. Otto could not recall his sister looking so radiant. Pete looked like the happiest man in the world.

The rest of the reception passed quickly, with the throwing of the bouquet (Polly caught it) and the garter (Pete threw it at Jimmy, who let it bounce off him and fall to the floor). The newlyweds cut the cake, which Mrs. Crocker snatched up once they had fed each other a mouthful and took it to the kitchen, from which it emerged as cut slices on small plates. The room quieted considerably as the crowd ate their pieces.

As the noise started to build, Jimmy whistled for attention. "Everybody outside for the throwing of the rice!" he called, and the multitude filed out to the entrance of the church. There they formed two lines with a space between and held small mesh bags of rice. Pete and Mata held hands, hesitated at the door, and then ran toward the drive and Pete's waiting 1939 Chevy, which Jimmy had pulled up. The car was decorated with streamers and messages sketched in soap: "Just Married!" "On Our Way!" and "Honeymoon, Here We Come!" They reached the car, and Pete pulled the door open for Mata. Betty helped her pile her skirts and train inside the car, and the couple drove off to cheers and applause from the assembled crowd.

Otto and Betty stood there for a moment. "Well, that's that," Otto said.

"Come on, mister," Betty said as she took him by the arm. "We have cleanup to do."

Otto shrugged and followed her back into the church. Mata and Pete were flying in the J-4 to Minneapolis and staying in the Minneapolis Hotel for a few days. The remaining M & M pilots would cover Pete's flights until he returned. Otto wanted to talk to Mata about starting service with the

Beechcraft to Madison since the DC-3s were covering Minneapolis these days. Ah well, it would wait until the lovebirds got back.

With the church cleaned up and flowers and gifts stowed in their car, Betty and Otto set out for home. They took the arrangements and presents into the house and stored them in the living room. They would have a grand opening when Mata and Pete returned.

They didn't feel like eating, so they sat on the sofa holding hands. "It's too soon to go to bed," Betty said.

"Yeah, it's too soon to go to bed to *sleep*," Otto offered, "but it's not too soon for something else." He pulled Betty over on top of him. "You know that baby we've been wanting? Let's try making one."

Betty kissed him, stood up, and pulled him to his feet. "You're on, mister," she whispered, and they moved smoothly together to the waiting bed.

***

Two days later, Otto and Jimmy brought the 6:30 flight back to Pioneer Lake. Betty was in the operations room filling in daily reports. Jimmy headed to the couch for a nap, Susan got a soft drink and flopped down in the chair, and Otto went over and kissed Betty. "Hello, Mrs. K. So good to see you!"

She put her hand up to his face. "And I'm glad to see you, too, Captain! Could I speak to you privately?"

Otto wondered what she had to tell him, but he said, "Certainly, madame. Your wish is my command!"

"You are so full of it," she laughed. He followed her into the office and closed the door.

She turned to him with a huge smile on her face. "I'm expecting!" she exclaimed.

He held her tightly in his arms and kissed her. "Wonderful! When are you due?"

"Dr. Heaton says next February! We'll have a little Valentine!"

"I'm just so happy! Let's tell Jimmy and Susan!"

"All right! I was waiting to tell you first. Then we'll call my parents. They'll be so excited!"

Otto and Betty came back into the operations room. "We have an announcement!" Betty said, waking Jimmy and bringing Susan out of her reverie. They turned toward Otto and Betty. "We're going to have a baby in February!"

Jimmy and Susan jumped to their feet, hugging the couple and shaking their hands.

Yes, Otto thought. This is what it's all about. He smiled broadly.

# Chapter 7
# Day of Labor, Days of Toil
# February 1948

Otto pulled back on the wheel of the first flight of February 1948. The M & M DC-3 climbed smoothly into the air. Jimmy pulled the levers to retract the twin gears into their housings underneath the engines. Otto liked the '3. It didn't have the power of the B-17's four engines, but it was quieter and more responsive. Jenny and Susan complained about needing a ladder to climb up the aisle when they were on the ground. Otto listened carefully and then told them that there was a sad land where flight attendants didn't have aircraft of any kind to work in. They stuck their tongues out at him and went out to the aircraft to preflight it by pulling themselves up by the seat backs, Otto supposed.

 He wondered what it might be like to fly a ship with a tricycle landing gear. He had flown taildraggers all his life. Jimmy had flown the B-29 in the war, and he said it was a whole lot easier to control on the ground. He said it was a nice, high-flying aircraft with a pressurized cabin and shirt-sleeve environment for the crew. The engines did have a tendency to catch fire, but good fire-suppression equipment was on board, and crews managed to put the fires out before they burned through a wing. Otto thought about asking Pete if he had ever been on an aircraft whose wing had burned through and decided it was a stupid question. He had seen any number of Forts take a shell to the wing root and fall five miles to the earth like a maple tag, twisting the whole way down so the crew was plastered to the fuselage by centrifugal force. There were no 'chutes to count with those wounded aircraft.

 Otto shook his head to clear it of the terrible images that filled his mind. They climbed to altitude, bound for Minneapolis an hour away. The faster speed of the Douglas gave them more time at the turnaround. Of course, it was more expensive to operate, but it also carried more paying customers than the Beeches, which were used for the four daily flights to Madison. There was a surprising amount of traffic to and from the capital, although Otto shouldn't have been surprised. Business was good for everyone in postwar America as GIs came home wanting to start families and buy cars, houses, and appliances.

 He thought of his own little family in the offing. Betty was due any day now, and Otto half expected her to have already delivered at the clinic in

Pioneer Lake. Old Doc Carter had died late in 1947, at the age of eighty, and his practice was taken over by his young assistant, Dr. Heaton. Betty and Otto both liked the young doctor, who attended to all kinds of medical conditions, including pregnancy. Like Doc Carter's wife before, Dr. Heaton's wife served as his nurse and assisted with births. More and more babies were being born in clinics and hospitals, with the number of established medical facilities growing to meet the need. Doc Carter and Dr. Heaton had started the clinic early in 1947 to take care of their burgeoning patient load. Treating patients in the Carters' home wouldn't work anymore.

With the airliner at cruising altitude, Otto engaged the autopilot and left Jimmy to tend the controls and radio. He went back into the cabin, greeting passengers who seemed happy to see him, even if some did look away after catching a glimpse of his face. He found Polly near the rear of the cabin serving drinks and snack. She looked up and saw him. "Captain! What brings you back here?"

"Just wanted to witness some of that famous M & M Sky-High Service," he said, using one of the advertising phrases Mata had come up with for some newspaper and radio ads. "What was the line for the entire sentence? 'M & M Airlines—professional service to Madison and Minneapolis aboard the finest aircraft around. Come join us for some of that famous M & M Sky-High Service.'" Polly looked around quickly and crossed her eyes when she saw none of the passengers could see her.

"Would you like something to drink, Captain?" she asked sweetly.

"Yes, I'd like some coffee," he told her. "And a cup for my coworker in the cockpit."

"Yessir, coming right up," she trilled, and made her way up the aisle to the galley. Otto followed her and she quickly poured two cups of coffee with practiced ease. "Careful, they're hot," she said seriously.

"I'd be disappointed if they weren't." She screwed up her face briefly and went back down the aisle. Otto took the cups into the cockpit, handing one to Jimmy over his shoulder. "Thanks, Boss," he murmured.

"Joe's on me," Otto replied, and they both laughed quietly. Below them, the farm fields lay dormant underneath a thick blanket of snow. Otto knew that in not too many days they would be shades of green and gold. He saw a herd of cattle and thought how cold they must be, but marveled at how they survived the cold by huddling together like that. He wondered idly what the temperature was outside the thin aluminum skin of the Douglas. During the war, the outside temperature in the thin atmosphere was minus thirty degrees

Fahrenheit, necessitating heated electric suits and gloves, oxygen masks, and leather helmets. Having a pressurized, heated cabin like the B-29 or the DC-3, for that matter, made a difference.

The flight went quickly, and they made the turnaround at Minneapolis Airport, which was bustling as usual. Otto let Jimmy fly the trip back, watching for traffic. They were cleared into Pioneer Lake by the new control tower. Mata had arranged for the control tower to be built and had worked with the CAB to staff it. She was amazing, Otto thought. She and Pete were happy, walking on air, it seemed.

Jimmy made a smooth landing and the aircraft taxied up to the terminal right at 11:00 AM. Otto clasped him on the shoulder. "Good landing, co-pilot!" he exclaimed.

Jimmy grinned. "Thank you, Captain!" They shut down the flight systems and secured the controls, undid their safety harnesses, and went back to greet the deplaning passengers. Polly had opened the door and was standing at the foot of the stairs saying good-bye to the people, who were walking briskly to the terminal in the chilly wind. He said good-bye to the few remaining passengers getting off and then went down the steps behind Jimmy. "You know, Polly, it is awfully steep when we're on the ground. It's nice and level in the air, though."

Polly rolled her eyes. "Thanks for noticing, Boss," she intoned. Just then Otto noticed Mata running toward them and sensed something had happened. He hoped nothing had occurred on the flight to Madison. Jimmy and Bob had taken that over this morning. Mata looked excited but not upset, so he guessed it was something else.

"Otto! Otto!" Mata called when she got close enough. "Betty went into labor! She's at the clinic! I took her over about an hour ago!"

"Let's go," Otto told her, and they ran for Mata's car. She drove, which was a good idea, since Otto was so charged up he would have gotten several speeding tickets had the local constabulary been out. They pulled up in front of the clinic after a fast fifteen-minute drive. Otto didn't wait for Mata to switch off the engine before he leaped from the seat and ran into the clinic.

The waiting room was empty except for a receptionist who sat behind a small desk. "Captain Kerchner," she greeted him. "Mrs. Kerchner is doing well. She's dilated about four centimeters, so she has a ways to go."

"Can I see her?"

"You'll be able to see her after the baby is delivered. We ask fathers to wait here in the waiting room. In the meantime, please have a seat. Could I get you some coffee?"

Otto stood there for a moment. He wiped his brow. "Yes, please. And some for my sister, as well." Mata had come through the door.

"Hi, Mata," the receptionist called. "How are you and how is Pete?"

"We're fine, Joan, thanks. How are Fred and the kids?"

"Oh, you know, this and that."

Mata laughed. "Yes, I do know." She went over and sat by Otto. "What's the word?"

"Joan said she was four centimeters and she had a ways to go. I don't know why they don't let husbands be with their wives."

Mata studied the ceiling. "Custom, I guess. Fathers might faint or get too worked up."

Otto snorted. "Well, I was there when I placed the order, so I should be able to be there for the delivery."

Mata blushed and rolled her eyes. "Have a nice magazine. And here comes our coffee. Might as well get comfortable. We have a wait ahead of us."

Joan did keep them updated through the rest of the morning and assured them that it would be all right for them to grab some lunch at Spencer's. Otto had arranged for Pete and Jimmy to fly the legs to Minneapolis the rest of the day, with Bob working the Madison flights and Pete and Jimmy alternating as his co-pilot. They needed more pilots, he thought. They'd have to get to work on that. A little after noon, Mata and Otto drove to Spencer's. He hadn't been there in a long while, but the place hadn't changed much since before the war. They went in and took a seat. Otto ordered his usual cheeseburger and Coke; Mata had a salad. She smiled when their meals came. "One day I think you're going to turn into a cheeseburger," she chided him gently.

"Just trying to help the local dairy industry," Otto offered.

Mata cut her salad up. "You still going with the same names?"

"Yes—Hans if it's a boy, and Maria if it's a girl."

"That's nice," she murmured.

They ate in silence for a while, and then Otto asked, "So you and Pete are doing well?"

"Yes, we just love the house he and his brothers built for us. Verner and Erik are thinking of going into the construction business. They're so talented at it."

"What would they do with the farm?"

"Sell it. They asked me to help them write up a contract with the same outfit that bought our dairy. I think it's the right time to make a move. As the town expands, the land will be more valuable if used for housing. I read an article about a place in New York called Levittown where they put a bunch of houses on farm property. It's called a subdivision, and you know what a demand there is for housing. I think the Peterson brothers could do the same thing around here, but on a smaller scale."

"Sounds like you could be a business consultant."

Mata winked at him. "I think I already am."

They finished eating quickly and made their way back to the clinic. Joan reported that Betty was "progressing nicely" and that they should have a baby by early evening. Otto and Mata settled down to wait, reading all the magazines and dozing on the chairs.

About six o'clock, Jimmy and Susan showed up with some carryout spaghetti. The friends ate in the waiting room, and Joan joined them.

About 7:30, Becky Heaton came out of the doctor's room. "You have a baby girl," she told Otto. "In fact, you have *two* baby girls!"

They all stood up, although Otto felt faint. "What? How? When?"

"Two healthy baby girls, born in the usual manner, a few minutes ago. We'll get everybody cleaned up and then you can come in to see them."

Mata, Susan, and Joan hugged Otto, and Jimmy shook his hand. Just then Pete walked in. "Has the baby been born yet?" he asked.

"You mean babies," Mata told him. "You're an uncle twice over."

Pete shook Otto's hand. "Congratulations, old man. You don't do anything halfway, do you?"

Otto muttered, "I guess I don't." He was still trying to get used to the idea of two babies. Becky came back out.

"Otto, you can come back now, and then the rest, but one at a time. Betty is exhausted."

Otto pushed through the door and followed Becky down the hall to the delivery room. Dr. Heaton had changed out of his scrubs into a shirt and tie. He also looked tired, but there was a smile on his face. He stuck out his hand.

"Congratulations there, Papa! Everything went well; they're both healthy and active and Betty did very well. Go on in and see your family."

Otto walked softly to the side of the bed where Betty lay with her eyes closed. He thought she looked so beautiful. She had a twin nestled on either side, and they were asleep, swaddled tightly in white blankets. They both had light hair, he could tell that.

He kissed Betty lightly on the forehead. She opened her eyes and smiled at him. "How are you?" he asked softly.

"Tired," she said, "but not too tired to hug you." Otto wrapped his arms around her and held her for a while, trying not to disturb the babies. He stepped back and looked at the three of them.

"They're beautiful," he whispered.

"Now we need *two* girls' names," Betty whispered back.

"We have one," Otto recalled. "And so we need another."

"We have Maria"—she indicated the infant to her left—"and who is this young lady?" She nodded toward the baby on her right.

"What about 'Marion' after your mother?" Otto asked.

Betty's eyes shone. "She will be so pleased." He put his hand on each of the girls and then bent down and kissed them.

"You'll make a great mom," he told her.

"And you'll make a great dad," she responded.

"Well, there are some other people out here who want to talk to you, so I'll tell them to come in one at a time. And I'll call your parents. I'm sure they're anxious to hear something."

Betty nodded and closed her eyes again. Otto went out into the waiting room.

"Well, how do they look?" Mata wanted to know.

"They're beautiful. You can go in and see them now, Aunt Mata!" Mata glided through the door. "May I use your phone?" he asked Joan. "I need to call Betty's parents."

"Certainly," Joan said. "Dial nine to get out."

As Otto dialed the number, he thought that this was his first call as a family man. It was a role he thought he was going to like.

# Chapter 8
# Hard Times
# December 1948

It was the day after Christmas, and Otto was sleepy. They hadn't run flights on Christmas Day, and a heavy snow had fallen throughout the daylight hours and into the night. Since he lived closer to the airport than Mata, Otto had called "Spud" Jenkins, who used his surplus Jeep fitted with a blade to keep the runway clear. Jenkins was a bachelor who lived alone and didn't mind being called out Christmas evening He also liked the money, although as far as anyone could tell he didn't spend much on anything, including clothes and the ramshackle farmhouse he lived in that badly needed a coat or two of paint. But he was reliable and, although he was also irascible, he did good work. He also plowed the town roads, so he would probably work all night.

Otto thought that they would have to see about weather conditions the next morning before Pete took Flight 220 to Minneapolis. It was scheduled at 8:00 AM. Mata had arranged the installation of a Telex a couple of months before so they could get weather information from the Minneapolis Airport. Pete had been commanding flights for a couple of months with a new young fellow named Stan Wallace, who had been through flight school on the GI Bill. Otto wasn't sure which branch of service he had been in, but he thought it was the army. Stan was a nice young kid who flew well. There were getting to be too many new pilots to know much about them.

Otto was glad to have the day off, even if it was a busman's holiday where he went to the office and did crew scheduling. He had enjoyed the first Christmas with the twins, who were six months old and doing so many things on their own. He and Betty had helped them tear off the wrapping paper from their presents, and although they were more interested in the paper than the presents, Betty said that was what babies did. They had a nice meal with John and Marion, who had come over after presents, but had to cut the conversation short so Betty's folks could get back home in the snow. After they had left, the girls took a nap while Otto helped Betty with the dishes. Then Otto stretched out in his chair and Betty lay down on the couch, and both enjoyed naps themselves.

They awoke in the evening, which looked more like night with the heavy snow clouds still pouring down their load. The girls got up, and they all had a light meal and then recessed to the living room and listened to "The Railroad Hour." The twins played on the floor and Otto and Betty sat on the couch and held hands, happy to be together with their new family. The girls went to bed about 9:00, and their parents followed an hour later. Five o'clock comes awfully early, Otto thought as he turned out the light.

***

Otto sat at the operations desk, drinking another cup of coffee and trying to become fully awake. Although Betty tended to the girls when they awoke at night, Otto still woke up with them. Interrupted sleep did make a fellow drowsy, he thought, as he looked at the latest Telex to come in from the weather service. It looked like the storm had blown through about midnight, and the skies should be clear with some westerly winds during the day. Good enough to go flying.

Pete and Stan pushed through the door with Susan not far behind. "Good morning, Boss!" the pilots called. Susan headed for the coffee pot.

"Good morning, crew!" Otto returned. Susan flopped down on the sofa, put her coffee cup on the table, and put her head in her hands. She groaned softly.

"What's the matter, Little Miss Sunshine?" Stan asked her. "Too much Christmas cheer?"

"I had a lovely Christmas with Jimmy and his family, thank you," Susan muttered. "We just ate a little too much."

"And drank some?" Otto asked.

"Just a few holiday spirits," Susan whispered.

"Well, if you just had your coffee straight up, it might help you wake up," Stan offered. "Instead of that sugar/milk mix you call coffee. But there's no cure for a hangover other than time."

"I don't have a hangover," Susan moaned. "I'm just tired."

"Well, crew, here's the briefing. Looks like the weather should be clear the rest of the day. The runways are clear and I expect the aircraft should be ready to go in time for an eight AM takeoff. So, you have about an hour to recover from the holidays. We've got a good load factor on two-twenty with all the people coming back from Christmas there."

Pete and Stan nodded. Susan closed her eyes.

"Did you have Spud clear the runways?" Pete asked.

"Yep. Gave the guy some extra money."

"He does a good job."

"That he does. Did you and Mata have nice Christmas?"

"The best. It was just what we both wanted." Otto knew they had spent the day at the Petersons'. Pete and Mata would come over Sunday after church to exchange presents and have another holiday meal. If they kept this up, Otto would have to order the next-size-larger uniform.

He stood up. "There's likely to be icing at all altitudes today. Stan, remember to run the boots every ten minutes or so. Take a look every once in a while to see how the wings look from the cabin. Be casual about it; we don't want to alarm the paying customers. Stroll down the aisle and pretend to enjoy the view. You can say something about the landscape like, "There are a lot of dairy farms down there."

Pete and Stan laughed, waking Susan. "Let's go, Goldilocks," Stan laughed. "The bears have arrived!"

Susan yawned and stretched. "Who's Mama Bear today?" she asked. "Is it your turn, Stan?"

Stan pulled her to her feet. "Well, you're Baby Bear and Pete is Papa Bear, so I guess I'll take what's left." The three crew members went out into the cold where Flight 220 was waiting.

\*\*\*

Otto studied the latest Telex and didn't like what he saw. A sudden storm was blowing up off the lake with higher winds than predicted and snow, sleet, and ice. He called the Northwest ops office in Minneapolis.

"Captain Kerchner here, of M & M," he said into the mouthpiece. The Northwest folks were good about helping them out at the other end. "Yes, I'm calling to see if you would make sure that the crew for two-twenty gets the word about this storm that's coming along? Tell them to expect a rough ride back and to be extra careful. Yes . . . thank you. Good-bye."

He put the phone back in the cradle and went over to pour a cup of coffee. He had gotten into the habit of drinking it black in the service. At least this was pretty good stuff, unlike the bitter swill the army seemed to brew. Oh well, they had done the best they could, considering the number of troops they fed. And the air corps got at least two hots a day, unlike the ground pounders who might exist on C rats for a week before the feeding units caught up with them. Or the shower units. There were, as he thought about it, a few compensations for being shot at every time they went up and having a long way to fall if something went wrong. At least he didn't have to experience that, although he had his own little crash. That was a long, slow fall.

Otto shook his head. Strictly in the past, he reminded himself. Life was good. What more could he want? He turned to preparing the paperwork for the turnaround back to Minneapolis.

Mata came in about the time Flight 220 broke ground. She looked somewhat sleepy, although not hungover. As far as Otto knew, his sister only drank on rare ceremonial occasions. She said she didn't like the taste. He had to agree with her, for the most part. Wine was OK, and he had been known to have a scotch or whiskey after a particularly hairy mission. Thank God there had been precious few of those.

"Good morning, Brother," Mata said softly. "Did you have a good Christmas?"

Otto got up and kissed her on the cheek. "We sure it. It was nice with the twins."

"I can't wait to see them. They're growing like weeds."

"Yes. It makes a definite difference in Christmas with them around."

Mata nodded. "I bet."

Just then Bob and Jimmy came through the door to take Flight 320 out to Madison. The twice-daily service had proved popular since its start a few months before. M & M would have to add yet more crew members. "How's the weather, Boss?" Jimmy asked.

"Not good," Otto frowned. "There's a bad storm coming through. I think it was a surprise to everyone. Pete and Stan are bringing 420 back. I called to tell them to be careful.

"We're always careful," Jimmy said thoughtfully, "but we'll keep an eye on it."

Jenny came in to complete the crew on 320. They drank some coffee and then went out to preflight the aircraft. Otto followed to check.

The snow was starting up, heralded by increasing winds. We're going to have to think about cancelling four-twenty, Otto thought, and calling Pete and telling him to return to Minneapolis. This was looking extremely nasty. He saw ice on the wings and decided to call the flight off. He went over to Jimmy. "We're going to cancel four-twenty. You can take three-twenty out if the weather improves."

Jimmy nodded and waved Bob back into the office. He went up the steps to the cabin and told Jenny they were cancelling. She shrugged on her coat and walked with him to the office.

"I'll call Pete and tell him not to come back until the weather improves," Otto said. He lifted the receiver and dialed the Northwest number again. He waited a few seconds and then spoke. This is Captain Kerchner of M & M Airlines again. Would you tell Captain Peterson to hold on bringing four-twenty back until the weather improves? Yes, I know. Thank you." He put the receiver down. "OK," he said. "Stand by for further instructions."

Jimmy, Bob, Jenny, and Mata all saluted him. Otto rolled his eyes.

Outside the storm was mounting in its fury. The snow had increased to the point they couldn't see all the way across the field. The flakes were driven sideways by gale-force winds. I'd hate to be out in this in anything, Otto thought, much less an airplane.

Jimmy and Bob sat down at the table and started a hand of poker. Susan went over to talk to Mata. Otto busied himself with making some notes for airport expansion. Maybe that way Northwest could bring in some long-distance flights. The office felt warm and cozy with the storm howling outside.

The phone rang about half an hour later and Mata answered it. She looked troubled as she listened to the other person, and then handed the phone to Otto. "It's the tower. Pete's on the horn with them, and there's trouble."

Otto took the phone. "Captain Kerchner here. Yes, yes. Yes, I see. I'll be right over." He put the handset down and looked at Mata and his crew members. "Pete is having trouble with the aircraft. He didn't get the word to stay in Minneapolis. Mata, you come with me. The rest of you stay here to handle calls."

Mata and Otto put on their heavy coats and went into the storm. Otto held on to her as they lowered their heads and struggled against the wind. They were out of breath when they reached the control tower. Otto forced the door open and they ran up the steps to the control room. Roger Scott, the controller, handed Otto a headset. "We just heard from him. He has icing and one of the engines keeps cutting out."

Otto put the headset on. "Flight four-twenty, this is Pioneer Lake. Come in."

# ON THE WINGS OF EAGLES

He heard Pete's voice distantly through the headphones. "Otto, we're icing up at all levels. We're about half an hour out, but number one keeps sputtering. I'm open to suggestions."

Otto thought for a moment, then keyed the mic. "Have you tried ascending?"

"No," came back Pete's voice. "I've been dropping, trying to find a warm layer. I'm presently at ten thousand feet."

"The storm has the surface levels frozen. Try climbing to thirty thousand and see what happens. If that helps, do a combat descent when you get above the airport. I'll stand by."

Otto took off the headset and gave it to Roger. He turned to Mata, who looked stricken. "I heard of pilots during the war who were iced up and found a warm band of air by going higher." She nodded. He hugged her and said, "Don't worry, Sis, we'll get them down." She nodded again, fighting back tears. Otto indicated a seat near the wall and took one himself. There was nothing to see with whiteout conditions outside.

After about ten minutes Roger nodded to Otto. He put the headset back on. "Otto, that worked," Pete said. "We're at thirty thousand and the ice is coming off. I don't know what happened to the anti-icers. The ship was getting hard to control at ten thousand."

Otto silently blamed himself for not training Pete better about handling icing conditions. "Great, Pete. I estimate you're ten minutes away from your descent. Have Susan make sure everyone's strapped in tight. That kind of spiral dive really generates some g's."

"OK, Boss," Pete came back, sounding more confident. "Thanks for the help. See you on the ground."

"Roger," Otto returned. "Good luck, Pete. Pioneer Lake over and out."

Otto handed the headset back and sat back on the chair. He took Mata's hand. "They'll be on the ground in ten minutes. Wait and see." Mata nodded again, and then closed her eyes, her lips moving in a silent prayer. Otto bowed his head briefly. *Lord, help my friends. Help me be a better pilot and instructor and person. Amen.*

The three people in the control room sat in silence for about five minutes, and then Roger put his hand to one of the headphone receivers and listened intently. He handed the spare headset to Otto. "More trouble," he said.

Otto put the headset on. "Come in, Pete. What's going on?"

Pete's voice came back faintly. "We can't get one gear down. The hydraulic and emergency won't work. Again, I'm open to suggestions."

In spite of the cold in the control room, Otto felt himself starting to sweat. He bowed his head again, thinking and praying. "The gear could be frozen in the 'up' position. Try bouncing the aircraft to see if it will fall into position." There was a momentary pause while Pete pulled the DC-3 up sharply and then brought it down and then up again.

"No dice, Boss," he said.

"OK," Otto said. "You'll need to circle to burn off fuel if you have to make a one-gear landing anyhow, so you have time. I assume you've cycled the gear selector and checked the breakers."

"Several times."

"All right, let's see if the ice will melt enough for the gear to come down. Then bounce it again. Call me in five minutes."

"Will do, Captain."

"We'll get you down, Pete, in roughly the same condition as you took off in."

Pete laughed a short, sharp laugh. "Hope so, Boss. Back in five."

This time Otto sat down with his headset still live. He took Mata's hand. "He's going to try a couple of things and check back in a few minutes."

"Thank you," Mata whispered. She held Otto's hand tightly.

"So, how do you like married life?"

"It's wonderful. Pete treats me so well. We have the best time together. And the Petersons treat me like the daughter they never had."

"They're lucky to have you as a member of their family. And so am I. We'll get 'em down. Please try not to worry so much."

Mata nodded and smiled weakly through her tears. "I know you will. But this brings back all the worrying I did while you were in the air corps over in Europe. We didn't get much news about you, although you were very good about writing me."

"I tried to, as much as I could. I couldn't write much for a while after my accident because I was either in a morphine haze or being treated or on a ship. It wasn't until I got to the hospital in Boston that I was able to write more regularly."

Mata bit her lip and smiled slightly. "I know. I still worried about how the war and your injury had changed you."

"Well?" Otto asked, raising one eyebrow.

"You came back the same wonderful brother I knew from the time you left. I'm so proud of you and am just crazy about you."

Otto blushed. "Love you, too, Sis." Just then his headphones crackled.

"Pioneer Lake, this is M & M four-twenty ten miles from the airport."

"Come back, four-twenty. This is Pioneer Lake."

"No joy, Boss. Gear's still stuck."

Crap, Otto thought. "All right, try raising the extended gear and then lowering both again. Worst comes to worst, it'll be better to try to land wheels up than on one gear." Otto remembered trying to land his bomber on one wheel. Look how that had worked out. Of course, he was by himself with no radio and had his hands full just trying to land the plane, much less diagnose and fix a stuck gear.

There was a pause on the other end of the connection. Pete came back on. "No dice. Left gear won't retract."

Some days it doesn't pay to get out of bed, Otto reflected. Then he remembered something. "How's that port engine doing?"

"It smoothed out when we got to altitude. Apparently the ice melted and it's running strong."

Glad that problem fixed itself, Otto thought. A bad engine and a stuck gear would be about one problem too many. Not that one wasn't more than enough just by itself. "All right, burn your fuel down to five percent and then come in. We'll have the crash equipment standing by, but I hope we won't need it." The field had a small fire truck and war surplus ambulance with a couple of rescue workers who had done that in the military. They had never had to use them until today. "When you land, hold your starboard wing up as long as you can. Full up aileron on that side. Chop the engines when you touch down and stay off the brakes so you won't spin it. If you have time and space, have Susan move the passengers to the port side of the cabin. Have her instruct them in emergency landing procedures. Make the announcement just before you set down. Do you have that?"

"Sure do, Otto. Thanks. It helps to have you go over the procedure."

"All right. I'll leave you alone to do your work. You're cleared straight in after you descend to final approach altitude. There's no traffic but we've declared an emergency for you anyhow. Good luck, Brother."

"Thanks, Otto. See you on the ground."

"You got it, Pete. Safe landing! Over and out."

He handed the headset back to Roger. Mata stood and the three of them went to the big control tower windows to watch for the first sight of the approaching aircraft. They could see the flashing lights of the emergency vehicles about halfway down the runway, but little else since the snow continued to come down in buckets, still blowing sideways.

They could not hear the engines over the roar of the wind, but soon Roger cried, "There they are!" The silver, white, and blue bird drifted into view, driving into the wind, one gear down, the landing lights punching a hole through the blowing snow.

God help them, Otto prayed. God help us all. He put his arm around Mata, who had both hands to her mouth. "Ohhhh," she moaned.

The DC-3 dropped lower and lower and then touched down, throwing back twin rooster tails of snow. Otto could see Pete was fighting with the rudder to keep lined up on the slippery runway. Spud had gone on to clear the town roads since they hadn't expected this new storm. Darn the luck, Otto thought.

The aircraft rolled out, moving gradually more slowly, going past the usual place where it would have slowed to use the taxiway. Otto could see Pete had the right aileron full up. The ship held up until it had slowed considerably. Then the right wing dropped and the airplane slid straight down the runway for about forty feet and then spun around, facing back where it had come from. They could hear the metal of the wing and wheel housing crunching in spite of the wind and watched as the starboard prop folded back over its nacelle. It slid backward for a few feet and then came to rest. They could see the rescue equipment speeding down the runway, skidding to a stop as the workers piled out. The two firemen ran to the fire truck, pulled the hoses out and hauled them toward the stricken airplane.

Just then Otto saw a yellow flash under the starboard nacelle. "Oh hell, they're on fire!" he shouted, as Mata screamed. They and Roger threw on their coats and pounded down the stairs.

Two firefighters stood off a distance and sprayed foam on the flames because they didn't have fire suits on. *We never counted on a fire this big,*

Otto thought. Guess we should have. Dammit. Too late for it this time. He and Mata and Roger ran toward the craft, which was now burning brightly on the right engine and wing. The flames were moving toward the cockpit area. They were fortunate that the cabin door was on the port side and the pilots could go out the cockpit window on the same side.

As the firefighters continued to spray foam, the threesome ran around to the port side of the fuselage. Otto saw out of the corner of his eye Jimmy, Bob, and Jenny running from the ops shack. They had enough presence of mind to grab some blankets from the closet.

Otto saw that Susan had the door open back of the wing and was at the bottom of the fold-down stairs helping passengers down. As each one reached bottom, she shouted, "Run! Get away! Keep going!" and they did not hesitate to do so. They were met by the three from the ops office and given blankets, which they threw over their heads and continued to move toward the terminal building.

Otto noted nineteen people who had gotten off, so if that was the count, they were all off except for the pilots. Two more passengers appeared and made their way down the stairs. The cabin door stood open. Susan started to go back inside. "Susan," Otto shouted as they made their way up to the door. "Stay out here! We'll go in!"

Otto and Roger climbed the steps. Thick, heavy black smoke was now billowing from the top of the door, and the cockpit was fully engulfed in flames. The foam couldn't keep up with the fire. Otto and Roger dropped down to the floor and crawled forward up the aisle. Otto saw what Jenny meant about needing a ladder. They could hear Stan somewhere ahead of them. He was pulling Pete with his hands under Pete's arms. "C'mon, Stan! Keep coming!" The aisle was just wide enough for one person at a time.

Stan called, "I'm coming! Pete's been burned! He's unconscious! He was helping passengers off when it happened." Stan dissolved into a coughing spasm.

Here it is all over again, Otto thought, dismayed. He hoped Pete's burns were not too bad. Of course, he hadn't been conscious for his own rescue, either, so he had no idea how bad they were. He and Roger backed out the door and stood waiting for Stan and Pete. Stan appeared, pulling Pete to the edge of the door and then handing him down to Roger and Otto. They took him onto the runway. Mata ran up with a couple of blankets and laid one on the snow covering the runway. Otto and Roger laid Pete on the blanket and

Mata covered him to his neck. His face was an angry red and he was moaning. His eyes were swollen shut.

Mata knelt down, weeping, with her arms around Pete's torso. "Mata!" Otto called, "go around and have the rescue worker bring a stretcher!" She looked up and, nodding quickly, ran around to the other side of the wreck, which seemed to be burning less violently. Otto grabbed the top of the blanket beneath Pete, Roger grabbed the middle, and Stan took hold of the bottom. They lifted Pete up and walked back away from the airplane. George, the ambulance driver, came running with a stretcher and dropped it on the snow for them to place Pete on. He then ran back to bring the ambulance up. Mata came back from where the ambulance stood. She reached them as they were lifting Pete up in the stretcher. She took Pete's hand and walked with the group to the ambulance that had pulled up.

The worker came around and opened the rear doors. Mata climbed in the back with Pete and Otto took the passenger seat. George closed the rear door, jumped in the left side, started the engine, and they were off for the clinic. George called in on the radio to Dr. Heaton's practice. "This is Airport Rescue," he said. "We're inbound with a burn case. Please stand by to receive the patient in about twenty minutes."

Joan's voice came back over the radio. "We're advised," she said. "Who is it?"

"Pete Peterson."

"Oh, no," Joan said. "We'll be ready for him. Clinic out."

"Roger that," George said into the mic. "Airport Rescue out."

As George sped off down the runway and onto the airport road, Otto looked back at Mata, who was bending over Pete. He was increasingly agitated, rolling back and forth on the stretcher, which was locked down to the floor of the ambulance. Mata looked at Otto pleadingly. "Can't we do something for him? He's in such pain."

Otto looked at George. "Do you have morphine syrettes?"

"Yeah," said George, his eyes on the near-whiteout conditions on the road. "They're in the white medical kit behind the seats."

"All right," Otto said and turned to Mata. "Take out a bag with small plastic containers with a plastic cover over a needle. Take one out, take off the cap, roll up Pete's sleeve, and jam the syrette into his upper arm. That'll relieve the pain in just a few minutes."

Mata did as Otto told her, and in a few minutes Pete quieted down. She turned her eyes back to Otto. "Was it like this when you were burned?"

Otto shrugged. "I was unconscious for a couple of days. When I woke up I was in a world of hurt, so they kept me sedated for about a week. I had some strange dreams, I tell you." He had not even told Mata about seeing their father in the bright garden after his crash.

"Isn't morphine addictive?" Mata looked troubled.

"It is, and I was addicted to it for a while, but they got me off it. The military had a lot of experience with burns and addiction. What a way to learn how to treat them."

"I'll be there for him," Mata said.

"So will I," Otto replied. "So will I."

The ambulance plunged on through the snow, its red lights flashing and siren screaming against the uproar of the storm. They sped through town and slid to a stop in the clinic's lot. Dr. Heaton and Becky were standing just inside the doors waiting for them.

Otto and Roger jumped out and went around back to open the doors. They slid the stretcher out and carried it through the doors Becky held open and into the examination room, followed closely by the doctor. Joan, the receptionist, came around her desk and hugged Mata, leading her to a chair to sit down. Otto knew she would ask Mata if she wanted something to drink.

"Can you stay and help if I need you?" Heaton asked Otto. Otto nodded as he and George helped slide Pete onto an examining table.

"He's had one syrette of morphine on the way here."

"How did this happen?"

"Crash landing. Apparently he was trying to help evacuate passengers instead of going through the cockpit window."

Heaton grunted. Becky started cutting Pete's clothes off. Heaton handed Otto some rubber gloves, a mask, and a pair of scissors. "Get washed up and help us cut his clothes off. Try not to pull any skin off when you do, but you might not be able to avoid it. My main concern is his face and his eyes."

Pete's face had continued to redden and his eyes were swollen tightly shut. Becky stopped cutting his clothes off as Otto started, wet a gauze sponge with sterile water, and gently laid it over Pete's face. He groaned slightly and stirred. *Lord, I know how that feels,* Otto thought, and continued cutting Pete's pant leg.

\*\*\*

An hour later, Otto was sitting in the waiting area with Mata. Pete's parents had joined them about half an hour earlier. No one said much.

Dr. Heaton walked through the door from the back area. The four stood, but Heaton motioned them down.

"Well, at least some of the news is good," he started, and Mata winced. "His burns except for his face are first-to-second degree. The face I would call a bad second degree burn. And he can't see."

Otto gulped. "You mean his eyelids are swollen shut and he can't see?"

Dr. Heaton shook his head. "No, I mean his eyes don't work. I'm not sure why, but I was able to examine his eyes and they're burned out. I can't treat a case of this severity. We'll have to take him to Minneapolis to the hospital. Can you fly him there? I think the storm's just about blown itself out. We gave him some more pain meds and he's not feeling any pain."

Mata dissolved into tears. Otto nodded. "Sure. We can leave as soon as he's ready."

\*\*\*

The ambulance came back, and once again Mata rode in the back with Pete. She laid her torso over on his. "Careful, Sis," Otto warned. "You don't know what damage you might do by putting pressure on his burns." Mata straightened up, nodded, and put her right hand lightly on Pete's chest. They rode the rest of the way to the airport in silence.

Otto had called ahead to have Jimmy preflight one of the Beeches. All flights had been cancelled since most people would have found it difficult to get to the airport. Jimmy had told him that there were no other injuries on the flight, for which Otto was grateful. They worked it out so that Jimmy would fly co-pilot and Jenny would come along as an extra pair of hands. An ambulance would meet them at the Minneapolis airport and take Pete to the same hospital where Hans had been taken years before. It seemed like such a long time ago, and so much had happened since then. Otto remembered making that flight in the J-4, which still sat with the J-3 in a hangar. He idly thought that they needed to have them checked and restored if necessary.

They arrived at the airport, and George and Otto carried Pete on the stretcher to the waiting Beechcraft. Jimmy had the engines running and came back to help them load the stretcher. Jimmy had some of the ground crew take a couple rows of seats out, and they were able to secure the stretcher to the seat clamps with cargo straps. The Beech was used as an air ambulance during the war, so it wasn't much of a stretch to configure it for one patient. Mata and Jenny sat across the aisle. Once they were belted in, Otto and Jimmy made their way to the cockpit.

"So everyone else on the flight is all right?" Otto asked.

"Yes—shaken up, but all right. Stan breathed a little smoke. He said Pete insisted on going back to help evacuate the passengers rather than bailing out the windows. Stan got back into the cabin but Pete was throwing switches to try to cut off the fuel to the fire and it flashed around him. That's why he was burned and Stan wasn't. Stan feels awful about it."

"Well, we don't need two burned pilots," Otto remarked grimly. "One is one too many." He sat in the left seat and belted in. "Let's get going!"

Otto advanced the throttles and the Beech taxied to the end of the runway. The storm had blown through and conditions were what pilots called "severe clear." Otto heard Roger in the tower: "M & M Special Medical Flight, you are cleared for takeoff. Good luck, Captains."

"Acknowledged," Otto answered. "Thank you, Roger." He released the brakes and ran the engines up to takeoff speed. The Beech rolled down the snowy runway and lifted into the air, bound for the hospital in Minneapolis, an hour away.

# Chapter 9
# Aftermath
# December 1948

Otto and Mata sat on two of the hard wooden chairs that lined three sides of the waiting room for friends and family of surgical patients. Jimmy and Jenny had gone out to try to find something to eat, but Otto and Mata weren't hungry. They stared at the doors leading to the operating rooms. They had been waiting for nearly two hours, their anxiety growing with every minute. When they had brought Pete in, they were shuffled off to a room where an aide took information from them. Mata answered all the questions, with Otto sitting beside her, his hand on her back. By the time they finished, Pete had been prepped for surgery and moved to the OR.

Otto kept thinking of the irony of Pete being burned in an accident involving an aircraft with a stuck landing gear. The accident was eerily similar to his crash in the B-17. He prayed that Pete would not have the degree of damage to his body that Otto did and that he would recover his sight. The clock on the opposite wall ticked loudly as the minutes crept by.

Mata did not speak, occupied by her own thoughts. Otto knew she was strong, but something like this was so hard to take. He reached over and took her hand, and she gripped his strongly. He smiled tightly at her and she smiled back, her face then lapsing into a vacant and troubled expression.

Jimmy and Jenny came back and the group sat silently for another hour. The doors to the OR swung open and a surgeon came out, still dressed in scrubs. He went over to Mata, who stood up, as did the others.

"Mrs. Peterson?"

Mata nodded.

"Your husband came through fine. He's resting comfortably now and should recover well. He'll need treatment and physical therapy and should recover, well, fine except for his vision."

"What about his vision?" Otto asked.

The surgeon regarded him gravely. "I'm not a specialist and we'll have one look at him, but I don't think he will ever see again. The flare-up of the flames literally burned his eyes out. I'm sorry." He looked at his feet. "Do you have any questions for me?"

"When can I see him?" Mata asked.

"One of the nurses will come out and take you to recovery when we have him situated."

No one said anything else, so the doctor turned and went back through the doors.

The four friends looked at each other and then sank back into their seats.

"I was hoping . . . " Mata started but then lapsed into silence.

After half an hour, a nurse came in. "I can take you back to see Mr. Peterson, two at a time."

Mata and Otto stood and followed her out the doors and down a hallway to the recovery room. The long space was lined with beds separated by curtains. Few of the beds were occupied. They came to the bed where Pete lay, his head swathed in white bandages. Mata rushed over to him and laid her torso on top of his. He reached around with bandaged arms to hold her.

"I'm so glad you're alive," she whispered. Otto stood at the foot of the bed.

"Yeah, I'll be OK, except for this sight business," Pete murmured.

"You're still my love," Mata told him, and she kissed him on the exposed lower part of his face. "Sight or no sight."

"I'm so sorry about this," Otto told Pete, who lifted his head toward the sound of Otto's voice.

"Sorry about the aircraft, Boss. I tried everything I could think of."

Otto put his hand on Pete's. "I'm sorry I couldn't figure out some better way to get you down. That landing was incredible considering what you were facing."

Pete smiled ruefully. "Not incredible enough, I guess."

"The passengers and other crew came through it fine," Otto told him. "You paid the price."

Pete dropped his head back.

"I'll go send in Jimmy and Polly." Otto started to leave.

"I don't blame you, Boss. Sometimes these things happen."

Otto hesitated. "Yes, they do. Unfortunately."

# Chapter 10
# Back Home Again
# March 1949

Pete sat in a chair at the table in the ops office. Mata was feeding him some soup. He took a few spoonfuls and then said, "I think I can do that myself."

"Go ahead," she told him, and put the spoon in his hand. "The bowl's right here."

Pete guided the spoon into the bowl, took a spoonful of soup, and guided it into his mouth.

Mata clapped her hands. "Very good!" she exclaimed. Pete grinned. After two weeks in the hospital and two weeks' physical and occupational training, he had been released to come home late in January. The adjustment to life without sight had been slow and difficult, but Mata thought that he was doing well making his way in the world. He came with Mata to the airport. He soon found ways to make himself useful in the day-to-day operations of the airline, which was booming as warm weather crept closer.

Otto came into the room. "Good morning, Petersons!" he called.

"Good morning," Pete and Mata chorused. "How are the twins feeling?" Mata asked.

"They're better, I think." Otto frowned. "Betty was up most of the night with them, but they had all fallen asleep as I left. I hope what they've had is just a shared cold."

"They're certainly growing," Pete added.

"Yes, they're a lot of fun. Betty will bring them over when they're recovered. I know they'd enjoy some aunt and uncle time. How's the flight schedule?"

"Two-twenty left a few minutes ago, and four-twenty is on time for departure at eight thirty," Mata said, looking at a sheet in front of her. "We have good load factors all day, so all's well."

"Very good," Otto noted. He sat down. "And how is Bill working out as a pilot?" They had hired him to take Pete's place.

"All the crew like him. He plans to have his family join him as soon as he finds a house for them. I have a few people I'm going to call."

Otto nodded. He continued to be amazed at all the details Mata took care of in addition to working with Pete as he learned to cope with his blindness. They had been talking about getting a seeing-eye dog in a few weeks to give Pete more independence.

Mata consulted some notes. "You left early yesterday, and a General Rackham from the air corps called."

Otto lifted an eyebrow. "I wonder if that's Colonel Rackham from the Eighth."

"It must be. He said he was a ghost from your past. Very commanding voice."

"Well, it will be good to talk to him. Did he leave a number?" Mata handed him a piece of paper. "Thanks, Sis. You do good work. And by the way, it's the air force now. It's been a separate branch of service since September of 1947."

"Well, who knew?" Mata smiled.

Otto went into his office, picked up the phone, and dialed the operator. "Operator, I'd like to make a long distance call. He gave her the number, heard a series of clicks and pops, and then heard the sound of a phone ringing as if from afar.

"General Rackham's office, Corporal Evans speaking."

"My name is Captain Otto Kerchner, and I'm returning the general's call."

"One moment please," the woman on the other end of the line told him.

Otto looked out the window at 420 taxiing for takeoff. And another day begins at Pioneer Lake Airport.

"Kerchner!" Rackham's booming voice was unmistakable. "How the hell are you?"

"I'm fine, sir! Congratulations on your promotion!"

"Aw, hell, it's the general-officer equivalent of a shavetail. I do all the work and catch all the hell while the three- and four-stars take all the credit. But that's how it is in this man's army. I mean air force. About time we got our own branch. But anyhow, I see you're doing good work with your airline. You were a damn fine pilot. Damned shame about that accident. But that's in the past. How would you like to come work for me again?" "Rip" Rackham hadn't changed much since the days of the Eighth, Otto thought.

"Well, sir, I'd have to talk to my wife."

"Well, of course. Gotta keep 'em happy at home. Or as happy as you can, right, Kerchner?"

"Yessir."

"I'm Stateside after running the Candy Bomber Express into Berlin. More like the Candy Butt Express. Damn Ruskis turned on us after the war. I knew they would. FDR gave the farm away to Stalin, but that's above my pay grade. I'm here in Nebraska at Offutt Air Force Base. We're cranking up a new command to be called the Strategic Air Command. We need bomber pilots. Lots of bomber pilots. So I'm calling some of my boys from the Eighth to come work with me as instructors. Talk to that wife of yours and give me a blast back, OK, Kerchner?"

Otto paused to breathe. "Yessir. But you're not using the '17, I take it?"

"No, son, we're flying B-29s until the air force gets a jet bomber on line. Don't know how soon that will be, but in the meantime it's the Superfort."

"I've never flown a '29, sir."

"Piece of cake. You'll catch on. Pretty good bird except for an unfortunate tendency for engine fires. But we'll bring you up to speed. Get me an answer ASAP, Captain, all right?"

"Yessir," Otto stammered, feeling as if he should salute. The phone clicked and Rackham was gone. Otto put the phone down, thinking hard. He went back into the ops room.

"That was my old CO, General Rackham. He wants me to come instruct on B-29s."

Mata and Pete turned their heads toward him. "Where would you do that?" she asked.

"Nebraska. Offutt Air Force Base. It's a voluntary assignment. I'll have to talk to Betty about it. Although if things heat up with the Russians, I could be recalled to active duty."

"Haven't you done enough?" Mata asked.

"Apparently there's more to do. Rackham's a good man. He wouldn't have asked if he didn't need me." Otto put his coat back on. "I'm going to go talk to Betty. I'll be back shortly." He went through the door into the bright sunshine.

Mata and Pete sat there for a moment. Pete put his hand over on hers. "You're probably thinking, 'Here we go again.'"

Mata nodded. "I am, Pete, and I don't have a good feeling about this."

# Chapter 11
# Offutt Air Force Base
# April 1949

*My dearest Betty,*

*Well, I arrived at Offutt AFB this afternoon about five o'clock. The train was packed about like they were during the war. I got to the station from the airport in plenty of time to catch the ten o'clock. I got a sandwich from the dining car for lunch and ate it at my seat because the diner was so crowded as well. We went through Des Moines about two and got into Omaha about four. Of course, there was a bus at the station, which looked like it was left over from the war, to take air force personnel to the base. It was me and a bunch of enlisteds, but they let me ride in front. Rank has its privileges, huh?*

*I reported to General Rackham's office. He looks about the same, a little grayer, a little heavier, but still the same old "Rip" Rackham. We talked a bit, and then he took me to the officers' club to eat. He has gathered some of the best pilots from the old outfit to instruct on the B-29. I told him I had never been near a '29, but he said they were in the training business and that they would get me up to speed. He is very concerned about the Russians and the threat they pose to us.*

*After dinner, Rackham's aide took me over to the bachelor officers' quarters. Offutt is a huge base and the accommodations are a cut above what I was used to during the war. My apartment is a nice size and I can do some cooking, but I'll probably just eat in the mess hall most of the time. I've unpacked and put out my pictures of you and the girls. I miss all of you so much and hope I can get leave soon to come visit. I think I'll fly home, though, instead of taking the train!*

*I'd better turn in. Things get started here early.*

*Holding all of you in my heart until I can hold you in my arms, I am, forever, your*

*Otto*

As Otto lay in bed waiting to fall asleep, he thought back to his meeting with the general. He had gone directly to Rackham's office from the bus. Rackham's aide sent him into the inner office immediately. Rackham sat behind a huge desk. He jumped up, came around, ignored Otto's salute and the little speech he had prepared, and enveloped him in a big bear hug. My gosh, Otto thought, the man is still strong.

"Kerchner! You old dog! It's great to see you! Come on, sit down and take a load off! You want something to drink? A smoke?"

"I'm not much of a drinker, sir, thank you, except after a hard mission, and I don't smoke, but I would like some water." Rackham sighed, called his aide in, and ordered a whiskey and a pitcher of water be brought in. The aide came back posthaste. Rackham took the whiskey and Otto took the glass the aide had poured out of the pitcher. "A toast!" Rackham boomed. "To the Eighth and all her fliers!"

"To the Eighth!" Otto returned, and he took a drink from his glass. Rackham pounded down about half of his and set the glass on his desk.

"So, how was your trip, Kerchner? Any problems?"

"No, sir. I took one of our flights to Minneapolis and the train the rest of the way. It was crowded."

Rackham frowned. "Yeah, hell, war's over and everybody thinks they have to run their asses all over the place. Well, there's another kind of threat that we have to be ready for, and that's why you're here. And don't call me 'sir' when we're alone like this. Call me 'Rip'!"

Otto took another sip of his water. "All right, s—I mean, Rip. Back in the squadron we didn't think you knew about your nickname."

Rackham threw back his head and laughed. "Do I look like I fell off the cabbage truck yesterday? Of course I knew about my nickname. A good leader has to know everything he can about his men. Like I know you are one of the finest fliers I've ever seen. That's why you're here—to pass along some of that knowledge and skill to the young fellows coming up. I'm assembling some of the best boys we had in our outfits to teach on the B-29. You'll turn out some fine pilots, and we're going to need them with what we got coming up."

"Sir, one thing?"

Rackham looked at him sideways. "I mean, Rip, I have never been near a B-29, much less flown on one. I've certainly never instructed someone how to fly one."

Rackham laughed again and pounded his open palm on his leg. "Hell, boy, we'll teach you! That's what we do around here. You'll be horsing one of those big mothers around the pattern like you've been doing it all your life. C'mon, let's go get some chow!"

The next several months are going to be interesting, Otto thought as he drifted into a dreamless sleep.

***

Otto yawned and looked around at the briefing room. He was used to rising early, but the trip and unfamiliar bed seemed to have made him sleepy. He glanced around at the other pilots assembled for an initial briefing from Rackham. Some of them looked familiar, but he didn't recognize most of them. At that moment, Bob Donovan walked in wearing captain's insignia. He didn't see Otto at first but rushed over when he caught sight of him. "Otto! How are you, bud? So good to see you!" Otto half rose to greet him and they embraced briefly.

"Bob! How have you been? Wow! Imagine us meeting like this! Who would have thought it?"

Otto became aware that someone was standing on the small stage at the front of the room. Rackham had come in as he and Donovan were embracing. The rest of the room was standing at attention. Otto and Bob quickly snapped to.

Rackham motioned them down. "At ease, men. Be seated. On behalf of the Strategic Air Command, I want to welcome you to the Forty-First Bomber Training Command. Each of you has been selected by me personally for a task which has been deemed essential to national security. You will be learning the ins and outs of the Boeing B-29 Superfortress. Pilots with wartime experience flying the '29 already have been assigned to combat squadrons and will be given their missions. You fellows will eventually, sooner than later, be instructing green pilots yourselves. You're all excellent aviators who can fly the wings off anything in the sky and have a knack for teaching. I'll turn you over to Colonel Marshall, who will brief you on the first day's activities. Good luck and good flying!"

Marshall, a short, dark fellow in an immaculately pressed uniform, pulled down a screen at the front of the room. "We're going to see a short orientation film about the B-29. You will want to take notes."

Well, no BS about you, fella, Otto thought. Let's cut right to the chase. He pulled out his notebook and began writing rapidly.

# Chapter 12
# On the Flight Line
# April 1949

*My dearest Betty,*

*Today I got to fly a B-29! After three weeks of ground school and orientation, they actually put us in one. Of course, an instructor pilot and a standby pilot sat in the jump seat. Four of us trainees (that's a funny word to use to describe those who have five thousand hours in command of an aircraft, but that's what they call us) took turns as co-pilot. Our pilot, Jim Foster, put us through our paces, demonstrating the best way to do each maneuver. The '29 is a beast with incredible power and is so much more comfortable than the Fort. We fly in shirt sleeves since the cabin is pressurized, and the ride is smooth and comfortable. We are way above most weather, and Nebraska this time of year is beautiful, although we soon will be getting into tornado season.*

*The procedures for the '29 are different. I don't mean to worry you, but the aircraft is prone to engine fires. There are ways of dealing with them and they work very well. Each engine has a fire-suppression unit that we can trigger and put out fires. Unlike pilots in the Pacific, like Jim, who flew forty missions over the ocean to Japan, we are over land with plenty of fields to put down on in an emergency. So far, we don't stray too far from Offutt for that very reason. We'll make longer cross-country flights, but those will come later.*

*I can't write much about our mission since it is hush-hush, but I can say that we will be training pilots for very long flights with an extremely lethal load. And should the Communists start a shooting war somewhere, I imagine our fellows will be called on to deliver conventional payloads. There are some faster bombers in the works, but I can't say much about that here either.*

*Well, time to hit the books. I thought my student days were over, but if I'm to be an instructor, I have to be the person in the aircraft who knows more about flying it than anyone on board.*

*I am your devoted husband who misses you and the twins very much. Hope to get home in May. Will write more tomorrow.*

*All my love,*

*Otto*

\*\*\*

Otto grabbed the throttles on the console and pulled them back. "That's it," Jim said. "Nice and easy. Glide slope looks good. I'm pulling on a few more degrees of flaps. Remember, you're not in a taildragger."

Otto had come in nose high the first few times he had attempted landings. Jim was sitting in the right-hand seat with his hands resting lightly on the wheel. He pushed the nose down as the main gear made contact. Otto remembered, wincing. "Sorry, Jim."

"No problem," Jim returned. "Just don't do it that way again. Go ahead and stop her and we'll go around and try it again."

This time, Otto brought the big bomber in slightly nose up and the main gear kissed the tarmac, followed by the nosewheel. He pulled the throttles back and lightly tapped the brakes. "Bellisima!" Jim exclaimed, kissing the fingertips of his right hand like an Italian chef. "That was one primo touchdown! You touch those brakes like you're paying for the pads."

"Well, I do run an airline, and I do pay for those pads."

Jim laughed. "Good landing is what I'm trying to say. Now let's taxi in and we'll get out and let you take 'er up for a turn around the pattern."

"Thanks, Boss," Otto said. He thought, Wow, time to solo already. Hope I'm prepared.

They reached the hard stand and Jim undid his harness. "Donovan, you fly co-pilot. I understand you fellows knew each other in the Eighth."

"Yep," Donovan said, sliding into the right seat. "I was the OK Kid's co-pilot then as well."

Jim looked at Otto. "The 'OK Kid,' huh? I get it. Well, we'll switch off after OK makes a couple of rounds, and then you can play pilot."

Donovan grinned as Jim exited the cockpit. The two other trainees stayed on board. "Just like old times," Donovan remarked. "Let's do this." Otto and Donovan cleared the area around the aircraft and taxied out to the end of the runway. They held there, checking the gauges that told them the condition of the four Wright Duplex Cyclones that were roaring outside the cockpit windows. Otto advanced the throttles and released the brakes. The B-29 began its takeoff roll.

To minimize the possibility of an engine (or two or three) catching fire, they had been instructed to climb out slowly, gaining altitude gradually to minimize the strain on the engines. The sooner they reached cruising speed, the sooner the engines were able have a greater airflow and not run as hot. This practice was contrary to Otto's experience, where he had learned to gain as much altitude as he could as quickly as he could to give himself more time and height to react to any engine problem. Of course, if the slow, flat climb was to avoid an engine fire, that trade-off made sense.

They climbed out in a nearly flat ascent, reaching operational altitude after about twenty minutes. Bob leaned out the engines and they described a large "racetrack" shape in the sky. After a couple of laps, Bob took the wheel for the descent. Otto took it back for the cross leg and turned on the downwind leg and then the base leg. The big ship lowered toward the runway, and Otto planted it right on the numbers of runway thirty. They rolled out with Bob handling the throttles and Otto lightly riding the brakes. They taxied up to the hangar.

Jim came out to the cockpit window as Bob cut the engines to idle. "Your turn, Donovan! Let Smith fly co-pilot. A couple of times around and then bring her back and we'll see what happens next!"

Bob moved over to where Otto had been sitting and set off back down the taxiway. The Superfort rolled out and climbed out into the bright blue Nebraska sky. Otto sat in the jump seat and smiled.

# Chapter 13
# Building Time
# May 1949

Otto and Bob were forty thousand feet up somewhere over Kansas. Otto keyed his mic and called, "Pilot to navigator."

"Yessir," came the answer from Second Lieutenant Johnston, who looked as if he had finished high school a couple of weeks ago. Maybe he had, Otto thought, although he knew Johnston had been in navigators' school for the past six months.

"Where are we, Lieutenant?"

"Sir, we're over Topeka."

"Good. Give us a course back to base."

"I'm on it, sir."

"Pilot out."

"Roger that, sir."

"Johnston, you're a young guy, but don't say 'Roger.' It gets confusing if there's a Roger in the crew. Say 'Navigator out.'"

"Yessir! Navigator out."

Otto smiled slightly. Well, Johnston seemed to learn quickly enough. Maybe. Habits were hard to break. He would have to see.

He and Bob were building time and ferrying the new crop of navigators around to give them practice. Otto hoped they were practiced enough because he did not want to end up in Chicago the way a crew did a month ago. The kids seemed to be trained fairly well, though, and no one had gotten badly lost for a couple of weeks. Of course, they would soon start night flights, and that was a whole new ball game.

Donovan horsed the big aircraft around in a one-eighty and straightened it out. They were on a track directly for Offutt, which lay about an hour away. Otto scanned the skies for traffic. They were under radar control from Omaha, but it didn't hurt to be careful. A mid-air was not a pretty thing. Huh, he thought. That's the understatement of the year.

"What are you going to do after we graduate?" Donovan asked. The ceremony was scheduled at the end of June. Then they would be able to instruct green pilots. Otto supposed they were about ready. It had been a challenge, but they had good instructors and a good instructional program. More than anything, he would be glad to have a week after graduation to go home and see his family.

I'm going to go home and spend the week with Betty and the girls. How about you?"

"I'll go back to Chicago and spend the time with Frances." Bob and his wife did not have any children. "We'll go visit her mother in Minneapolis. She's not well and Frances is worried about her."

"Hey, give me a call when you get there and I'll come down and see you both."

"You got a deal, Captain."

"All right, Captain." They both laughed.

The navigational-training flight bore on through the warm afternoon. Otto never ceased to be amazed at what he could see from this altitude. Farms and highways and even cars moving along them were clearly visible. Lakes and dams and rivers slid into view and then passed back under their wings. Twenty miles out, Otto cut the engines back and started his descent into Offutt. The tower cleared them in for a straight approach.

As they descended through twenty thousand feet, Donovan said suddenly, "Number three's temperature is climbing."

Otto looked at the inboard starboard engine. He couldn't tell any difference from how it looked, but he'd have to act fast to avoid a fire.

He keyed his radio mic. "Offutt Tower, this is Gray Goose Six declaring an emergency. We have an engine that's starting to overheat. I'm shutting it down and feathering the prop. Please have the crash trucks standing by. Gray Goose Six."

In his headphones he heard, "Gray Goose Six, Offutt Tower. Understand you have an engine overheat. Will have crash equipment out to meet you. You are still cleared straight in, runway twenty-one-L. Good luck. Tower out."

"Goose Six out."

Bob was working the engine controls. "Crap!" he exclaimed. "The prop won't feather!"

Otto looked over. Without the prop feathered, the engine would create drag on the starboard side of the aircraft, making it more difficult to control. Worse yet, the spinning prop would continue to draw fuel into the engine, increasing the chance of fire. That they didn't need, Otto knew.

Just then Bob called, "Engine overheat! It's gonna ignite!" They had seen the films in training of engines on fire, and knew that it was a bad situation. Of course, those films were made by crews who made it back to base. The ones in which the engine fire burned through the wing did not bring back any film or anything else, including themselves.

"There it goes!" Bob exclaimed. Otto had the controls wrenched over to port to compensate for the added drag on the starboard side.

"Fire the bottles!" Otto said calmly, and Bob punched the fire-suppression button for the number three engine. The engine was now fully engulfed, and Otto looked over quickly to see the white foam billow out over the nacelle. The prop was still spinning.

The foam blew away but flames still licked at the joint between the nacelle and the wing. Otto had a dilemma: he needed to get on the ground, and fast, but a higher speed would fan the flames. They were at five thousand, sinking rapidly and boring straight for the center line. Otto decided to push it and jammed the throttles to military power and then clamped his hand back on the wheel. The '29 juddered and shook. Bob also had the controls in a death grip.

The tower broke in. "Goose Six, say your status."

"We have a fire. We're coming in. Busy now. Goose out." Otto saw the field approaching rapidly. The fire continued to grow. Bob looked out the window. "It's getting worse," he intoned.

Otto nodded grimly and flew the '29 down to the runway. They touched down hard, with the shocks on the gear compressing and then springing the fuselage up. Bob slammed the throttles back, and Otto stood on the brakes, pads be damned. The big bird decelerated precipitously. Crash trucks sped in from their port side, lights flashing and, Otto assumed, sirens screaming, although they could not hear them. The bomber continued to slow, and when it neared a stop, Bob unbelted and opened a hatch in the floor. The aircraft bumped to a stop; Otto killed the engines. The other trainees jumped through the hatch and then he and Bob dropped down through the nosewheel compartment and onto the runway. They ran away from the stricken aircraft, whose right wing was now blazing away.

The crash trucks roared up and began spraying foam on the fire. Otto saw that they would have it under control in a matter of minutes. He and Bob and the trainees stopped at the edge of the runway. An ambulance screeched to a stop. Two young corpsmen jumped out.

"Are you all right, sirs?" one asked breathlessly.

"Yes, we're fine, son," Otto answered. "We're going to need a new aircraft, though. Can you give us a ride back to the ops building?"

Black smoke continued to billow from the right wing, but the fire was diminishing. The crew of the burning aircraft got out of the ambulance and walked into the ops building.

Rackham was there to greet them. He pounded them on the backs. "Well done, men! What a fine piece of flying! I thought you were going to break the gear off when you slammed that thing onto the runway! But you brought it back, and, more importantly, you brought yourselves back! Outstanding!"

"Thank you, General," Otto murmured. "Can we have something to drink?"

Rackham threw back his head and laughed loudly. "So you still drink after a hard mission, eh, Kerchner? We'll take you over to the officers' club. Whatever you want is on me!"

"Thank you, sir, but I just want some water."

Rackham laughed again. "Water! You're one of a kind, Kerchner! I'll tell you that!"

# Chapter 14
# Going Home
# June 1949

Otto looked pensively out the window of Northwest Flight 500 from Omaha to Minneapolis. He was very tired. He and twenty others in their group had received their certification as instructors on the B-29 the day before, and they were given a week's leave with instructions to report back ready to go. Otto felt as if they were all up to the task. If they weren't, Rackham wouldn't hesitate to pull them from instruction and have them fly tugs for target practice. There were jobs in this man's air force and then there were jobs. He would prefer not to fly a target tug with inexperienced gunners shooting at it, even if there was a long cable connecting the target to the tug. He'd never heard of a tow plane shot down by green gunners, but the odds would say it happened at least once. The army probably didn't publicize it widely if it did happen.

The green fields of the Midwest slipped by beneath the wings of the Martin 202. The aircraft was being touted as a replacement for the DC-3, but Otto was not impressed. Something about the way the aircraft handled bothered him. Or maybe it wasn't the aircraft but the pilot. Easy to second-guess when someone you didn't know was flying. Otto had on his air force uniform with the new major's gold leaves on his shoulders. He had thought of wearing his M & M pilot's uniform but didn't want to call more attention to himself on the Northwest flight.

He could hardly wait to get home and see Betty and the girls. Three months was a long time to be away from them, and he didn't know how long his instructing post would last. Not long, he hoped. He knew they were growing up fast in his absence. They'd be a year old soon.

The pilot came on and announced their descent into Minneapolis. Otto tightened his seat belt and looked around the cabin. It was nearly full, which was good news for the airlines. If Flight 500 was on time, he should be able to catch the noon M & M flight to Pioneer Lake. He wondered who would be flying that leg. Probably Jimmy, or maybe Bob. He would see.

The aircraft slid down the approach slope and bounced twice on landing. Otto frowned. If he'd been instructing, he would have made the pilot go around and shoot about five more landings until he showed he could get it right. No sense in shaking up the paying customers. He shook his head. The plane ran down the runway, slowing to a walk and then turning onto the taxiway. They reached the terminal, and Otto let the other passengers deplane ahead of him. He had plenty of time to make it to the gates that M & M used, and he might even have time for lunch.

He made his way down the steps that had been rolled up to the Northwest Martin and went through the double doors into the terminal building. Crowds of travelers surged this way and that, and it was with great difficulty that Otto made his way to the snack bar where he and Jimmy had eaten lunch three years before. So much had changed during that time. It didn't seem possible that it had, but the airline had grown, Mata and Pete had gotten married, he and Betty had welcomed twins, Pete had been blinded, and Otto had been called to active duty. And he thought he would lead a calm life after coming home from the war. He guessed that wasn't in the cards.

Otto stepped up to the counter. A young fellow he had never seen before looked at him. "What'll it be, Major Kerchner?"

Reading the name tag off the worker's uniform, Otto answered, "I'll have a cheeseburger with fries and a Coke, Steve. How do you know my name?"

"My brother worked here before me until he went to UM. He talked about seeing you about once a day for the past several years."

And I am a distinctive-looking fellow, Otto thought. "Thank you, Steve. And say hello to Jerry for me." He turned away and looked for a place to sit and found one at a two-person table. He sat and watched the people pass by. A Northwest captain came to the other seat. "Mind if I sit here, Major?"

"Not at all, Captain," Otto returned. "How's flying?"

"We're full up," the captain mused. "Say, you wouldn't happen to be Captain Kerchner of M & M Airlines, would you?"

Otto nodded. "One and the same." The Northwest captain extended his hand.

"I'm Fred Roberts. Pleased to meet you. I've heard so much about you and your service in the war. I also hear your operation is going well."

"We're paying the bills. I've been in Omaha getting ready to instruct on the B-29."

Roberts looked down briefly. "I've heard about that. I take it that's why you're wearing the air force uniform and you're a major."

Otto laughed lightly. "Yes, but I'm still a captain with M & M."

Otto's food came, and he waited to see if Roberts' food would also show up. Roberts motioned to the burger and fries. "Go ahead and eat. I know you want to make your connecting flight."

Otto looked over his shoulder. "Yours is coming now; we can eat at the same time." The waitress placed Roberts' order at this place. His meal was exactly the same as Otto's. They both tore into their burgers.

"So, Captain or Major Kerchner, you might be interested to know that Northwest is working to acquire some smaller airlines to expand our service into smaller airports."

"Really?" Otto asked. He did not concern himself with the larger business picture with the industry. Mata kept an eye on that for them.

"Yeah. We might be interested in buying M & M. Don't know if you'd be interested in selling. We'd keep the name and operate it as a subsidiary of Northwest. We'd hire all your personnel and take over the upkeep on the aircraft. The livery would stay the same. Anyhow, just a heads-up for you."

Otto took a sip of his drink. "Thank you. I'll talk to my manager about it and have her call the people at Northwest. I appreciate the info."

"Your manager's a woman?"

"Yep," Otto said. "She's also my sister."

"Well, who knew?" They had both finished their meals and stood up at the same time to let some other people use their seats. Roberts extended his hand again. "Pleasure to meet you, Major. Good luck and smooth landings to you."

Otto shook his hand firmly. "And to you, Captain. Take care."

They turned and went in opposite directions. Otto made his way to the M & M gate, where he could see Flight 422 had come in and was waiting out its turnaround before it would become Flight 423 to Pioneer Lake. He had half an hour to wait before boarding, so he had a seat in one of the chairs at the gate.

Shortly, Jimmy, Bob, and Jenny came through the crowd. Otto stood up and waved. They came over, all talking at once. "Otto! So good to see you! How are you? We heard you'd be riding with us!" Jimmy and Bob shook his hand while Jenny gave him a big hug.

"Well, I'm glad to see you," he told them. "How are you all doing?"

"Fine," they answered in unison. "Want to come help us preflight the aircraft?"

"If I remember how," Otto told them. "It's been a while, and I'm used to four engines."

"Oh, I think you'll figure it out," Jimmy laughed. "Let's get on board, Boss."

He followed the crew out to the waiting DC-3 and followed the pilots on their walk-around. Jenny went into the cabin to do her preparation work. The three pilots finished and climbed up the familiar stairs to the cabin. He let Jimmy and Bob go ahead to the cockpit. Jenny was in the back checking the refreshments. The two pilots settled into their seats and belted in. Otto took the jump seat. The cockpit looked small compared to that of the B-29, and the distinct slant of the floor struck him since he had become accustomed to the level floor of the Superfort. Jimmy and Bob ran through their prestart checklist. Otto could feel the fuselage shaking as passengers began boarding. Jenny would settle them in their seats.

After a few minutes, she knocked on the cockpit door. "We're ready to go," she told them and then closed the door and went back into the cabin.

"All right, gentlemen," Jimmy announced, "Let's get this show on the road. Major, would you help us look out for traffic on the taxiway?"

"Of course, Captain. It would be my pleasure." Jimmy flipped switches and turned knobs as Bob read the start checklist. The twin Wright Cyclones turned over, puffed white smoke and then caught, settling to a smooth roar. A tug pushed them back from the gate, and they set out along the taxiway. Otto and Bob looked left and right for other aircraft. The DC-3 turned onto the end of the runway and held. Jimmy pressed a hand to his headphones, evidently receiving clearance. Otto was not plugged in, so he could not hear the tower.

Jimmy nodded, released the brakes, and advanced the throttles. The silver, blue, and white bird sped along the runway and lifted into the clear blue June sky, headed for Pioneer Lake and home. At last, Otto thought. Coming home at last.

# Chapter 15
# A Week in the Life
# June 1949

"Otto!" Betty called. "I need help!"

Otto put down his paper and went into the girls' room, where Betty was changing diapers on both girls, or attempting to. She looked around to see him come in. "Here, you take Maria and I'll take Marion." She was holding Marion on the changing table while Maria toddled around the room.

"I don't know how to change a diaper," Otto muttered.

"Would you like to learn, mister?"

"Frankly, no," Otto said.

Betty sighed. "Well, let me do this one and then I'll fix Maria. Honestly, Otto, it's not that hard."

"I don't have the necessary skills."

Betty snorted, cleaned Marion up, got out a fresh diaper, folded and pinned it with an expert hand, and put her on the floor. Otto carried Maria over to her. Betty quickly changed her diaper and put her down. Both girls ran to Otto, holding up their arms to be held. He picked them up and kissed them both.

Betty pushed her hair back from her face. "Honestly, Otto, I think you have no idea of what's involved keeping up with these girls."

"I help as much as I can."

"Yes, you're here to play with them, but you're not here enough when they're wet or sick or tired or cranky. You get to be with them when they are their best."

"I have to make a living, Betty."

"You didn't have to run off to play with your big-boy toys in Omaha."

"That's my duty to the country. I go when I'm called."

"Well, yes, and I'm stuck here."

"I'm sorry, Betty. We do what we have to do. Don't you get help from Mata and your mother?"

"Mata is busy helping Pete adjust to a condition caused by your precious airline. And my mom has her own life. They've been good to help me as much as they can, but they can only do so much. It all falls on me, and I'm sick of it!" She dissolved into tears.

Otto put the girls down and went over to her. He held her until she stopped crying. "I don't want you to feel like this. We can get you some help, a nurse to come in or a sitter. We can afford it. Would that help?"

She looked up at him. "What I really want is to have you here again. It's hard without you, and soon you'll go off again and who knows for how long?"

Otto chewed his lower lip. "You and the girls could join me on the base. There's plenty of housing. It would be an adventure for all of us. I'll likely be there for a year, and would have some leave, but not enough to be around very much."

"I . . . I think that would work."

Otto kissed her. "All right, then, I'll set it up when I get back and send for you as soon as I can. I'm sure Susan and Jenny would be delighted to house sit for us. All right, my love?"

Betty nodded. "Yes, yes."

\*\*\*

Betty stood with Otto in front of the small, cheaply-built house on a treeless street with dozens of other identical houses as far as she could see. The girls tugged at her hands.

"So this is it?" she said to Otto.

"Yes, this is a family housing unit."

"Otto, there's no *grass*! There are no *trees*! Does this place even have a *school?*"

"There's a school, and grass and trees are scheduled for planting soon."

"In the meantime, I'll have to do laundry all the time to keep up with the dirt."

"I'm sorry, Betty. At least this way we can be together."

"When I became your wife I didn't sign up to become a military wife."

"It's temporary," Otto said and picked up their suitcases and took them to the front door. Betty and the girls trailed behind. Otto fished in his pocket for a key and used it to open the door. They went inside.

"Uh, I have to get over to the office," Otto mumbled. "Maybe you can set things up."

Betty looked around as if she smelled something bad. She sniffed. "I'll do my best. Otto"—she placed her hand on his arm—"I'm sorry to complain so much. This is just totally different from anything I've ever done."

He kissed her. "I know, dear. It'll work out. I'll be back as soon as I can." He went back to the car and drove off to the ops building.

He parked in front of the two-story structure and walked through the double doors. Rackham's aide was seated at a desk with a stack of large envelopes in front of him. "Good afternoon, Major Kerchner. Did you have a good leave?"

"Yes, thank you," Otto told him. "You have my schedule?"

The corporal handed him one of the envelopes. "Here you are. Briefing here tomorrow at zero seven hundred hours. General Rackham will be conducting it himself. Then you get to go flying with some new pilots."

"I can hardly wait," Otto returned. The doors opened and Bob Donovan came in.

"Otto!" he called. "How are you?"

"I'm good, Bob. How are you?"

"Good. Glad to be back. Anything different?"

"I brought the family with me."

"I want to meet them. Is Betty happy to be here?"

"Actually, no. It's a big change for her and she has care of the girls constantly."

Bob pulled a face. "Well, maybe she can meet some people and it won't be so bad."

"I'm sorry we didn't get to see you while you were in Minneapolis."

"Yeah, well, as I told you when I called, Frances' mom was in the hospital, so that wouldn't have been a good situation for visiting."

"I understand. How's her mom doing?"

"She's better but is still in the hospital. We hope she'll get out this week. Frances' dad died in an accident a couple of years ago, so her mother might have to come live with us. We'll see."

"I hope she's much better soon."

"Thanks, man. Catch you on the flight line."

"All right," Otto told him. "See you tomorrow."

He took his envelope and went out into the June heat. This should be a very different experience, he thought, but then he had been having different experiences the past several years. He got into his car and drove back toward their new home. He was hoping for the best.

# Chapter 16
# Back on the Flight Line
# June 1949

Otto was used to rising early, so getting up at 5:00 AM posed no problem for him. The girls had come and gotten in bed with them. Normally Betty would have taken them back to their cribs but she figured they were in an unfamiliar place and wanted to be with their parents. Betty didn't sleep as well as Otto did, so she was still sleeping soundly when he arose. He dressed in his flight suit and made his way to the kitchen to scramble a couple of eggs, fry some bacon, and put the coffee pot on the burner to perk. He made toast on the griddle beside the eggs and made a mental note to have Betty buy some orange juice at the post exchange later that day. They had brought some staples from home but not everything they would need.

He put his food on a plate and poured some coffee and was sitting at the table as Betty came into the kitchen yawning, tying her bathrobe around her. "Good morning," she said. "Looks like you're off to fly."

"Yes, ma'am, I am," Otto murmured as he stood up to kiss her. They both sat down. "Would you like some coffee?"

"I'd love some," Betty answered. "That would be great." She smiled at him.

Otto took a cup from the box they had packed with some plates and other kitchenware. He poured the steaming liquid into the cup and put it in front of Betty with a spoon and the sugar bowl. "Sorry, no cream. Can you go to the PX and get some and also some orange juice?"

"I've been making a list in my head. I'll need the car to go shopping."

"There's a bus I can catch," Otto told her. He looked at his watch. "Oops. I'd better get going. Don't want to be late the first day of my new job. He bent over and kissed her. "I instruct Monday through Friday from zero seven hundred to fifteen hundred hours. We'll do something special Friday night."

"What will we do with the girls?"

"If there's a drive-in, we'll take them along. They can fall asleep in the back seat. Or I can ask some of the other guys if they have daughters who babysit. We'll work it out. Gotta go, kiddo. See you later!"

Betty waved as he went out the door. Otto walked two blocks over to the base bus stop. One bus made a more or less continuous loop around the clock about every half hour. The work and business of a major base went on around the clock, twenty-four hours a day, seven days a week, three hundred sixty-five days a year. He hit the bus schedule exactly right, as one pulled up just as he reached the stop. It was just a ten-minute ride to the ops building, so he was there nearly an hour early. He'd coordinate his schedule with the bus better so he wasn't there so early in the future. Still, it didn't hurt to be early the first day on the job.

He walked through the doors of the ops center where he had been the day before. A corporal directed him to the entrance to the auditorium, where he saw seven or eight instructors and what must have been about ten pilot candidates scattered about. He settled down in a seat and in less than ten minutes, Bob Donovan eased into the seat beside him. "Hey, Major OK," he breathed in a sleepy voice. "Fancy meeting you here."

Otto grunted. "Yep, I like to come here early and often."

Donovan looked around. "Sure could use another cup of coffee. Did you see any on the way in?"

"Nah." Otto shook his head. "I'm not sure the swill they serve here qualifies as coffee anyhow."

"If it's hot and it's black it meets my standards," Donovan returned. He got up. "I'm going to see if I can scout up some hot, black swill."

Otto waved one hand as Donovan moved quickly up the aisle. The auditorium began to fill rapidly. Otto recognized the other instructors dressed in flight suits and appearing much more relaxed than the trainees, who were in fatigues and looked anxious. They had just finished ground school the Friday before and were about to get their hands on some big iron. Otto hoped they were ready. He hoped he was ready, but somehow he thought he was.

Donovan came back with two mugs of coffee and gave one to Otto. "Best I could do, Major. Drink up."

Just then General Rackham strode onto the stage. It was the same gait he used for briefings back at Polebrook—confident, with just a bit of swagger. Rackham flew lead every so often. Otto couldn't think of a leader more respected by his men. Eisenhower, maybe.

The airmen jumped to attention. Rackham motioned them down. "Be seated, men!" he boomed. "I want to welcome you to orientation for Class 49-6 of the Forty-First Heavy-Bomber Training Command. We're going to teach you to fly the B-29 so you can take the fight to the Ruskis if they want one. And if they do, they'll get one. You'll be learning all aspects of the Superfort, and you'll be instructed by some of finest flyers in the world. I handpicked them for this job, so you listen to them and do what they tell you. Your life and the lives of everyone on your aircraft will depend on it. Welcome to our little summer camp. Learn a lot, listen hard, practice hard, and get ready to kick some Russian ass!"

Rackham's speech was greeted with cheers and applause. "All right," he said when the uproar had died down. "I'll turn it over to Colonel Burns for the nuts and bolts. Good luck, men, and good flying. My door is always open to you." He snapped off a salute and the room jumped to attention once again as he strode off stage. There goes a leader, Otto thought.

Burns took over the briefing, which was mostly for the benefit of the candidates. Otto's mind wandered. He wondered how Betty was getting along and hoped her day was going well. He would find out this evening. Burns finished the briefing and the assembled airmen rose and made their way outside to waiting buses, which would take them to the flight line. It was getting hotter by the moment. That would mean longer takeoff runs and more attention to engine temperatures. Not that they didn't pay close attention to those anyhow, especially after their experience with the navigation flight.

Otto and Donovan took adjoining seats on the first bus. The instructors got on buses together, while the candidates took those further down the line. Rank has its privileges, Otto thought. After a short drive, the buses pulled up to the familiar flight line. Ten B-29s were parked in a line. "Look at that!" Otto exclaimed. "They've painted the tails orange."

"Yeah," mused Donovan. "That means 'student driver—stay far away!'"

Otto laughed. He and Donovan jumped out of the bus and made their way to the number three bomber. Otto was lead pilot and Donovan would ride the jump seat as an auxiliary pilot if he were needed. They would have four candidates who would take turns learning the aircraft from the co-pilot's seat.

Otto took a clipboard from the crew chief and signed off on the bomber. Their four students walked up. They stopped and saluted. Otto and Donovan shook hands all around, exchanging names. The candidates looked very young and very concerned, although they were not much younger than Otto and Bob. "Welcome to heavy-bomber training," Otto told them. "We'll work with you to get you up to speed on the Superfort. Be sure to ask any questions that occur to you, and don't hesitate to sound off if you see something that doesn't look right. Clear?"

The four men mumbled their assent. "Sir," one named Olson said. "I've read about what you did during the war. It's a pleasure to meet you, sir."

"Well, no autographs today," Otto told him. "We're here to fly. Let's start with a walk-around."

He led the group around the Boeing, pointing out what they needed to be aware of. "The ground crew has been all over this aircraft for hours, but its condition and operation are *your* responsibility. Never forget that." With their walk-around concluded, they climbed one by one through the crew hatch near the nose. Otto settled into the left seat, Donovan took the jump seat, Olson climbed into the right seat, and the three others sat in seats behind the flight deck.

Otto opened his window and indicated startup to the crewman. The corporal nodded and unplugged some cables from the fuselage. "We'll run the prestart checklist," he told Olson. "You read it off and watch what I do."

"Yessir," Olson stuttered. "First item is 'fuel boost pumps ON.'"

Otto threw a switch on the left side of the panel. "Boost pumps ON!" And so his first day as a heavy-bomber instructor began. "Number one START." The four huge engines started with a roar, one after another. Otto taxied them to the end of runway nine, held until he heard the clearance call come through, advanced the throttles, and released the brakes. Training aircraft number six forty-nine three, call sign Mother Goose Three, rolled down the runway and lifted into a cloudy sky.

# Chapter 17
# A Letter to Mata
# August 1949

*Dear Mata,*

*This is like during the war when I wrote you from wherever I was. I hope you and Pete are doing well. We are here. Betty and the girls are settled and have made some friends. I'm about to finish instructing my first group of pilot candidates, and they've learned quickly. I think they'll be all right. I feel as if I'm making a real contribution to our defense, regardless of where a threat comes from.*

*The bombers we're flying are B-29s, like the ones that dropped the atomic bombs on Japan to end the war. They're bigger and more powerful than the B-17 I flew in Europe and easier to fly, in one sense, although I do have to keep on my toes.*

*The base here is HUGE. I forget how many acres it covers, but there are all kinds of operations groups. We're just one, involved with training new heavy-bomber pilots. I'm not sure specifically what the other operations are, but there's something going on here around the clock.*

*The base has a lot of amenities, including stores, a social hall, a movie theater, a chapel, and a hospital. It's like a small self-contained city with its own water supply. We're not that far from Omaha if we want to go out someplace special, but mostly we stay on base. There's plenty to do with barbeques, baseball games, card nights, and dances. This weekend we're having a World War II hangar dance, just like we had during the war. The fellow who took over for Glenn Miller is bringing his band to play. We're looking forward to it. We haven't "cut a rug" for quite a while!*

*I hope the airline is doing well in Pete's and Jimmy's and your capable hands. That's great that Pete is learning Braille and you are learning it with him. That's my sister!*

*I like your sketches for the new livery for M & M. We could use an update using the same colors, but that's just what you did. Maybe you should go into the design business! I don't know when you would have time, with Pete to take care of and the airline to run. We'll talk about it when we visit next week. I have a week's leave at the end of this training cycle and then come back for another six-week stint and so forth until we run out of trainees. Scuttlebutt is that we'll run right up to next June, depending what the Russians do. A year plus will be enough for me. I'm glad to do my duty and will be even gladder to get back home. I know you miss seeing your nieces, and they ask about Aunt Mata and Uncle Pete every day. I think Betty took some pictures of them and had them developed, so I'll get some copies and send them along to you.*

*That's about all for now. Please take care and we look forward to seeing you next week. We should be able to fly out early Saturday and be home on the 2:00 PM.*

*Your brother,*

*Otto*

\*\*\*

Otto sat in the jump seat behind Olson, who was making what he and Otto hoped would be his final qualifying landing with an instructor on the aircraft. Olson was about as ready as he was going to be, Otto thought. They were descending through one thousand feet. Olson's co-pilot, a kid named Jones, was calling out altitude.

Nine hundred feet. Looking good, Otto thought. He wondered idly what they were having for dinner.

"Gear down," Jones called, and toggled the gear switch. "We have three ge—no we don't. Nose gear is showing red."

Otto didn't speak. He wanted to see how the crew handled this problem.

"Cycle the switches," Olson said. Right response.

"Cycling," Jones muttered. "No dice."

"Declaring an emergency," Olson said tersely. He keyed his radio mic, "Offutt Tower, this is Mother Goose Three declaring an emergency."

"Understood, Goose Three." Otto heard the tower in his headphones. "Say the nature of your emergency and fuel on board."

"We have a stuck nose gear and about thirty minutes to bingo fuel."

"Roger, stuck nose and thirty minutes to bingo. Stand by."

The tower came back almost immediately. "Goose Three, you are cleared to circle in the standard pattern while we get this little glitch fixed."

"Roger, Tower. Goose Three climbing." Olson said into his mic. Then he called, "Gear up; ascending to one thousand feet." Jones punched the gear switches as Olson advanced the throttles and pulled back on the column. The engines roared, and the ship accelerated as she climbed. Otto still sat quietly. They were doing all the right things. His job was to observe and not to interfere unless they did something really stupid or dangerous. The worst thing they could do was panic, and he didn't see any tendency to do that with either flyer.

Olson pulled the bomber into a climbing turn to intersect with the traffic pattern. All other aircraft were holding at different altitudes, staying out of Three's way. Jones threw the gear switches to "down." No luck. He tried the EMERGENCY position on the switches. Still nothing. "Franck, would you check the fuse for the nose?"

"Sure thing," the third of four trainees in the aircraft answered. The fuse for the nose gear was located at the top of the wheel well. Franck left to climb down from the bombardier's station to the fuse location. He was back in half a minute. Goose Three droned on.

"Fuse is burned out," he reported.

"All right," Olson said, "Get out the crank. Franck, you're elected."

The second lieutenant unclipped a long piece of metal from the co-pilot's armor plate stanchion, pried up a plug in the floor, put the crank in the socket and started turning.

"Does anyone remember how many turns?" Franck.

Olson spoke over his shoulder. "Two hundred fifty-three."

Franck kept cranking, counting under his breath.

"You don't have to count," Jones said. "The light will tell us when the gear is down."

Otto looked on approvingly. The crew had it all memorized and figured out.

The Superfort continued on its huge "racetrack" pattern in the clear sky. Otto could see other aircraft keeping their distance, waiting their turn to land. They'd have to get the gear down quickly because everyone in the ten-airplane training unit had about the same amount of fuel left, about twenty-five minutes' worth now. He checked his watch.

As they passed parallel to the runway, he could see the crash trucks standing by. He had a brief flashback to the horrible day Pete had been blinded and quickly discarded it. He needed to concentrate on what was going on.

"Offutt Tower, Goose Three," Olson said into the mic.

"Offutt here. Go ahead, Three."

"We're cranking the nose manually. Should have it down in a couple of minutes. Will advise when it's down and locked. Goose Three."

"Roger that, Goose Three. Offutt standing by."

The five men on the flight deck flew in silence for about two minutes. Jones looked at the gear panel. "Bingo!" he exclaimed. "Three green lights."

Olson reached for the mic. "Offutt Tower, Goose Three, we have three good gears. Over."

"Goose Three, Offutt Tower. Roger that. You are cleared for landing, runway niner left. Over."

"Understand cleared to land, niner left. Thank you, Tower. Over."

"We didn't do anything, Three. Happy landing. Tower over and out."

Olson turned on the base leg, descending sharply, then continued on to the final approach. He called out flaps settings, which Jones pulled in. Olson trimmed the throttles back and the big Boeing settled smoothly onto the runway, rolling out to the second taxiway.

"Landed a little long," Otto said, "But a good landing nonetheless, considering the circumstances."

Olson trundled the big bomber down the taxiway. "Major, have you ever had to land with a gear up?" he asked Otto.

"Yes, I did. It didn't work out very well."

"What happened?"

"The aircraft crashed and caught fire."

"So that's how—"

"Yes," Otto intoned. "That's how. And my brother-in-law was blinded when the DC-3 he was flying crashed when he had to land with a gear stuck in the retracted position."

"Wow. I guess we were lucky," Olson said.

"Lucky and well-prepared," Otto observed. "You've studied and trained hard for six weeks. Today it paid off. As soon as the ground crew replaces the fuse on the nosewheel, take her up. Jones is your co-pilot. Smith will ride jump as a third set of eyes and hands. Take a couple of circuits around the field and after you've done that about three times, let Jones have a turn, then Smith. I'll watch from here."

"Thank you, sir."

"Don't thank me. You're earned your seat. All of you have." Olson brought the plane to a stop in front of the hangar and they climbed out as four maintenance men and a fuel truck converged on the aircraft. Otto and Donovan faced the three candidates. "Good work today, men," Otto told them.

The three stood at attention and saluted. "Yes sir," they said together. "Thank you, sir!"

"We'll be in the ops shack if you need us. Your call sign is 'Mother Goose Three.'"

"'Lone Goose Three,'" Olson repeated. "Thank you, sir."

The three candidates turned toward the bomber, while Otto and Bob headed for the ops shack. It was air conditioned, thank goodness. They went through the doors and stopped at the Coke machine on the way in. "I'm buying," Bob told Otto. "You were as cool as ice up there."

"It doesn't look good for the instructor pilot to panic and scream during an emergency. The crew followed emergency instructions to the letter, so I knew there was nothing to worry about."

"Still, you never know which way a green pilot is going to jump."

"Olson's not the jumpy kind, so I knew we were good."

"You did good work, Chief."

"You were pretty calm yourself, there, Donovan." They sat down at a small table from where they could see the flight line to drink their sodas.

"Yeah, well, maybe I was frozen with fear." They both laughed.

"Bob, don't you have any confidence in your instructing or in mine?"

"Oh, I have plenty of confidence in our instructing. It's the green pilots that worry me. They can get you killed pretty fast. So can that big silver bird out there."

"Well, there are always risks associated with flying," Otto observed.

Bob lifted his bottle high. "I'll drink to that, Boss."

Otto raised his Coke. "Hear, hear! And may all your landings be smooth ones."

"I'll drink to that, too!" And they laughed again.

As they finished their drinks, Otto and Bob could see the Superfort they had just left heading down the taxiway for takeoff. "Let's go watch our boy take off," Otto said, and they rose and went back out into the heat. They could see the entire length of the runway from in front of the ops shack. Procedure called for them to go to the tower to listen to transmissions to and from the air force's newest heavy-bomber pilot, but they didn't want to miss the takeoff from this perspective.

Lone Goose Three turned onto the active runway, facing into the wind. Even from a distance they could hear the big engines run up as Olson and Jones checked them before applying takeoff power. The engines dropped to idle for a few seconds and then climbed back in a thunderous crescendo. The aircraft shimmered in the heat waves off the tarmac and then bobbed upward briefly as the pilots released the brakes. The '29 rolled down the runway, slowly at first and then faster and faster. At just the right spot, Olson pulled back on the control column and the big bird slipped into the air. Olson held it flat to build speed at the expense of altitude as he had been taught. Otto nodded approvingly.

In a matter of seconds, the aircraft had flown out of sight, with Goose Three slowly gaining altitude. Otto and Bob went over to the tower entrance and climbed up the stairs to the control area. The two controllers nodded at them when they came in and handed each man a headset. Otto and Bob could hear the calls between the controllers and the aircraft.

"Goose Three, turning on downwind."

"Roger, Goose Three, this is Offutt Tower. Continue normal pattern and you are cleared to land. Traffic at nine o'clock high."

"Roger, Tower, we are cleared to land, and traffic is at nine o'clock high."

Otto picked up a pair of binoculars from the shelf that ran around the perimeter of the control room. From his hours in the pattern, he knew where Goose Three would be. He saw it in the field of the glasses, boring steadily on and descending slowly. It turned on the base leg of the pattern and then onto final, lowering smoothly toward the runway. It touched and rolled out to the first taxiway. Olson turned down the taxiway and moved to the runway for another takeoff and turn around the pattern.

"Looked good," Otto said to Bob.

"Yep, sure did," Bob grunted.

The silver Superfort stood at the end of the active runway for a few seconds and then was off on another turn around the circuit.

"Let's go over to the hanger to pour some champagne," Otto said.

"Yep, I got the necessary equipment," Bob told him, taking some glasses out of his flight bag. "I haven't celebrated with champagne in a long time."

"Neither have I," said Otto as they walked down the tower stairs.

"As in forever?" Bob asked him.

They crossed the tarmac to the hangars and waited in the shade for Goose Three to complete its circuits. After about half an hour, the big aircraft taxied up to the hangar and shut off its engines.

Otto had arranged with the crew chief of the airplane to cool down some champagne. The chief brought it to him, and Donovan poured seven flutes of the golden liquid. The four new pilots piled out of the '29. "I propose a toast!" Otto called.

The four came over and each took a glass.

"To the newest B-29 pilots in the air force!" Donovan said.

"TO US!" the four men answered and downed their drinks.

"Hear, hear," Otto, Donovan, and the crew chief answered, and they threw down their champagne. They shook hands all around.

As Otto and Donovan walked away from the excited group, Bob said, "A good day's work, I'd say."

"I would, too," remarked Otto. "Now for a week off. Let it begin!"

# Chapter 18
# Back Home in Pioneer Lake
# August 1949

"Otto," Betty said seriously, "We need to talk."

"When a woman says that to a man, it's never good news," Otto replied. "So what's the bad news?"

They had been home for five days on a week-long leave before the next round of instruction started for Otto back at Offutt. Betty had enjoyed being with her family and friends. It was also clear that she was not enjoying the prospect of going back to Omaha.

They sat down at the kitchen table. Maria and Marion were taking their naps. "Otto, I don't want to go back to that base with you. I want to stay here where our family and friends are."

"I can understand that," Otto said. "I know there's not much for you to do."

"Yes, and everyone's about the same age. I like being around people of all ages."

"I can try to get home on weekends. My hours are fairly regular."

"That would be good. How much longer do you think you'll have to do this?"

"Rackham says we should be caught up about next May. So, nine months more. Could be less, but I don't think it will go on any longer than that. That would be about six more training cycles. After that, SAC should have enough instructors that they won't have to use old warhorses like me."

She bent across the table and kissed him. "You're not old, my wonderful warhorse."

***

Otto found himself days later taking the bus back to Offutt. This would be Class 49-9 he would put through their paces. So far, no one had washed out. Whoever was doing the selection of pilot candidates was doing a good job. It was probably Rackham. He seemed to be a presence everywhere, although he picked the best men for the job and then stood back and let them do that job. Still, he seemed to know everything and everyone.

Otto wondered how his trainees were faring. Some of them went on for advanced training to deliver atom bombs. Others had further training in dropping conventional weapons. It wasn't clear where or when such weapons would be needed, but it was obvious that such a necessity could arise anywhere around the world. SAC was truly a global command, and its people had to be ready to go anywhere at a moment's notice. Otto was glad he got to stay in the States. Of course, that could change at any moment. As always, it was impossible to know what the future held.

Otto went by the house they had lived in to make sure everything was ready for the movers to come. They hadn't brought much, and they'd sold the furniture to another couple moving in down the street. He let himself in and looked around the quiet rooms. He couldn't say that he had a lot of good memories of this place. Betty was usually worn out and the girls were as often as not cranky and argumentative. They had gone to ball games and dances and picnics, but it didn't seem their hearts were in it. Their hearts were at home, and it was good that they were there. He missed them terribly and hoped the next few months would pass quickly. He went out, locked the door, and went over to the stop to catch the next bus for the BOQ.

# Chapter 19
# A World-Wide Reach
# April 1950

Otto dropped his bag on the bed of his quarters. The arrangement whereby he flew home Saturday morning and came back late Sunday had worked well for the past several months. Betty and the girls seemed reasonably contented by it, and now he would be embarking on what he trusted was his last training assignment. He quickly got ready for bed and slept dreamlessly until the early morning. He arose, readied himself, and caught the bus to the ops building. He expected to receive his training assignment, but instead the corporal directed him to Rackham's office. Otto wondered what was up.

He opened the door and saw about ten other instructors sitting in chairs around the room. Rackham wasn't there, but Otto was sure he would make a timely appearance. Bob waved him to an empty chair beside him.

"Hello there, amigo," he said. "Good to see you."

"Likewise, mon ami," Otto returned. "Any idea what this is about?"

"Not a clue, Major. We'll find out soon enough, I'm willing to bet."

Just then Rackham strode into the room, trailed by an aide. The men in the office sprang to attention. Rackham waved them down, as usual.

"At ease, men. I won't take a lot of your time. The brass is expecting something big in Southeast Asia somewhere. Don't know where, don't know when, don't even know who, but something's coming. Anyhow, our job is not to question why and all that shit. Here's the bottom line. We need a bunch of Superforts staged to our base at Okinawa, and you, gentlemen, have been elected to ferry them there. You'll have a briefing at the time you usually receive your assignments. Any questions?"

There were no comments as the men tried to digest the information. This was totally unexpected. They thought they would carry out one more round of instruction and then be released to go back to their lives about the middle of May. Rackham looked around the room.

"I know this is surprise and even a shock, but we need it done and we need it done *now*! If there are no questions of me, Colonel Burns will fill you in on the details." Rackham walked off the stage and through the door he had entered by.

Burns lowered a screen mounted on the wall and started going through the mission file on it. The pilots took out their notebooks and began writing the information down. Otto wrote rapidly along with the rest. He wondered with one part of his mind what Betty would have to say about this development. Plenty, he would bet, and none of it favorable. Well, maybe things would work out for the best. He would have to see.

Burns pointed to the place on the map representing Offutt. "You'll take off tomorrow at thirteen hundred GMT, zero seven hundred local. You'll stop at Fairfield Air Force Base, about sixteen hundred miles away. Estimated flight time, depending on winds, is seven hours plus or minus. You'll stay overnight and then depart at twelve hundred GMT, zero seven hundred local, for the first big leap—Hawaii, twenty-six hundred miles and about twelve hours. You'll again stay overnight and then depart Hawaii at seventeen hundred GMT, zero seven hundred local, again, for Okinawa, the big jump—fifty-five hundred miles and twenty-five hours. Obviously, each aircraft will fly with two crews, one active, one relief. Each crew will fly four hours on, with four hours off. We haven't worked out how you'll get back, but that will be in place by the time you get there. Any questions?"

The men sat silently, still digesting the news, no doubt thinking of how they would tell their families about the change in routine.

"All right," Burns said. "You have twenty-four hours to put your affairs in order. If you don't have a will, have one drawn up. The legal office is on call to facilitate that for you. Tell them you're with Operation Reach and they'll see you on a priority basis. Take clothes and effects for a week's days. It might be more; it won't be less. It'll just depend when MATS can bring you back. As the general said, this is highest priority, so we're depending on you. If there are no questions"—he hesitated and then plunged ahead—"you are dismissed."

The twenty pilots jumped to attention and saluted Burns, who returned the salute and went through the same door Rackham had used.

Otto and Donovan sat down. "What do you think?" Bob asked.

"I think this is another fine mess you've gotten us into," Otto told him.

Bob laughed. "Yep. I know. Well, I need to call Frances and tell her about the change in plans."

Otto sighed. "And I need to call Betty. I'm just imagining how happy she'll be."

"Buck up, buddy. 'We live in fame or go down in flame,' remember?"

Otto winced. "Tried that once. Didn't work out so well."

Donovan looked instantly chagrined. "Sorry, Otto, I wasn't thinking."

Otto waved his hand. "I know, it was an offhand comment. See you later." He walked out of Rackham's office and headed for the communications office to make a call to Betty on their line. He didn't have enough quarters to use a pay phone. It was official air force business, after all. As if that would impress her, he thought.

He stepped into the office and addressed the Women's Air Force corporal at the reception desk. She looked at him a little longer than was necessary.

"I'm Major Kerchner, and I need to make a long distance call to Wisconsin—official business."

The corporal handed him a clipboard. "Please fill out the top of the form. I'll call you when a line is available." Otto could see small desks behind her, each with a phone on it. No one was at any of the phones, so Otto supposed that the lines were being used elsewhere.

Otto sat down and filled out the top part of the form as instructed. Name, rank, serial number, reason for call. He wrote: "Otto Kerchner, major, 2391829, inform family of assignment." He took the clipboard, went over, and gave it to the corporal. She took it and smiled briefly at him. Otto went back to his seat and made himself as comfortable as he could. He didn't know how long this would take.

After about fifteen minutes, a private came from deeper in the office and gave a slip of paper to the corporal She looked at Otto and nodded. He went over to her desk. "Station two. First desk to the right," she told him as she indicated the desk next to hers. Not much privacy, but Otto supposed it didn't matter. It wasn't like it would be a sentimental call dripping with emotion. No such luck.

Otto lifted the receiver. "Dial zero for operator," the corporal told him. Otto did so. The operator came on the line.

"Operator," she said. "How may I help you?"

"I'd like to make a long distance call," Otto said. He gave her their number at home.

"Thank you," the operator replied. "Connecting your call."

Otto heard a series of clicks and pops and then the distant sound of a phone ringing. He hoped they got a good connection. This was not going to go easy even with one.

He heard a click as Betty picked up the receiver. Her voice was sleepy, and he had to remind himself it was about 7:45 AM. "Betty," he said quickly. "It's Otto."

"Otto! What's wrong? Why are you calling?"

"Nothing's wrong; I'm fine. I'm calling about new orders we just received."

There was a dead silence on the other end of the line.

"Betty? Are you there?"

"What new orders? Is it for another two years for you?"

"No, but we're taking some aircraft out of the country. I can't say where, but I'll be out of touch for about a week. I should be able to call you from our jumping off point."

"Is it the Middle East?"

"I can't say anything about our destination. I just wanted to let you know. We leave at seven o'clock tomorrow and I didn't want to call you too early."

There was another long silence, and then she came back on. "You go ahead and do what you have to do, Otto. You always have. I'll be here with the children."

There was a click and then the dial tone. All right, that went well, Otto thought. Or not. He put the handset down and walked back out of the comm office. He probably ought to hustle over to the legal office to see about a will. Should have done that earlier, but that was one of those things he didn't think about. He supposed that plenty of airmen thought about dying and had insurance policies, but surprisingly few had wills. He pushed his way through the pilot candidates headed for the flight line. This was going to be a busy day.

# Chapter 20
# California or Bust
# April 1950

Seated at the controls of the B-29, call sign Conestoga Four, six hours out of Offutt, Otto leaned back and stretched. With the constant drone of the engines and the autopilot engaged, there was precious little to do except for monitor the radio and look out for traffic. Donovan was interested in something below and to his right. "How ya doin', Bob?" Otto asked.

"Just enjoying the scenery. It's amazing there's so much desert in this part of the country."

"Yep, guess it's been there for a long, long time."

"Ever since we've been flying, I bet."

"Seems like it. Why don't you give Fairfield a call? Let them know where we are." They were supposed to report in every hour and it was close to 1100 hours local, 1900 hours Zulu.

"Roger that," Bob replied. He pressed this mic button. "Fairfield Tower, this is Conestoga Four reporting in."

"Conestoga Four, this is Fairfield. What is your position?"

Bob took the chart handed him by the navigator a few minutes earlier. "Fairfield, Conestoga Four, we are presently about fifty miles east of Carson City and estimating arrival at twenty hundred Zulu."

"Conestoga Four, Fairfield. Thank you. See you soon. Over and out."

"Conestoga Four out," Bob said and then clicked off. "Almost there."

"Yep, although this is a piece of cake compared to a combat mission."

"You got that right, my friend. Only seven hours in the air instead of ten or twelve."

"Yeah, and I've only been flying for two of those on this leg," Otto said.

"We'll make up for it on the last leg. Whew. Twenty-five hours. Glad we have some relief."

"Speaking of relief, I have to hit the head. You got the controls?"

"I got 'em," Bob said, although with the autopilot on that just meant that he was in charge of the aircraft. Otto unbuckled his harness and went back to the catwalk above the bomb bay, a tunnel really, to the chemical toilet in the rear compartment. The bunks for the relief crew were back there, and they were sacked out, although the navigator was reading a paperback. Otto was glad two of them were asleep since there were no walls around the toilet. "What you reading, Fred?"

Fred showed him the cover. "It's *The Thread that Runs So True*, by a Kentucky schoolteacher named Jesse Stuart. I'm from Kentucky, and I've been through some of the backwoods places he writes about. Talk about isolated! But he writes well."

"I'm working on *Death Be Not Proud* by John Gunther."

"What's that about?"

"Gunther writes about his son who had a brain tumor."

"Does he survive?"

"No. He dies at the end of the book. Or so I've been told."

"Sounds sad."

"Yes, but Gunther writes with hope and compassion. I like that."

"We all could use some of that," Fred said. "I doubt you're here to visit, so I'll vacate the premises while you do your business. Take your time."

"Thanks," Otto replied, and took care of what he had come back to do. He arranged his clothes when he was finished, filled the small thermos he had brought back with him, and started through the tunnel back to the cockpit. Fred was coming back.

"If you finish, I'd like to read the schoolteacher book," Otto told him.

"I'll swap with you. The book about the kid sounds interesting."

"It is. I'll catch up with you at some point."

Fred laughed. "I'm not going anywhere off this aircraft for a while."

"Not without a parachute, I hope."

"You got that right."

Otto crawled back to the cockpit. Bob was looking around.

"Want me to take it back?" Otto asked.

"Nah. I got it. Read your book. Leave the flying to me."

Otto settled into his seat and pulled his copy of *Death Be Not Proud* out of his flight pack. He read a bit at a time, looking up to scan the skies. He knew Bob and Frank, the navigator, were watching constantly, but he could not check out completely. Conestoga Four droned on through cloudless western skies.

About twenty miles out of Fairfield, Bob put in another call. "Fairfield, this is Conestoga Four, reporting twenty miles out."

"Conestoga Four, this is Fairfield with you. We're reporting clear, calm conditions. You are cleared into the pattern to land on runway thirty-seven left."

"Roger, Conestoga Four is cleared to runway thirty-seven left. We'll call when we're about to enter the pattern."

"Roger, Conestoga Four. Report upon entering the pattern. Fairfield over and out."

Bob began descending slowly. Otto put away his book. The other crewmen sensed the gradual descent and made their way through the tunnel to the space behind the cockpit. They strapped themselves in the jump seats so they could see the landing.

Bob keyed his mic. "Fairfield Tower, this is Conestoga Four, entering the pattern on the downwind leg."

"Conestoga Four, you are cleared to land. Regular pattern, runway thirty-seven left."

"Roger, Tower, cleared to land on thirty-seven left. Conestoga Four out."

Bob ran the various legs of the approach and greased the big bomber onto the tarmac. He slowed to a walk and turned on the first taxiway. They were greeted by a jeep with a sign that read "Follow Me" on the back. Bob steered the aircraft to a parking place on the apron where five other '29s stood in a line. He pivoted on the gear and parked it next to the last bomber. Otto cut the engines off and there was silence for the first time in seven hours.

Bob and Otto ran through the shutdown checklist, unstrapped, and made their way with their navigator and the relief crew to the forward hatch. They deplaned and were greeted by a corporal with a clipboard. "Welcome to Fairfield-Suisun Base, gentlemen. If you'll follow me, I'll take you to the transport to your quarters." He led them by a hangar to a waiting bus. I'm going to be riding buses the rest of my life, Otto thought.

"Where can we get something to eat?" Bob asked.

"The officers' club is located very close to your quarters. You'll see it on the way in. You'll be able to get a decent meal there. Or, should I say, an edible meal."

The six men boarded the bus and the corporal climbed aboard and started the engine. They drove away from the hangar and soon came to some familiar-looking buildings. The military must have one set of plans for its facilities, Otto thought. The bus stopped into front of the bachelor officers' quarters. "Here's your home for the night, gents," their driver called. "OC is further down this row of buildings."

As they got off the bus, Bob muttered to Otto, "Wonder what's on the menu?"

"It's Tuesday, so it's probably mystery meat."

"I could use a steak."

"So could I."

"Well, we'll find out. Let's dump our stuff and go see."

# Chapter 21
# The Long Reach
# April 1950

"Bob, what time is it?"

"Which time you want?"

"How about Zulu?"

"It's twenty hundred Zulu. We're about three hours out of Okinawa."

"Man, the Pacific is a big place."

"You got that right, buddy. Say, don't you have a watch?"

Otto held up his wrist. "Yeah. It's not as big as yours, though."

"So why do you ask me for the time?"

"So you can use your big watch."

"You know, they say size matters."

"Hhmph."

Otto peered straight ahead through the darkness. It was about 5:00 AM local time in Japan, which meant that sunrise should start catching up with them soon. He would be glad to see something after flying during darkness for a long period. With the crews alternating four hours on and four hours off, he and Bob were on their third shift of the flight. He had managed to nap some during the times they were off, but it wasn't a good sleep. He kept dreaming he was back over Germany, piloting the *Mata Maria*. What sleep he did have had been interrupted by nightmares of attacking German fighters. He woke several times in a cold sweat before he realized where he was. The last time he had given up and come up and sat in the jump seat behind the flight deck and read *Kon Tiki*, which Fred had traded him after he had finished the Jesse Stuart book. Talk about a long journey—Heyerdahl and his crew had spent 101 days crossing the Pacific, at an average speed of one and a half knots. Conestoga Four's total travel time was 37 hours, and their average speed was a hundred and ninety knots. A world of difference. Otto wondered at the courage it took to set out across the trackless Pacific on a balsa raft. He supposed that there were all kinds of challenges in this world. Piloting a modern aircraft nearly five thousand miles was a kind of challenge, although they had a lot of help. Still, if they ran into trouble somewhere over the ocean, help would be a long way away.

Conestoga Four droned on into the first light of dawn over the vast ocean.

***

"Bob, time to call Okinawa and let them know we're in the vicinity."

"I think they have us on radar, but I suppose that would only be polite."

They were an hour out from Japan. The relief crew had joined them behind the cockpit for the last part of the long flight. Bob keyed his mic. "Yokota Base, this is Conestoga Four of Operation Reach with you. Come in, please."

Amid bursts of static Otto heard through his headphones, "Conestoga Four, this is Yokota Base. Welcome to the Orient, gentlemen."

"Thank you, Yokota Base. We are estimating our arrival in an hour, at twenty-three hundred Zulu."

"Roger that. Give us a call when you're half an hour out and we'll set you up for approach and landing. Say your fuel, please."

Otto studied the gauges. "We have two hours' fuel," he reported.

"Two hours' fuel remaining," Bob repeated.

"Thank you, Conestoga Four. You should be fine. This is Yokota Base over and out."

"Conestoga Four out."

Otto flexed his fingers on the controls. Another hour and they'd be on the ground. He wondered how long they'd be there and how long it would take them to get back. At least they didn't have to go by boat like some poor schlubs. That would truly take forever, like a slow boat from China. That made him think of the song:

> *I'd love to get you on a Slow Boat to China*
> *All to myself alone.*
> *Get you and keep you in my arms evermore,*
> *Leave all your lovers*
> *Weeping on a far away shore.*
> *Out on the briney*
> *With the moon big and shiney*

*Melting your heart of stone*
*I'd love to get you on a Slow Boat to China*
*All to myself alone.*

Recalling the melody and the lyrics made him remember that he and Betty had danced to that just a couple of years before. A happier time. Then, somehow, he thought of Alice, who hadn't come to mind for years. Maybe it was the line, "Lovers weeping on a far away shore." Except he was the one left weeping. Well, water under the bridge, he reminded himself. He wondered what Betty and the girls were doing. Let's see, the local time in Wisconsin was 4:00 AM, so they would be asleep. He would have to see about some nice gifts for them to make up for his extended absence. He wasn't sure how long they'd be in Japan, but he thought it would be long enough to get to the PX and pick out something distinctive.

Otto was lost in his thoughts as Bob keyed his mic and called, "Yokota Tower, this is Conestoga Four reporting half an hour out. We're in the vicinity."

"Conestoga Four, Yokota Tower here. You are cleared for a direct approach to runway eighteen. Winds are ten knots from the north, visibility is good, and we have severe-clear conditions. Please contact when you are a mile out."

"Roger that, Yokota Tower. Runway eighteen, straight-in approach. Hope you have a nice, soft bed for us. Conestoga Four, over."

"We do have that, Conestoga Four. Happy landing. Yokota over and out."

Otto began a gradual descent and made a gentle turn toward the north to set up his landing. The big bomber slid down to the air field as if it were on rails. The runway came into sight when they were a mile out. Bob keyed his mic again. "Yokota, Conestoga Four. We are on final, a mile out. Thanks for the straight-in approach. We are a bunch of tired puppies. Over."

"Conestoga Four, Yokota Tower. Apparently the brass thinks you are important puppies since they ordered all Conestoga flights cleared directly in. Come on down! Yokota over."

"Yokota Tower, Conestoga Four, roger that. See you on the ground. Conestoga Four over and out."

The field gradually grew larger, and Otto dropped the Superfort right on the numbers. The big Boeing touched down without a jolt and rolled out to the first taxiway. Again they were met by a jeep with a sign reading "Follow Me!" Otto followed and was directed by a ground crewman to park, again next to Conestoga Five, which was lined up with the four earlier Conestoga flights. Otto stopped the aircraft, set the brakes, and shut down the engines. He and Bob ran through the shutdown checklist. With that done, they removed their headsets and harnesses and stood up. Bob stuck out his hand. "Another great piece of flying, Major OK!" he exclaimed.

Otto shook Bob's outstretched hand. "Fine job, Major Donovan!"

They went back behind the cockpit and exchanged handshakes and thumps on the back with their navigator and the relief crew. Both crews quickly exited the bomber. It was no longer their responsibility.

They were met by another corporal with a clipboard. He checked off their names and then said, "Gentlemen, if you'll follow me, I'll take you to the BOQ so you can relax or get some breakfast at the OC if you'd like."

Otto thought, they must have a factory where they turn out these identical corporals. Maybe they manufacture them in the Midwest. Nah, too expensive. He decided he probably needed to read less science fiction. He had read something about robots gone bad in a short story by Isaac Asimov in some science fiction magazine. So maybe identical corporals weren't such a bad thing after all. He had also read that Asimov's stories were going to be collected into a book, maybe to be published the next year. He liked Asimov's writing as well as Bradbury's. Maybe he would just lay off the cheesy science fiction. Yeah, that was a plan.

The bus deposited them in front of the now familiar-looking BOQ building. Otto and Bob were sharing a two-person room that looked like the ones in Nebraska and California. They threw their travel bags beside the beds and lay down. "I don't think I'm ever going to get up," groaned Bob. "Except I'm so hungry I'm going to have to."

"Well, we know where to eat," Otto chuckled. "The officers' club is right down the way."

"Hope they serve something besides fish and rice," Bob ventured.

"Somehow I think it will be just like the meals in Omaha and California and Hawaii," Otto sighed.

"Probably so, but right now I could eat a horse!"

"I don't think that's on the menu, but let's go see what is," Otto said, standing up. With that, they went out the door in search of something edible.

# Chapter 22
# The Layover
# April 1950

On the third day of the layover, Bob and Otto reported to the ops shack at 0700 hours, bags packed, to see if their transport back was available. The bored-looking corporal told them the same thing he had told them the previous two days: no transport available today, but try again tomorrow, same time, same station. Bob and Otto went to breakfast and then back to the room to read, Otto his book and Bob one of the lurid mystery magazines he enjoy so much. He read them during the war when he could get hold of them and was quickly engrossed in one showing a buxom lady on the cover being threatened by a big tough-looking guy with a large black gun. It was about the biggest handgun Otto had ever seen, and he wondered if it really existed. Oh well, with fiction you can get away with just about anything.

Otto finished *Kon Tiki* about ten o'clock. "I need something else to read," he told Bob.

"Here, try one of my magazines," Bob offered, tossing him one of several he had brought along.

Otto caught it and looked at the cover. It had a typical cover. Otto wondered if they had an artist who cranked out variations on the dame threatened by the big guy. He opened the magazine and began reading the first story, something called "Death & Company," by Dashiell Hammett. He had heard of Hammett and seemed to recall that he had written *The Maltese Falcon*, which he had enjoyed when he had seen it at the base theater in England.

He started reading:

*The Old Man, meaning the head of the Continental Detective Agency, introduced me to the other man in his office—his name was Chappell—and said, 'Sit down.'*

Hmm, not bad, Otto thought, and kept reading. He read through the story in about five minutes and found it interesting and inventive. "This isn't bad," he told Bob.

"Yeah, it's like anything else. There's a lot of junk, but if you choose your authors, there are some gems out there. I know you like science fiction, and occasionally these mags publish things by the likes of Theodore Sturgeon.

Otto read the rest of the magazine but didn't find anything as good as the first story. He put the magazine down and said, "I'm going to the PX to see if I can find something else to read. You want to go with me?"

"Nah," Bob said. "I'll stay here and see you at lunch. About twelve thirty, OK?"

"Yep, that's fine." A clerk had told Otto that they might have some silk dresses come in. If he could figure out the sizes, they would make ideal gifts for his girls at home. He found himself hoping this would be his last assignment and he could go home and get back to a normal life.

Otto walked out of the BOQ and took the now-familiar route to the PX. It was as big as a department store in Minneapolis. For that matter, the base was huge, as far as he could tell from what he had seen of it. He pushed through the double doors and went to the book section. They had a good selection, and he picked out *Red Planet*, by Robert Heinlein. He enjoyed Heinlein's short stories and, flipping through the book, it looked like he would like it. He paid for it and went over to the dress section. "Did the silk dresses come in?" he asked a clerk.

"Yes, sir, and we have a good selection. Do you know the sizes you need?"

"I'm sorry, I don't, but they're for a lady who's about your size and two girls who are nearly two years old and a typical size for their age. Or so I'm told."

"Twins!" the lady exclaimed. "What fun! Well, from what you've said, I think we can fit your ladies well. Please come with me."

She took him over to a display of about six kimonos on mannequins. "As you can see, they are loose-fitting, so even if the size is a bit off, they'll still work. We have them in children's sizes as well."

The robes were made of silk, and they were absolutely beautiful, Otto thought. He knew Betty and the girls would be happy to have them. It would be especially good to give Betty something that would make her happier. She had been through a lot in the past year with him being gone. He looked at the mannequins for a while and decided he liked the one with a lot of red in it for Betty, the green one for Maria, and a yellow robe for Marion. He said to the sales clerk, "I'll take the woman's size in red, and for the girls, a green one and a yellow one."

The clerk nodded and smiled. "Yes sir, it'll just take me a minute to get them from the stock room." She turned on her heel and hurried off.

Otto saw that the store was beginning to fill with shoppers. Well, it was getting on toward 11:00, and people were out and about. There were men in uniform, of course, but there were also women and children walking up and down the aisles. A low conversational hum arose in the store.

The clerk came back bearing the kimonos on hangers. "I can have them sent to your quarters if you'd like, Major."

"Thanks," Otto told her. "I'm here on temporary duty assignment. Home is Wisconsin."

"Well, we can ship there but it's quite expensive. So you're not local. I didn't think I had seen you before."

"I'm home based in Nebraska. We hope we're going back on MATS sometime soon."

"Then let me put these in some sturdy bags. They'll weather the trip back to Wisconsin just fine that way."

She strode off in the same direction as before and returned with two cloth garment bags. "We can put your wife's kimono in one and the girls' will fit in the other."

"Thank you," said Otto. "You're very kind."

The lady smiled and put the robes in their respective bags. She handed them to Otto.

"That will be one hundred dollars, please."

Otto took out his wallet and counted out five twenties. "There you go."

The lady took the bills and punched some buttons on her cash register. The drawer opened and a bell rang. She put the bills in one of the drawers, pushed it shut, tore off the receipt, and handed it to Otto. "Is there anything else I can help you with?" she asked.

"No, thank you. You've been most helpful already. Good-bye."

"Have a pleasant flight back, Major. Stop by and see us again."

"I will if I'm ever back here." Otto picked up his bags and made his way out of the store. He quickly walked the distance to the BOQ, where he found Bob still reading his mystery magazines.

"How was your shopping trip?" Bob asked absently.

"Fine. I got some nice kimonos for Betty and the girls and a Heinlein book."

"I hear he's good. Let me see the kimonos."

Otto unzipped the bags and showed the dresses to Bob. He whistled. "I'd better get one of those for Frances. You'd make me look bad otherwise."

Otto laughed. "They're right over at the PX. Some nice colors to choose from, too."

"I'll go over right after lunch. Say, you want to see a movie tonight?"

"What's on?"

*Twelve O'Clock High* with Gregory Peck and a cast of thousands."

"What's it about?"

"A B-17 bombing group in the war."

"Think we know anything about that?"

"We'll go see it to see if they got it right!" Bob exclaimed. "We can go by the store on our way back from lunch, get Frances' kimono, and then head over to the OC for a little billiards."

"I don't know how to play billiards."

'You know, Otto, that's what you get for reading and flying all the time. I'll teach you."

"All right, I'll play for fun. I get the feeling you're probably a hustler."

"Perish the thought, Major OK. Let's go to lunch!"

# Chapter 23
# Twelve O'Clock High
# April 1950

Otto settled into a seat next to Bob. The theater was about half-filled on a Tuesday night. They had spent the day looking around the air base and concluded that American air bases were like BOQ architecture—they must be much the same the world over. Bob had a big box of popcorn. He offered some to Otto. "No, thanks, Bob. I don't like the taste."

"C'mon, man, you're from the Midwest. You have to like corn."

"I like corn, just not popped."

The lights dimmed and the film started. Otto watched carefully, thinking that the film makers had done a good job depicting life on the air base during the war. The combat scenes were well done, with actual film of attacking German fighters cut into the combat scenes. While the film was realistic, Otto knew they couldn't show the blood and gore—the men torn up by bullets or shells or shrapnel. So, all in all, he would have to say it was accurate but distanced from the experiences he and Bob had.

Afterward, as he and Bob walked back, Otto asked, "So, what'd you think?"

Bob shrugged. "They got it right, mostly. They just didn't get all of it."

"Yeah, that's Hollywood for you."

"I guess so."

They walked back to their quarters and sat at the small table for a while. Otto never thought he would tire of reading, but he hadn't done much else for the past several days, and he could tell Bob felt the same way.

"Do you think much about our days in the Eighth?" he asked Bob.

"I do some. Sometimes I have nightmares."

"Yeah, me, too. I just want to put all that behind me."

"I bet you do, buddy. I do, too."

They talked for a while and packed once more against the possibility that tomorrow would start them on their way home and then went to bed.

\*\*\*

The next morning they reported at 0700 hours to the transport command. The corporal recognized them and called, "Majors, it's your lucky day! We have a flight leaving for Honolulu at zero nine hundred, so you'll have time to get some breakfast if you haven't already. Report back here at zero eight thirty for boarding."

"All right!" Bob exclaimed. "About time!" Since the two men had eaten breakfast, they decided to wait in the assembly area. Otto pulled out his Heinlein book, and Bob took another magazine from his stash. The time passed quickly, and then their flight was called. As they walked out to the aircraft, Otto saw it was a C-124 Globemaster, a four-engine craft. Otto had never flown on one, and he was anxious to see how it compared to other four-engine craft. It was an ungainly machine, obviously built for carrying loads rather than for speed. They walked on and found seats near the front. The interior filled quickly since this was the first flight out in several days.

Promptly at 0900 hours, the doors were closed and the engines started. They taxied out, held at the end of the runway briefly, and ran through the clear morning air for liftoff, bound for Guam, six hours away. Otto supposed that the transport flight broke the trip into shorter legs for crew relief. They would fly from Guam to Wake Island and then to Midway and finally to Honolulu. Total flight time was about twenty-eight hours, so Otto knew they would be good and tired when they got there. He pulled out his book and started to read. They had been promised sandwiches in about four hours, so he decided he had better get comfortable.

About six hours later, they began their descent into Guam. Otto couldn't see land anywhere, but he hoped the pilots could. As the transport turned, he finally caught a glimpse of the tiny speck that had to be Guam. It didn't look big enough to hold an airfield. The aircraft lowered and lowered until Otto could see individual waves. Still no land in sight. Finally, just before it seemed as if they would fly into the ocean, a runway appeared under his window, and then they were down. They taxied to a hangar and the doors opened, letting in some of the most humid air Otto had ever experienced. *We are in the tropics,* he reminded himself. The steward announced a half-hour layover, so he and Bob started for the exit to stretch their legs and have a quick look around.

Half an hour later they were back in their seats and taxiing out for the next leg of their trip. Bob had bought a couple more magazines at the little shop at the air base. Otto was still working on *Red Planet,* although he was sure he would finish before they reached Hawaii.

The big four-engine transport flew on through the afternoon and landed at Wake Island about 6:30 in the evening. They were let off to have dinner and then those continuing on for the flight to Midway, about five and a half hours away, boarded again. Otto noticed there was a new crew flying the aircraft. The other pilots had flown about twelve hours, so they were overdue for a break. Because the transport's route took them east, they would cross the International Date Line somewhere between Wake Island and Midway, and the day of the week would change from Wednesday to Tuesday. It was hard to wrap his mind around, although they had gone forward a day on the trip west. He supposed it all evened out in the end. Anyhow, they were due in to Midway about 5:30 AM local time. Otto and Bob tried to sleep as best they could, but it was difficult with the constant roar of the engines and the basic military seats that grew more uncomfortable with every minute. Ah well, military accommodations are supposed to be spartan, he thought as he tossed and turned.

They landed in the first light of dawn and taxied to a hangar that looked like every other air force hangar they had seen. They deplaned, got some breakfast, and then reboarded the aircraft for the next leg to Hawaii. Otto felt like his whole body was vibrating by this point. "How you holding up, buddy?" he asked Donovan.

"I'd like to stay in one place for a while," Bob replied. "I'm tired of reading and sleeping. Eating is about the only thing I look forward to. I never thought I'd get tired of reading and sleeping, but I have."

"Cheer up—there's only sixteen hours' flight time left," Otto told him. Bob groaned. "Then we'll be back in the good old U.S.A.!"

"I never want to leave again. I'm too old for this stuff."

"You're twenty-nine, Bob."

"I feel like I'm a hundred," he moaned, staring out the window at the featureless Pacific below them. "Man, this ocean is damned big."

"You got that right!"

The flight had been in progress for about four hours when the steward came up to Otto and Bob. "Majors," he said, "this needs to be kept quiet, so please keep your voices down. Is either of you rated for a four-engine heavy aircraft?"

Bob and Otto looked at each other. "We both are," Otto responded. "We just flew a B-29 to Okinawa and we're on our way back. We were instructing at Offutt in Omaha and were tapped to make one of the ferry flights."

The steward's face showed visible relief. "Both our pilots have come down with something. We don't know what it is, something they ate or a bug, but they're feeling pretty bad. They're barely able to fly, so we wanted to find some guys with four-engine experience to take over for a while."

"We're your guys!" Bob exclaimed.

"Hold on," Otto told him. "We're not type-rated in the '124. We'll need manuals."

"There's a complete set in the cockpit," the steward told him.

"Let's do it, then!" Otto said. He and Bob got up from their seats and followed the steward into the cockpit. The pilots were slumped back in their seats with the autopilot engaged. The steward shook the pilot to alertness. "Major," he said, "I found a couple of guys who can fly the rest of the way."

I don't recall any "rest of the way," Otto thought. Maybe an hour or so until they recovered.

The pilot shook the co-pilot. "C'mon Jim," he mumbled. "Our relief is here."

The co-pilot moaned. "Aw, man, I feel so sick."

"C'mon, we'll go lie down in the crew-rest compartment."

The pilot stood up and Otto slid into his seat. "Thanks, Major," he said to Otto and went out of the cockpit. The steward helped the co-pilot up. "Steady, sir," he said. Just then the co-pilot retched and vomited on the cockpit floor. Bob jumped out of the way and thought he avoided being splashed by the nasty green stream. He backed out of the cockpit. The steward guided the co-pilot around the mess and reappeared a couple of minutes later with a bucket and mop. He cleaned up the rank pool and took it out in the bucket.

"Thanks, son," Bob said.

Otto heard the steward saying, "I would say it was my pleasure, sir, but it wasn't."

Otto had to chuckle. Bob sat down and rooted around in the storage area until he came up with a flight manual. He laid it open on his lap.

"Thank God for air force standardization on these aircraft," Otto reflected.

"You got that right, Boss," Bob returned.

"Looks like the controls are about in the same place," Otto noted. "Wheel, throttles, brakes, rudder pedals. Planes are a lot alike at their base."

"I think we're a little higher than the '29, from what I noticed as we got off and on," Bob offered.

"Yeah, we'll have to worry about that only if we have to land this thing. I'm hoping the pilots will recover in time to at least guide us, even if they're not able to land."

"From what just happened to the co-pilot, I wouldn't count on it," Bob mused.

"All right. You make the call to Honolulu and I'll sit here and look around. Even in this desolate air space, Otto's training told him to watch for other airplanes.

"What's our call sign?"

"Don't know. Use the tail number—it's here on the dash."

"Of course. That's where they all are. Stupid me."

"You might be stupid, but you're the best co-pilot I've got right now."

"I'm the *only* co-pilot you've got," Bob returned. "The other one is back there thinking about how he enjoyed his breakfast twice."

"You have such a way of putting things, Bobolink."

"We aim to please, Major OK. I wish my fellow co-pilot had aimed better. I got some of that crap on my shoes."

"Call for the butler to come wipe it off."

"I'm glad we have a butler on this flight."

"I'm glad we had *us* on this flight. Otherwise a bunch of airmen could have become navy men."

"Never did like the prospect of ditching."

"Me neither. Let's just fly this thing."

Donovan keyed his mic. "Hickam Tower, this is MATS two-one-zero-three-five inbound from Midway. We have an emergency on board."

There was a burst of static, and then a distant voice came on: "Zero-three-five, Hickam Tower with you. Say the nature of your emergency, please."

Donovan responded, "Zero-three-five, both pilots are incapacitated. That is our emergency."

There was a long pause. "Excuse me, sir, but who the hell are you?"

Bob chuckled. "I am Major Robert Donovan, United States Air Force Reserve, presently acting as co-pilot for this flight. Major Otto Kerchner, United States Air Force Reserve, is acting as pilot. We are declaring an emergency and would appreciate your assistance."

"Stand by, zero-three-five."

There was a long silence on the radio. Otto and Bob looked at each other and both shrugged at the same time. The flight bored on.

"MATS zero-three-five, Hickam Tower."

"Hickam Tower, MATS zero-three-five."

"Zero-three-five, this is General Stevens of the MATS Command here. Am I speaking to the pilot?"

"General, this is Major Otto Kerchner, acting pilot for zero-three-five."

"Major Kerchner, how did you acquire control of my aircraft?"

"Sir, the pilot and co-pilot both got sick and the steward asked us to take over until they were better."

"So you assumed command on the word of a staff sergeant?"

"No disrespect, sir, but he was the only one asking."

"How sick was the crew?"

"Sir, both of them were a funny shade of green. The co-pilot threw up on my buddy's shoes."

"I see. Is there anyone who can vouch for you? I don't mean to be suspicious, but you would be some yokel from Peoria who somehow has taken over the cockpit."

"Sir, you can call General Rackham at Offutt."

"Rip Rackham? Holy cow! I know Rip!"

"He's our CO for a special project. I can't tell you more because I don't know your security clearance."

"Hell, son, if you're with Rip, you're OK. I'll give him a blast on the horn anyhow to tell him what his boys are up to! Pleasure speaking with you, Major Kerchner, and thanks for the help!"

The tower came back on. "MATS zero-three-five, you are cleared in with priority. Give us a call when you're an hour out."

"Roger that, Hickam. MATS zero-three-five over and out."

Otto grinned and looked at Donovan. "Well, that turned out for the better."

"Yeah, for a few seconds there I thought we were going to have to turn command over to the sergeant."

"We'd better review landing procedures in case our ailing friends don't revive in time."

"Got it, Boss," Bob answered. "Let's see... page four-thirteen... uh..."

Just then static crackled in their headphones.

"Zero-three-five, Hickham Tower here. Stand by for General Stevens. Over."

"Roger, zero-three-five standing by."

Otto raised his eyebrows at Bob. What more could—

"Kerchner, General Stevens here. How you boys doing?"

"We're fine, sir. We're on autopilot and reviewing landing procedures in case your pilots don't feel better soon."

"Outstanding! Rackham tells me you're one hell of a pilot, Kerchner, and Donovan ain't bad, either. In fact, ol' Rip says you're a war hero, Kerchner!"

"Sir, I just—"

"I know what you did, son, and it was some outstanding flying! Don't try to BS a general! We wrote the book on the dairy farm, if you know what I mean."

"I do, sir. I grew up on a dairy farm."

"Midwest boy, I hear. Well, anyhow, you bring my plane in safely. Rackham said to buy you both steak dinners and I'm going to do just that!"

"Thank you, sir. We'll be hungry by then."

"I'm sure they're not serving lobster thermidor on that flight, so work up an appetite. And a thirst, too, if you know what I mean. See you on the ground. Stevens out!"

Silence descended on the cockpit. "What time is it?" Otto asked.

"About twenty-one hundred Zulu," Bob noted. "That would be, let's see, eleven hundred hours local."

"All right. Sounds like we'll have steak for lunch if the Princes of the Masque of the Red Death don't revive."

"Far be it from me to wish ill on a fellow airman," Bob murmured, "but I hope they stay sick."

"Yeah," Otto returned. "I'm in the mood for a nice steak."

\*\*\*

"Ah, that hit the spot," Bob remarked as he and Otto walked into the bright sunshine outside the Hickham Base Officers' Club. General Stevens had indeed wined and dined them. He was a general from the same mold as Rackham and, in fact, had told them some good stories on Rackham when they were in pilot training together.

"Rackham liked this girl, see, who was the daughter of the commandant. He had a strict rule that she couldn't date any trainees, because he knew what we were like. So, anyhow, Rackham managed to get her attention, and they started meeting off base. Her old man wouldn't have figured it out, but one day Rackham "borrowed" an L-4 and he and the girl flew off for a little R and R. Well, the engine wouldn't start when they got ready to come back, so they had to call for a mechanic to fly over and fix it. When it did start, guess who was waiting for them when they landed?"

"The girl's father?" Otto had guessed.

"You got it, Major, and ol' Rip said he was sure his next post was going to be in the Aleutians, that is, if he wasn't busted out of the corps altogether."

"So what happened to the girl?"

"Nothing. They kept seeing each other on the QT and she promised to write when Rip went on advanced training."

"Did they stay together?"

"I'll say. She married him." Stevens had thrown back his head and laughed heartily. "So Rackham had his old CO as a father-in-law. Don't you just love it?"

Stevens had plenty of other stories to tell, and it was getting on toward 2:00 when Otto interrupted him. "General, we have a plane to catch in about forty-five minutes, so we'd better get going."

Stevens stood and shook hands with both of them. "Hope you won't have to do any more pilotage on the next leg, Majors. If you do, I'm sure you're capable of it. Take care and tell Rip to go to hell for me."

"Uh, we'll say hello to him when we get back," Otto said carefully.

Stevens roared with laughter and pounded them on the back. "That's right—be careful! Your next promotion might be at stake. Take off, lads, and Godspeed to both of you."

Otto and Bob boarded the C-124 for the next leg to Fairfield. They would arrive at 3:00 AM local time, sack out, and then see what was available for the hop from Fairfield to Offutt. Some hop, Otto thought. Five more hours if they could get on a flight the same day. MATS had a wide reach, but it wasn't exactly M & M. Well, they'd see. He tried to calculate how long they had been traveling. Let's see—they left Okinawa at 9:00 AM local on Wednesday, which had turned to Tuesday when they crossed the date line and would change back to Wednesday after midnight on the flight to California. So they would arrive at Fairfield at 1000 hours Zulu Wednesday, but they would have spent thirty-three hours in the air getting there. Another five hours to Offutt, then, for a total of thirty-eight hours. Whew. No wonder he was tired. Otto opened his book, which he had nearly finished. Maybe he would try one of Bob's mystery magazines when he did.

# Chapter 24
# Winging Eastward
# April 1950

Otto was at the controls of the *Mata Maria* high over France. He knew the entire rest of the crew was injured and the ship was badly shot up. He had to bring her home . . . with all ten of them alive. He pushed the throttles forward on the two remaining engines and thought he saw the Channel out ahead of him in the haze. Not much further to go. Hold on, cowboy. You can do it.

He felt someone shaking his shoulder and turned around to see who it was. "Otto, wake up! You're having a nightmare!"

Otto opened his eyes and saw Bob looking at him with concern. "Wha— Oh, thanks, Bob. I dreamed I was back in the Eighth trying to bring a crippled ship back. Where are we?"

"We're a couple of hours out of Offutt. We're nearly home, buddy!"

I wouldn't call it home, Otto thought. More like a way station, but it was more like home than the places they'd been in the past ten days. What time is it?

Bob consulted his watch. "It's about nineteen hundred Zulu, about two PM local. We'll be in about four PM local."

"Thanks, Bobolink."

"You're welcome, Major OK."

Otto turned and looked out the window. They were over foothills, which no doubt climbed to the Rockies somewhere behind them. The land would soon change to flat prairie and farmland as they neared Nebraska, and then it would be a straight shot to Omaha at the eastern end of the state. It would be good to get back to familiar surroundings. He hoped Rackham would give them about a week off to visit their families. He missed Betty and the girls more than he could imagine. After that, who knew what military necessity would crop up? The situation in Asia was getting dire. Some were saying there would be a shooting war in Korea, which had been divided between North and South at the end of the war, just as Berlin had been divided into sectors by the Allies. The airlift had resulted from that division when the Soviets wouldn't let the Allies access their portions of the city by land. It was quite an operation, from what he could tell.

Otto stretched and fell asleep again, this time without dreams.

***

Otto was awakened by the thump of tires on tarmac. He yawned and stretched as the C-124 slowed to taxiing speed and turned off toward the hangar. The twelve or so passengers gathered their belongings and filed out the exit. Otto and Bob stood for a second at the top of the stairs. It was already hot, and it was only late April. They walked down to the tarmac.

"We made it!" Bob exclaimed. He and Otto shook hands. "You want to get some real food?" Lunch had been a ham sandwich on stale bread accompanied by warm water.

"Nah, I think I'll go back to my quarters after I check my mail. And I want to call Betty."

"Good idea," Bob said. "I'll do the same. I don't mean I'll call Betty. I need to call Frances."

The two men headed toward the ops building. As they pushed through the doors, the corporal at the front desk looked up. "Major Kerchner? Major Donovan?"

"We're Kerchner and Donovan," Bob told him.

"General Rackham has asked that you report to him in his office immediately."

Bob and Otto looked at each other and then went to Rackham's office. His aide looked up as they walked in. "Majors!" he exclaimed. "Please go in. The general is expecting you."

They walked into Rackham's inner office, where this expedition had started. He rose from his desk and came around to greet them.

"Donovan! Kerchner! I hear you had a little excitement on the way back! Welcome home, fellows!" He shook both their hands.

"Thank you, sir. Yes, we had a little extra flying that fell into our laps. We're glad to be back, sir."

"Sit down. Let's talk." They sat at the large conference table.

"So how is my friend 'Glide Slope' Stevens?"

"Uh, he's fine," Donovan said. "He was very pleased with what we did and treated us well."

"I told him to. Old Slope is a fine fellow. A little excitable, though. He about took my ear off when he called the other day. Thought you two had somehow taken over his aircraft like a couple of latter-day pirates! He's been reading too many comic strips!"

"Once he talked to you, he was quite helpful. Even treated us to a steak dinner."

"Hell, I told him to. The least he could do. Then he called me after you left and wanted you to work for him. You boys interested in doing that?"

Otto and Bob looked at each other. They had the same thought. "No disrespect to General Stevens, sir, but we'd like to finish this assignment and get home." Otto spoke for both of them.

"I thought you'd say that. Well, I have good news. With this ferry flight, your assignment is complete. We won't need you again unless things really heat up and we need a bunch more bomber pilots. So stay available. You're free to go, gentlemen! I've already expedited the paperwork."

"Thank you sir." Otto and Bob stood and shook hands with Rackham. "It's been a pleasure serving with you again, sir."

Rackham went around and sat behind his desk. "Hell of a lot easier when no one's shooting at you, huh, fellas?"

"Certainly is, sir." Otto and Bob saluted and went outside.

"Looks like this is where we part ways," Bob said.

"If you're ever in Minneapolis, give me a call and we'll get together."

"Same for you if you're going to be in Chicago. Take care, guy."

"You, too, Bobolink." Otto shook hands with Bob and headed for the comm building. He would call Betty to let her know he was in, eat something, pack up what little he had in his quarters, get some sleep, and catch the first flight out for Minneapolis in the morning. He was looking forward to that flight.

# Chapter 25
# The Return
# April 1950

Otto watched from the jump seat as Jimmy lined up the M & M DC-3 for their final approach to Pioneer Lake. Flight 220 was on time. Jimmy made a nice landing and taxied rapidly to the terminal. He parked the aircraft, unstrapped, and turned to Otto. "Welcome home, Boss!"

Otto shook his hand. "Nice landing, Jimmy. Thank you. It's good to be here." He stood in the cockpit doorway and waited until Polly had said good-bye to the deplaning passengers. He went down the aisle and she hugged him as he came to the cabin door. "It's so good to see you again, Captain. We've missed you!"

"Thank you, Polly. I'll be around for a while this time."

As he stood at the top of the stairs, he saw Mata, Pete, Betty, and the twins waiting for him on the tarmac. He bounded down the steps and enveloped Betty and the girls in a huge embrace. He kissed Betty and then turned to hug Mata and shake hands with Pete. "It's so great to see all of you," he exclaimed. "It's been a long time!"

"Too long," Mata told him. They walked as a group into the terminal. "Are you hungry? We have lunch ready at your house."

"I am so ready for some good cooking," Otto told them. "Let's go!"

"So, where did you go?" Betty asked as they walked along.

"It's in the news now, so I can tell you. Bob and I and a bunch of other pilots ferried some B-29s to Okinawa so they'd be there for use in case of a conflict in that part of Asia. We just got back last night. We were gone ten days."

"We thought maybe you had gone to the Middle East."

"No, it was definitely Okinawa. Anyhow, we're back, and I'm done with instructing. I shouldn't have to go back unless something big breaks."

"Let's just pray that nothing does," Betty said. "I like having you around."

Otto smiled at her. "I like hearing that, Mrs. Kerchner."

"And I like having you home."

***

The girls were playing quietly in the living room as Otto dried the dishes while Betty and Mata washed. "So, how's the airline doing?" he asked. During lunch they had mostly talked about his trip.

"It's doing well," Mata said. "In fact, I think we could expand service to Milwaukee. There are some more DC-3s coming up for sale, and I'd like to acquire them and add Milwaukee and a couple of other cities."

"Sounds like a plan to me," Otto replied. "Maybe we can go regional."

"I think we're attracting the attention of Northwest. Someone from there called me about our becoming a subsidiary. I'm not sure we're ready to do that yet, but it's a possibility in a couple of years."

"What would that entail?" Betty wanted to know.

"I'm not sure of all of it, but basically we would keep the M & M identity but operate under Northwest's control. There are a lot of advantages to us, but we do lose basic control of the company. I'm going to check into it more thoroughly this week and will let you know."

Otto nodded. "Thanks for keeping on top of all that. I'll go with whatever you recommend."

"Those are words I like to hear, Brother."

They all laughed and finished the dishes.

***

The next morning, Otto was at the M & M operations center. Mata had arranged for a radio to be installed so they could talk directly to their aircraft and not have to go through the control tower or depend on Northwest to patch them through. Pete had learned to operate it and kept busy handling calls from the flights. Otto sat and observed the activities for a couple of hours as crews came and went. He was impressed by the efficiency and friendliness of the office and the crews. There were a number of flight crews he did not recognize; Mata had kept hiring, she said, against the possibility of expansion of their routes.

"Have a seat at the table," she told Otto. "I have a couple of ideas I want to talk to you about."

Otto obediently took a seat. "What, running the airline by yourself? You're practically doing that already."

"No, about a role change for you. And for me."

"And what would that change be, pray tell?"

"I think you should be chief pilot."

"Your confidence in me is commendable and understandable, dear Sister, but we're not big enough for a chief pilot."

"We're getting that way. And if we become a subsidiary for Northwest, we'll need one."

"That won't be for a couple of years."

"Plan ahead, dear Brother. Seems I recall someone near and dear to me saying that one time."

Otto threw up his hands. "Guilty as charged, Madame Prosecutor! So if I became chief pilot, what would I be doing?"

Mata slid a piece of paper across the table to him. At the top Mata had typed, *Duties of Chief Pilot, M & M Airlines, May 1950.* An extensive list of duties followed.

"I see you've been busy."

Mata laughed. "You have been in and out for a year, you know."

"Touché!" Otto exclaimed, also laughing. "If I do all this I won't have time to fly."

"If you'll notice, you'll be supervising pilots and doing check rides."

"Well, there's that, but I won't be doing the day-to-day flying that I like to do."

"That you like to wear yourself out with, you mean. And this will give you more time with Betty and the girls."

"That would be nice." He hesitated and then sighed and pushed the paper back toward her. "OK, you've talked me into it."

"I thought I could. Next item on the agenda: career change for me."

"What? You want to be a pilot? We can work that out."

"No," sighed Mata as she shook her head. "We practically have pilots coming out of our ears at this point."

"Well, who hired all of them?"

"I did, and you know why. Now listen up to me."

"Yes, ma'am."

"I would like to train Polly for my position. I've sort of made her unofficial chief stewardess, and she has done very well with the management aspects of the job. She also did bookkeeping for her family on the farm, so I could train her for my job very easily."

"You make a persuasive case, ma soeur!"

"I've been practicing. So what do you think?"

"I'd like to know what you plan to do instead."

"I want to become a designer."

"A designer. Of what?"

"You know I designed the livery for our airline. I'd like to learn more about how to do that better. The University of Wisconsin has courses in industrial design and artwork. I want to go there."

"You know industrial design is a man's field."

"I want to make it a woman's field as well."

Otto thought for a long while. He took another sip from his coffee. Finally, he said, "All right, then. You've been doubly persuasive this morning, so let's do these things." He stood up. "The airline will pay your costs. I think it's only fair for all the hours you put in building the business. And I will try to be the best chief pilot I can."

Mata came around the end of the table, hugged him, and kissed him on the cheek. "Thank you, Brother! This is so exciting! You won't regret agreeing to do it!"

"I know I won't," Otto told her.

***

As April passed into May, Otto began his duties as chief pilot. He would fly out on the early morning flight to Minneapolis one day, stay around until the early afternoon flight back, and then ride both legs of the late afternoon flight. The next day he would do the same routine with the flights to Eau Claire. Wednesdays he caught up on paperwork and took care of other details, including answering for Polly any technical questions Mata couldn't handle. Thursdays he checked the facilities at Pioneer Lake and Minneapolis. Friday morning he did the same for Eau Claire and then was home for Friday afternoons which, with Saturdays and Sundays, were free for Betty and the girls.

They enjoyed each other's company, going on picnics and hikes through the countryside behind the house, reading books together, and letting the girls play on the swing and slide that Spud had put up in the back yard. Honestly, Otto thought, the man could build anything out of wood or repair anything mechanical. He would bring him on as mechanic for M & M but he wasn't sure Spud was literate, and he would have to read to pass the A&P exams. He also had a habit of drinking to excess when he didn't have a job, which wasn't often. Otto had seen plenty of drinking in the air corps. In fact, he was afraid Donovan was heading for a career as an alcoholic, but Bob managed to avoid it somehow. At least Otto didn't see any evidence in the time they spent together at Offutt. Donovan had managed to beat the demons that tortured so many vets. Being in combat would drive a man to drink, Otto thought, glad he basically never got started.

And so May passed into June with calm tranquility.

# Chapter 26
All's Come Undone
June 1950

By the third week in June, Otto had settled nicely into his routine as chief pilot. Mata had begun classes at the UW at the end of May and found them challenging and instructive. Her first project was to design a livery for an airline! She laughed and said she could have used her sketches for M & M, but they were too amateurish. She worked up some designs for a fresh livery for the day when M & M would be a subsidiary of Northwest, incorporating Northwest's red in with M & M's old logo colors of blue, white, and silver. The look was arresting and modern, Otto thought.

Mata had gone for the day to her class in Eau Claire. She was able to take an early flight and then come back on a late afternoon return. Otto had finished his check rides for the day and was helping Pete in the ops office. Pete was able to function on his own, handling calls from various flights and essentially bringing the workweek to a close. There were a few flights on Saturday and two on Sunday, so the load was considerably less. Otto didn't even go into the office on weekends since he lived so close to the field and could be there in a matter of minutes if he needed to.

Mata came back in on the last flight of the day from Eau Claire, carrying a box with papers and books in it. Otto met her at the gate and took the box from her.

"How'd it go?" Otto asked her.

"I think I won a prize for the longest commute to class," she smiled. "Most of the students live on campus or nearby, so they drive to class. I guess I'm special."

"You know you always have been special," Otto told her, and she made a face at him.

"So special I got to do all the work on the farm while you were gone."

"I know, and I appreciate that," he told her.

She grew serious. "I know. I'm just glad you came back in one piece."

"More or less," Otto reflected.

"I know, Brother, I know."

By this time they had reached the ops shack and went in. Otto deposited the box on the table. Pete heard them come in and got up out of his chair. He and Mata embraced and shared a kiss. "Glad you're back," he told her.

"Glad to be back," she said, removing a light scarf from her head.

"So, how did class go?" Pete asked.

"It was fine. Some interesting projects people are doing. We talked about our ideas, and it's clear some people have no idea of what they're doing. I guess that's why we're there," she shrugged. "Anyhow, I'm ready to have some fun! There is a big-band dance in town tomorrow night. Why don't we all go to it?"

"That would be great," Pete said. "I haven't danced for a long time."

"I know Betty would enjoy that," Otto said. "I'll ask her when I go home."

"It's settled, then. You and Betty come to our house for dinner. Bring the girls and I'll get Susan to babysit them. Then we'll be off to trip the light fantastic!"

"'On the sidewalks of . . . Pioneer Lake,'" Pete sang, and they all laughed.

***

The dance was held at the Pioneer Lake High School gym, sponsored by the local Veterans of Foreign Wars chapter, and featured a Glenn Miller–style orchestra led by Jerry Gray, who had played with Miller. The dance was a sellout, but Mata had some inroads to get four tickets. Mata, Pete, Betty, and Otto piled into Mata's 1948 Ford sedan that she had gotten for a good price a year or so before. They were as excited as high school kids and, in fact, this was the sort of dance they went to then.

"Seems like old times, doesn't it?" Betty said to the group.

"You know, that would be a good name for a song," Pete offered, and he began singing,

> *Seems like old times, having you to walk with*
> *Seems like old times, having you to talk with*
> *And it's still a thrill just to have my arms around you*
> *Still the thrill that it was the day I found you.*

"Frank Sinatra had better watch out," Betty laughed.

"You know it," Mata told her. "I love Pete's singing. He's done more of it recently."

"I think he's quite good," Otto said. "I didn't know about his hidden talent."

Pete stopped singing. "I don't want to spoil my debut," he told them.

They parked in the crowded lot and made their way past the ticket taker. The dance was in full swing, with a combination of teenagers jitterbugging and some older folks making more sedate moves. Just then the orchestra ran through the ending of a fast song. The bandleader stepped up to the mic. "Now we're going to slow things down with a song from the war I'm sure you all remember, "I'll Be Seeing You," sung by our lady vocalist, Vera Nelson." A woman in a silver evening dress stepped up the mic as the orchestra struck up the introduction and started singing,

*I'll be seeing you*
*In all the old familiar places*
*That this heart of mine embraces*
*All day through*

"May I have this dance?" Otto asked Betty, bowing slightly. She curtsied back.

"You may, sir." She slipped into his arms and they glided around the dance floor. "It's been so long since we've danced, Otto. I'm glad we came."

"So am I," he replied.

"I don't think I ever told you that whenever I heard this song while you were away at the war, I would think of you."

"Really? You thought of me then?"

"Well, of course, silly. You were so thickheaded when you left. You didn't seem to want to be my beau while you were gone, so I just gave up on that. But I still thought about you."

"I thought about writing you a hundred times, but I figured you were mad at me."

"I started to write you, but I thought you didn't care about me. Would have saved myself a lot of trouble if I had."

"Well, I'm glad things turned out the way they did. You took a big first step when you saw me on the street that day."

"There was still a spark burning for you, in spite of my marriage. Or maybe because of it."

They continued around the floor without speaking. "Well, I'm back now and we're together, and that's all that matters."

Betty smiled at him and held him closer. The vocalist closed out the song:

> *I'll be seeing you*
> *In every lovely summer's day*
> *In everything that's light and gay*
> *I'll always think of you that way*
>
> *I'll find you in the morning sun*
> *And when the night is new*
> *I'll be looking at the moon*
> *But I'll be seeing you.*

\*\*\*

Sunday morning, Otto was listening to the radio as the family got ready for church. The announcer came on with a news flash:

> *In this morning's headlines, from Seoul, South Korea comes this news: North Korean armed forces have invaded South Korea at eleven points along the border dividing the territory of the Communist regime from the southern republic.*
>
> *Seoul radio announced today that North Korea had formally declared war on South Korea. The American ambassador in South Korea (Mr. John Muccio) said that at four AM today the North Korean armed forces began an unprovoked attack against the defense position of the Republic of Korea at several points along the thirty-eighth parallel. Fighting was in progress. The South Korean defense forces were taking up a position and resisting aggression, he said. South Korean*

136

*officials and security forces were handling the situation calmly and ably. There was no reason for alarm as 'it was not yet' determined whether the North Koreans intended all-out warfare.*

*The acting premier of South Korea (Mr. Sihn Sun-mo) said that he had forwarded an urgent appeal to Washington for tanks, planes, larger-caliber artillery, and ships for South Korea. After a long cabinet meeting he had asked the Korean ambassador in Washington to appeal to President Truman to act quickly.*

"Betty!" he called. "The North Koreans have invaded the South!"

She came into the living room. "Oh no! I hope this doesn't mean war!"

"I'm afraid it does," Otto told her. "And I'm afraid we'll be drawn in."

"What about the United Nations?"

"We're a big part of that, so it's the same thing."

"I guess that's why you took those bombers to Okinawa."

"Apparently it was."

"Oh, Otto, I hope this doesn't mean you'll be called up again. You've done your duty. And you just got back."

"I'm still in the reserve, Betty. We'll see what happens. Are the girls ready for church?"

"Yes, they're ready to go."

"Let's get in the car, then. I wonder how many other people have heard the news."

# Chapter 27
# Call of Duty
# July 1950

Otto was checking over the statistics after the last flight of the day on July 3. July 4 was a holiday with just one flight out and back to each city. The remaining workers for M & M were going to the Pioneer Lake Fourth of July parade in the morning, a company picnic in the afternoon, and then fireworks over the lake. It was one of Otto's favorite days after Christmas and Easter.

As he was waiting for the last flight to come in, the phone rang. Mata answered it. "M & M Airlines, Mata speaking. Yes, yes, General, he's right here. I'll put him on, sir."

She held out the receiver to Otto, whispering, "It's General Rackham."

Otto took the phone. "Yes, General, it's Major Kerchner."

"Kerchner, it's Rip Rackham. Guess you've heard about the mess in Korea. Well, to cut through the BS, I need you again, son."

"Do you need more pilots trained, sir?"

"Hell no, we don't need any more damned pilots. We got pilots coming out our ass, thanks to you and the boys this past year. I need squadron commanders. I want you to command a squadron of B-29s based in Okinawa. You know, the same place you took the bomber a couple of months ago."

"Well, sir, I . . ."

"This is not a request, Kerchner. Truman's getting set to call up the troops. That includes some reservists. How soon can you report?"

"I'll have to talk to my wife, sir."

"All right. Let her know what's going on. I'll look for you here as soon as possible. Give me a blast to let me know when you're coming. Rackham out."

Otto heard a click and then the buzz of the dial tone. Mata studied him with a stricken look on her face. "Oh, Otto, not again."

"Yep, I'm afraid so. Rackham wants me to command a B-29 squadron in Okinawa. That will mean planning and possibly leading bombing missions. Betty is not going to be happy about this."

"How long would you be gone?"

"Depends on how long the North Koreans misbehave. The Russians will no doubt get involved, and maybe the Chinese. Could be at least a year. I need to go home and tell Betty. I don't have a choice this time."

"Good luck, Brother."

"Thanks, Sis. I'll need it."

Otto walked over to the small house. He found Betty in the kitchen working on dinner. The girls were playing on the floor.

"You're home early," she greeted him and then saw his expression. "What's wrong?"

He kissed her. "Rackham just called. I'm being called up to command a bomber squadron in Okinawa. Truman is calling up the reservists to supplement regular forces."

Betty's hand flew to her mouth. "On, no! Not again, Otto! You've done your part!"

"Well, there's more to be done, apparently."

"How long would you be gone?"

"I don't know, but I think it could be up to a year." He moved to her and held her in his arms.

"I can't take your being away for that long. I can't stand it happening again."

"I believe you and the girls will be able to join me on Okinawa. It'll be just like my day job."

"Except here you're not being shot at on your day job."

"I don't know what kind of air defenses the North Koreans have. Nothing to match what we have, for sure."

"I still don't like it, Otto."

"I'm not asking you to like it. I'm asking you to understand."

She clenched her fists. "I'm fresh out of understanding. I know you're going to do it, so go ahead. Just don't expect that I'll be here when you get back." She stormed out of the kitchen, ran into their bedroom, and slammed the door.

Otto stood motionless in the kitchen. He shook his head. Smoothly played, Kerchner, he thought. He went into the living room and got down on the floor with the twins.

\*\*\*

Otto did not have to report immediately to his duty station. It took time to put things in place, even with the B-29s deployed in the Pacific. The ones he and Bob had helped shuttle to Okinawa had been restaged to Guam. He would not have to be in Okinawa until the middle of July, so he had a couple of weeks before he left. Betty remained cool, so his last weeks at home were not pleasant. He tried to stay busy with his check-pilot duties and helped with the girls as much as he could. They were the highlight of his life, and their smiling faces and unforced innocence made him glad he was a father. The day arrived when it was time for him to leave. Betty did not come to the airport to see him off. He hugged the girls and told them he would see them soon. Betty had gone out of the room, so he called good-bye to her. He thought it would be awkward if something happened to him and she had not used her opportunity to say good-bye. She would have to live with that, he supposed.

Otto boarded the first flight to Minneapolis that morning, where he would catch a Northwest to Omaha. Mata, Pete, Jimmy, and Susan saw him off. Stan and Bob had the flight, with Polly as stewardess. The flights were uneventful, and soon he was on familiar ground at Offutt. He reported to the BOQ, left his gear there, and then went over to the ops shack. The corporal at the front desk told him that he would be on the first flight out in the morning at 0700 hours. Otto knew the drill from there. He just hoped the pilots on the transport stayed healthy.

He was standing in the lobby of ops looking at his travel orders when Bob came through the door. He feigned surprise. "Major OK! What are you doing here?"

Otto hugged Bob and shook his hand. "Same thing as you, Major Bobolink! We're on our way back to the tropical paradise of Okinawa."

"Did Rackham offer you command of a squadron?"

"Yep. You?"

"Yep. Did you accept?"

"Yep. You?"

"Yep."

"We sound like a couple of Gary Cooper imitators," Otto allowed, and they both dissolved into laughter.

"C'mon, Major, I'll buy you a drink. By drink I mean a Coke."

"You got a deal, Major. And I'll buy you one, something more to your liking than a soft drink."

"I read you five by five, Major. Let's go!"

They walked through the heat to the OC and pushed through the doors. The club was starting to fill up with some of the other instructors from their project. They knew most of them by sight, though few by name. They just didn't have that much contact with them.

Otto and Bob sat at a table close to the door. Bob got up and went over to the bar. "A Coke and a whiskey on the rocks," he told the bartender. The man nodded and fixed the drinks. Bob took them over to Otto.

"A toast," Bob called after he had been seated. He raised his glass.

"A toast," Otto echoed, and raised his.

"To a short deployment and a safe return."

"Second that motion, Brother."

They touched their glasses and each took a sip.

Bob put his glass down. "Now *that's* the pause that refreshes!"

"I thought that was Coke's slogan."

"Refreshment is where you find it, mon ami. Well, it's back to the Okinawa Astoria."

"Finest accommodations in the Far East," Otto put in.

"Yep, just like the Omaha Astoria, finest accommodations in the Midwest."

"Truer words were never spoken. So how's Frances?"

"She's fine. Her mother's not doing well, though. I might have to come back if she passes on."

"I'll pray for her and for all of you."

"Thank you. How'd Betty take the news?"

"Not well. She basically didn't talk to me after I told her I was being deployed."

"Sorry to hear that, pal. Makes it rough on you."

"Yeah, well, you do what you have to do. 'Ours is not to reason why / Ours is but to do or die.'"

"I think you flew one too many missions with Detwiler." Their navigator on the B-17, an English major, quoted poetry at what he considered appropriate moments. Otto didn't always consider his timing to be good, but apparently some of the poetry had rubbed off on him.

They finished their drinks and stood up. "Let's trip off to Shangri-La," Bob said.

"Can we get there by bus?" Otto wanted to know.

"It's just a short trip."

"I thought that was on the Good Ship Lollipop."

"That's to the candy shop."

"This won't be no candy shop," Otto reflected.

"You got that right, my friend. Nonetheless, let's push on. As Detwiler might have said,

>*That which we are, we are;*
>*One equal temper of heroic hearts,*
>*Made weak by time and fate, but strong in will,*
>*To strive, to seek, to find, and not to yield."*

"I see you were listening to him as well."

"It gets boring sitting in a bomber without someone shooting at you."

"Let's hope we're good and bored with this deployment."

"I'm afraid we're not going to be."

# Chapter 28
# Strangers in Paradise
# July 1950

Otto and Bob reached Okinawa with ten other squadron commanders from their training deployment. They would be part of the 92nd Bombardment Group, which, with 98th Bombardment Group and the 31st Strategic Reconnaissance Group, operated from Yokota Air Force Base near Tachikawa in Japan.

They walked out into the humidity at Yokota onto the tarmac. The flight had been uneventful. Rackham had greeted them after their arrival at Offutt. They were transferred from the training squadron under his command to that of Major General Emmett O'Donnell, who had taken control of the groups in Japan and Okinawa. O'Donnell had been in the Pacific during the war, but Rackham knew him. Otto thought all those generals knew each other one way or another.

He and Bob made their way to the now-familiar BOQ and quickly fell into a routine. They would meet their crews at the end of the week and begin missions a week after that. Otto wondered if there was special training for squadron commanders, but apparently there wasn't. He supposed that the air force thought he knew about flying and bombing, and that was what they would be doing.

At the briefing in Omaha, someone had asked about families deploying with them. Rackham had said that would depend on how long the deployment lasted but that he thought it would be at least a year, and under normal conditions their families could join them in about a month. "Of course," he thundered, "these are not normal conditions. But you've been with the air force long enough to know that there are no 'normal conditions.' Some bonehead higher up the chain of command thought of that phrase. We know different, don't we?" The men had roared their approval.

Otto and Bob went to the officers' club for lunch and then took a nap to combat fatigue from the long flight. They got up and visited the flight line, introducing themselves to the ground crews for the '29s. The flight crews were arriving all during the week, so they would have time to prepare for what they would say to them. Before they could do that, they would have a briefing from O'Donnell himself. Otto had heard that the bombers had been used in ground support missions so far in the "police action," as it was being called, since it was under the auspices of the United Nations. Apparently the UN didn't declare wars. Well, a rose by any other name, Otto thought. That led him to think of the speech from Shakespeare in which Henry V calls to his troops, "Once more into the breach, good friends!" Yep, here they were in another breach, all right. Otto wondered how long they would have to fill it.

*** 

Otto looked around the auditorium, which closely resembled the one at Offutt. General O'Donnell strode on to the stage, trailed by several aides. Generals must study striding, Otto thought, because they did it with such conviction. The men in the room jumped to attention, and O'Donnell motioned them down with another practiced gesture. A slide projector threw a map of the Korean peninsula on a screen at the front of the room.

"Gentlemen," O'Donnell began, "Perhaps you're wondering why I've asked you here." A ripple of laughter ran through the room. "Most of our business has been tactical in nature, and as you've known since the day you were born, the Superfort is a strategic bomber. I am authorized to tell you that your mission will be changed to a strategic role by the time you have your crews up and going. You'll be hitting the enemy's war production facilities. You know what I'm talking about from your experiences in the ETO and the PTO: railroad marshaling yards, explosives plants, chemical plants, road and rail bridges, fuel dumps, power plants, and the like. We'll hit these targets hard and we'll hit them often. We're here to do a job, and I'm sure you'll do us proud. Now Colonel Bryant will give you some information on the particulars."

Bryant took the stage and gave them more information about planning the raids. They would be conducted in daylight and would involve about fifty bombers each. Otto's thoughts wandered to the resistance they would encounter. There had been little against the tactical missions, but there might be more against strategic runs. The Russians would surely be involved, and he thought he had read they had fighter jets. He had talked to some World War II pilots who had run up against German jets and the results were not pleasant. The damage they did was limited by Allied air superiority and the limitations of the jets, but the Russians had gained more time to improve their models. It was something to be aware of. The colonel finished his briefing and called for questions. Otto raised his hand.

"What sort of resistance are we likely to encounter on these missions?" he asked. "Specifically, I'm wondering if we might run into jets."

"That's a possibility," the colonel answered. "We'll have to see if the Russians get involved with their air force. We'll just have to go from there if they do."

A murmur arose from the room. No one was eager to take on a MiG that could fly more than five hundred miles per hour in a bomber flying at two hundred thirty miles an hour.

There were a few other routine questions, and then the briefing was over. Otto met up with Bob outside the ops center. "What do you think?" he asked him.

"I think I don't want to be in a piston-engined bomber that meets up with a jet fighter," Bob told him.

"Me either."

"We got any jet bombers?"

"I hear one is in development, but I don't know when it will be operational."

"So we're stuck with the round motors."

"So it seems."

"Let's go have drink."

"Yeah. I could use one."

\*\*\*

*Tuesday afternoon*

*Dear Betty,*

*I know you were upset with me when I left. I wanted to write you as soon as we got here to let you know I arrived safely yesterday afternoon about 3:00 PM, which would have been midnight where you are. I love and miss you, as I do the girls, and hope you will be able to be with me soon.*

*I'm staying in the bachelor officers' quarters, which you saw while you were at Offutt. There is base housing, and my understanding is that they'll allow us to bring families over in about a month. I hope you decide to come so we can all be together again over here. Try to think of it as an educational adventure in an exotic foreign country, which it is. I never thought the Japanese would live peaceably under the Occupation government after the way they fought us during the war, but they are very respectful and supportive of American troops. There's talk of their becoming our allies. The same thing is happening in Germany, at least* in the western part. Incredible to think that they are now on our side against the Russians, who of course were our allies. And all that happened after we bombed the living daylights out of them. War is an odd thing, all right.

Okinawa is very beautiful outside the base (the base looks like any other air force facility in the world), and I think you will enjoy the sights and the food. The girls will love it! Please make plans to come soon.

I meet my pilots Friday. In the meantime, I need to learn about the missions we'll fly and the crews that service the bombers and work on my briefing for the fliers. I find myself wondering if I will have trained any of them. The odds are I did.

We're just back from lunch, and Bob is writing Frances. We'll probably go play some pool at the officers' club later on after we read for a bit. Bob regularly beats my pants off, but it's a friendly game with no money down. We play for drinks, which, if I win (which isn't often), is a good deal for Bob since I drink Cokes, as you know. If I lose, whiskey costs a bit more, but Bob's a good man and a good pilot. After dinner, we're planning on seeing a movie at the base theater, The Third Man, which is to Bob's liking since he's a big mystery fan. I'm glad to have him as my companion on this adventure. We've been through a lot together.

So have we, my dear Betty, and I want you to know I'm going to try to make this situation a good one in which to continue to raise our girls. I know that together we can do it.

With all my love to you and to Maria and Marion.

Your husband,

Otto

\*\*\*

Otto walked onto the stage in one of the smaller briefing rooms. He hadn't mastered the stride that Rackham and O'Donnell had, so walking confidently was the best he could do for the present. The pilots in the room sprang to attention. Otto motioned them to their seats. That he did convincingly, he thought.

"Good morning, gentlemen, and welcome to beautiful Yokota Air Force Base. You know why you're here, so I won't waste a lot of time telling you about that. Our mission is the same as it was during the war: strike the

enemy's means of production of war materiel until he is unable to wage war. We have the equipment and the personnel to do just that and we have the will. I will be counting on you to be professional, to use your skills, to watch out for each other, and to be careful. Take no unnecessary risks. Stick to the mission plan and be aware of everything going around you. Communicate with each other, and let's take the fight to the enemy!"

The pilots sprang to their feet, cheering and shouting. They quieted quickly and sat down.

"I'm going to turn the briefing over to Captain Lewis, who will fill you in on the details of our first mission, which we will fly in a week, after you've had a chance to practice and to familiarize yourself with the area and with procedures. You might have read in the papers that B-29s have been flying tactical missions. The '29, as you know, is not a tactical bomber, so we're shifting to strategic targets, hitting factories, rail lines, highways, bridges, and dams—anything to interdict the war effort on the other side. These are the targets the Superfort was designed for and for which you trained to deliver the goods. We'll be doing this in daylight, as Americans did during the war. The Brits bombed at night, as you've probably read, but we accomplished more by daylight."

Otto grew somber. "We don't know what kind of opposition the North Koreans or their friends the Russians and Chinese will put up. We know that so far it hasn't been effective, but that will change if they throw jets against us as we've heard they might. If they do that, we'll figure out how to counter it. We have good men, brave men, intelligent men, determined men, and together we'll get the job done.

"Captain Lewis will continue now, but know that my office door is open to you at any time. I don't plan to spend a lot of time in it, so look for me on the flight line or in a cockpit seat. I plan to fly with you when I can and when they'll let me. Good luck and accurate bombing!"

Otto walked off the stage to thunderous applause. He went back to his office and sat behind the desk. He hadn't had much of a chance to unpack, so he opened another box that had arrived the day before with his personal effects and took out a picture of Betty and the girls. He put it on the corner of the desk and thought how much he missed them. He emptied the box and then turned to some paperwork. In this man's air force there was always paperwork to be done. He labored on until it was time for lunch and Bob stuck his head in the door.

"Hey, Major, want to go to lunch?"

"Yeah, let's go. I've had enough paperwork for one morning."

They walked outside and down to the officers' club. "So, what do you think, Major OK?"

"About what, Major Bobolink?"

"About these missions?"

"I think they'll be bombing missions. What we don't know is what kind of resistance we'll run into. When the Democratic People's Republic realizes we're going after their infrastructure and means of production, they're going to beef up their air defenses. I don't think it will be too long before they have jets coming at us."

"And then?"

"Then I don't know. We'll have to try something else."

"Like what?"

"Well, like fighter escorts, but they would pretty well have to be jets as well and I don't know how that would work out with the difference in speed. We could use Mustangs or even twin Mustangs, but even then it would be props versus jets. That would be no contest."

They had arrived at the OC by this time and had lunch. Otto had not been back in his office for more than five minutes when a young lieutenant stood at the door. "Major Kerchner, sir?"

Otto looked up and immediately recognized him. "Lieutenant Olson! How are you!"

"I'm fine, sir. I'm in your squadron. You probably didn't see me for everyone else."

"No, I didn't, Olson. Sit down. Tell me what you've been up to."

"Thank you, sir." Olson took the chair across the desk from Otto. "Well, sir, when I completed basic bomber training, I took advanced training. Then I was a co-pilot on a SAC aircraft and flew practice missions out of Offutt. They were long but uneventful, which is good, I suppose. Then we got the call and, well, here I am."

"It's good to have you on board. I'm developing plans for our first mission, which we'll fly early next week. Do you have a good crew for your aircraft?"

"Yessir. We're not sure who the pilot is yet, but we'll find out soon."

"I plan to fly with the group, so would you like to be my co-pilot? Major Donovan has his own squadron, so I need a good right seater."

Olson couldn't speak for a moment. "Sir, I would be honored! Thank you, Major!"

Otto waved his hand. "My pleasure, Olson. I know I can depend on you, especially if a nosewheel won't deploy."

Olson grinned. "Yessir. Oh, do I remember that incident! I was so impressed with how cool you were. I was sweating bullets."

"Well, you didn't show your nerves. You kept calm and it all worked out."

"Yessir. That was an important lesson to me."

Otto stood, and Olson jumped to his feet. "Glad to have you as part of the team, Olson, and especially as part of *my* team."

"Yessir! I'm pleased to be here! And one other thing, sir!"

"Yes, son, what is it?"

"I got married last month, sir. She's a real sweet girl from Omaha. You'd like her, sir."

"I'm sure I would, Olson."

"Will we be able to bring our wives out here?"

"In about a month is my understanding. I'll let you know something as soon as I do."

"Yessir! Thank you for your time." Olson saluted, and Otto returned the salute.

"Carry on, Lieutenant." Olson turned and walked out of the office. Otto smiled. Things were looking up.

# Chapter 29
# Once More into the Breach
# August 1950

Otto held the controls of the *Mata Maria* lightly in his left hand. North Korea slipped under the silver wings of the flight of B-29s. He had wanted to command this first mission to see what would be facing his crews, and, as the saying went, rank had its prerogative. This raid was on munitions plants near Sunchon. The North Koreans had nearly overrun the South, and something had to be done, and fast. Otto got on the radio.

"Keep it closed up, group, and keep your eyes peeled for bandits." He hoped if any came they would be Lavochkins and not MiGs. They had no intel that jets were around, but that would come. He was certain of that. And they would be sitting ducks.

A few puffs of flak rose up ahead of them. No evidence of surface-to-air missiles, although there would be little warning of those unless someone was looking in the right place at the right time. The flight bored on.

The navigator's voice sounded in Otto's earphones. "Pilot, this is navigator. Approaching the IP."

"Roger, navigator. Understand approaching IP." Otto looked over at Olson, who was looking around rapidly. He reached over and touched him on the shoulder. "Keep it calm, Lieutenant. The other positions will spot any threats and sing out to us when they see something."

Olson's head stopped turning. "Yessir. This is just so different from our practice missions. There are real, live enemies down there!"

"Yes, there are, and we're going to take care of some of them in a few minutes."

"Pilot, navigator here, IP!"

"Nav, confirm IP, bombardier, it's all yours!" Otto took his hands off the controls and felt the aircraft move in response to input from the bombardier. The bomb run lasted several minutes, but it always seemed longer. Finally, they heard the call, "Bombs away!" The Superfort lurched upward as the munitions fell from the bomb bay. Otto took control of the aircraft and put it over into a right-hand turn. He knew that behind him the other airplanes in the flight were following suit.

"Tail, see if you can spot any impacts. Weather's clear, so you should be able to see something."

"Tail here. Roger that, pilot. Will report."

Half a minute elapsed, and then the tail gunner called in.

"Tail here, pilot. I am seeing a lot of smoke and flames on the ground, so I think we hit them pretty hard, sir."

"Pilot here, tail. How about our ships?"

"They're all there, sir."

"All right, tail. Thank you. Sing out if you see anything unusual."

"Wilco, sir. Tail out."

Otto looked at Olson, who was grinning widely enough to split his face. "What are you so happy about, Lieutenant?"

"Not happy, sir, just pleased that I was finally able to use what I know on a real mission and not on a training exercise. Nothing against the training program, sir, which you were a part of. I feel as if I'm well prepared. I just am glad to use my training."

Otto nodded and laid in the course indicated by the navigator. "You want to take the helm, Lieutenant? I want to stretch my legs." Otto unstrapped himself and went back to the space behind the cockpit proper to the engineer's, radio operator's, and navigator's stations. Even with these three men crammed into a relatively small space, there was still room for him. He couldn't help comparing it to a B-17, which was about six feet across at the same point. The '29 was nine and a half. Three and a half more feet made a big difference.

"Hey, Major, how's it going?" the navigator greeted him. He was a fellow named Showalter and was one of the best in the air force, according to his performance reports. The radio operator was busy with a transmission, and the flight engineer was pouring coffee from a thermos into the top. He raised it to Otto.

"Want some, Major?" he asked.

"No thanks, Lieutenant Selfridge. I appreciate the offer, though. I just don't want to have to crawl back to the toilet, which I will need to use if I drink too much of anything."

The radio operator had finished his transmission. "No need to do that, sir. We'll let you use our secret relief tube we had installed by the ground crew."

Otto laughed. "Thanks. I'll keep that in mind."

"Yeah," Showalter nodded. "It's great that when we use it on a mission, we can piss on the North Koreans."

Otto laughed again. "I'll remember that in the future." He stayed there for a while and then went back to the cockpit. "Want to take it the rest of the way in?" he asked Olson.

"You bet, sir! Thank you, sir! Wow! What an opportunity!"

Otto strapped himself back into the left-hand seat and watched as Olson skillfully brought the aircraft in. As they touched the tarmac, he thought, One mission down. Who knows how many more to go? It would be for the duration and of course no one knew how long that would be. Rackham had told them to expect to be deployed for at least a year, maybe longer. Otto prayed that it wouldn't be longer.

# Chapter 30
# Home Matters
# August 1950

*August 25, 1950*

*Dear Betty,*

*I'm writing you with good news! At least I hope you'll think it's good. Dependents are being transferred in and should start arriving in two weeks. That means we'll be able to see each other by September 10 at the earliest and the 17th at the latest. You will receive instructions for packing and moving in the mail in a couple of days. You'll have a weight allowance for what you can bring, but I know you'll choose wisely. The climate here is sub-tropical to tropical, and we have a rainy season from April to June followed by typhoon season from June until November. It's hot and humid with showers in the summer. I thought this information would help you pack clothes for you and the girls accordingly.*

*I've missed you all so much. Although I am keeping very busy, my thoughts keep returning to the three of you. We've flown about ten missions with little resistance and no losses so far, although I don't know how long that can last. We haven't seen that much opposition and I hope that will continue. We're starting to turn the North Koreans back, which is what we're here to do.*

*It should work out well to get the girls started in the dependents school here. The school has quite a good reputation, and I think Maria and Marion will enjoy getting to know people from various places. I hope you'll make friends with some of the other officers' wives. The club is open to you, and the ladies who are here enjoy lunching together, talking, and playing cards. There's also a happy hour, but I know you don't drink, but maybe you could come and eat the snacks! I pray you'll be happy here and that we will enjoy our time together. I can hardly wait to see you again.*

*It's Sunday afternoon here and it's raining. When I finish this letter, I'm going to read and then Bob Donovan and I are going to see a movie.*

*I am holding you in my heart until I can hold you in my arms, my darling Betty. I love you. Kiss the girls for me.*

*All my love to all of you,*

*Otto*

Otto read back over the letter, took an envelope from the desk where he sat writing, folded the letter, put it in the envelope, and addressed it. His return address was the San Francisco APO, but the reply would reach him just fine. He hope the answer would be quick and that Betty would be as excited as he was about coming to join him. He turned off the light above the desk and went over to the chair where his copy of *1984* lay. He picked it up and began reading.

Otto had read for about half an hour when Bob came in. He had been at the officers' club playing pool. "Hey!" Otto called. "How did the games go?"

"It's going to get to the point no one will want to play me. At least for friendly bets," Bob frowned. He was good, Otto knew.

"I'm going to rename you the Hustler," Otto allowed.

"Major Hustler. I kinda like that," Bob answered, flopping down on his bed. He held up a magazine. "The latest *Ellery Queen's* out. You can borrow it when I'm done with it."

"Thanks," Otto told him. "I'm working on my book. As usual."

"Hmm. What's that one about?"

Otto thought a moment. "It's about a future society where everything is controlled by the government. There's a character named Big Brother who is an all-powerful figure. One of the citizens, a fellow named Winston Smith, is resisting him and the government. I don't know how it turns out for him, but I have a feeling it's not going to be a good outcome."

"Sounds jolly," Bob remarked. "Is it one of those science fiction books you're always reading?"

"Well, it's set in the future, in 1984, but there are no spaceships or aliens. I think it's about the totalitarian system of government in Russia. It's not really about our society. We have freedoms."

"You got that right, my friend," Bob agreed, and with that he opened his magazine and started reading. After a while the magazine dropped to the bed and he began snoring.

Otto continued to read for a while and then, in the quiet of the Sunday afternoon, fell asleep himself.

\*\*\*

*September 8, 1950*

*My dearest Otto,*

*I received your letter and with it your explanation of the moving procedures and schedule. I have a few more days to have everything packed and am in good shape thanks to Mata coming over with Polly and Susan. My mom has helped with the girls. They are excited about seeing their daddy, and so am I.*

*I have come to terms with your deployment, especially after knowing that we can join you there. I am proud of what you are doing and love you so much. I can hardly wait to be with you!*

*Mata and Pete continue to run the airline and it is doing well. It's not like World War II with rationing and so forth. In fact, it's hard to tell there's a war going on since our daily lives are so little impacted by it. We pray for you and all our brave forces. The pastor at church has a special prayer for the troops every Sunday, and there's a bulletin board with a list of who's serving and their branch. You're at the top of the air force section: "Major Otto Kerchner, Squadron Commander, 22$^{nd}$ Bombardment Group, Okinawa, Japan." Any number of people at church tell me they're praying for your safe return. I wonder what they will think of our big adventure to join you!*

*The girls are doing well, growing quickly and able to do so many things for themselves. They really are good children, and I thank God for them and for you every day. The girls are not into the "terrible twos" yet, but my mother assures me it's coming. She said I was awful at that age, if you can imagine that, ha ha!*

*I've started talking to them about our trip and they understand they will take a big plane ride to see Daddy. That's all they care about. I think I'm going to take them to Minneapolis and back one day so they'll be somewhat accustomed to being on an airplane.*

*The nights have started turning cooler here with the beginning of September. Soon we will be going into a tropical climate, as you wrote me, and I am doing my best to bring suitable clothes, although we are limited as to what we can pack. You said the PX was big there and I can buy anything we need as far as that goes.*

*I hope you have a nice house or, should I say, quarters picked out for us. I'll be interested to see if it's like the one we had on Offutt. I hope it's an improvement! The important thing is that we'll all be together again.*

*I will write just before we leave. Hugs and kisses from all of us.*

*I am your love,*

*Betty*

Otto read through the letter again, folded it, and put it in his pocket. He was at his desk, waiting for the daily mission to come back. About a week before, O'Donnell had ordered squadron leaders to stand down from flying, citing increasing casualties from flak as the North Koreans had fortified their factories and infrastructure. There were no jets being deployed against the bombers as of yet, but intel said that it was just a matter of time. Otto chafed at not being able to lead his men, but orders were orders. Olson had done so well Otto had made him a pilot. He flew one of the newer bombers that had come in and had asked Otto if he could name it "The OK Corral," in honor of his former instructor. Otto gave his apparently grudging consent, but secretly he was pleased. He didn't know how Olson had found out about his nickname—probably from Donovan—but he took the naming of the bird as an honor. Olson now had five flights as pilot in command and was doing well. So far, so good.

Looking at his watch, Otto saw that it was about time to go to the control tower to watch the flights come in. He left his office and joined Bob, who left about the same time. "Time to go greet the troops," Bob remarked.

"Yep," Otto answered. "Hear anything from radar reports?"

"No, I'd have to go over to the radar shack for that, and this damn paperwork is about to kill me!"

"I know what you mean." Otto held the door open for his friend and they stepped out into the stifling humidity of Okinawa in September.

"Darned oppressive," Bob observed. "When do you expect Betty and the girls?"

"Any day now," Otto replied. "I just got a letter today in which she indicated they would be leaving about the tenth, so I figure that will put them in here tomorrow or the next day. It will be good to see them. I'm sorry Frances can't come."

Bob sighed. "Yeah, well, she has to take care of her mother."

"I understand."

By this time they had reached the door of the control tower and went up the stairs to the glassed-in observation area. One of the controllers looked up. Bob's and Otto's squadrons were the only ones out, so they didn't expect any other commanders. The controller nodded and handed them field glasses. "They're about twenty miles out, sirs. No problems, no damage, and no losses."

Otto relaxed visibly. He and Donovan stood there not saying anything, listening to the routine transmissions between the tower and the aircraft. Finally Bob tapped him on the shoulder and pointed toward the north. There was a tiny speck out there that, when Otto trained his glasses on it, resolved itself into a B-29 lowering toward the field. The two men watched as plane after plane landed and taxied to their hardstands. With the last aircraft parked, Bob and Otto gave back the field glasses and hurried over to the parking area. They met Olson and his crew walking toward them.

"Lieutenant Olson," Otto called. "How did it go?"

Olson looked weary. "The flak is increasing with every mission, Major, and they're dialing us in closer and closer. They're going to get at least one of us soon, and maybe more."

"Would escorts help?"

"No, sir, not unless they take out the flak batteries. Maybe deploy some B-26s against them. But you know, sir, that those are portable, so there's no telling where they'll set them up. No, I can't think of a thing that would help in this situation. Just keep doing it until they're done, I suppose, no matter what the cost."

Otto reflected. Air and ground forces were being effective in turning the North Koreans back. And word had come in about an invasion at Inchon to cut off supply lines and take back Seoul. He hadn't heard how it had gone but hoped it was successful.

"All right, men, get something to eat and drink and rest yourselves. We go out again tomorrow. We're making progress!"

"Thank you, sirs," the crews said.

Bob and Otto walked on down the line. "What do you think we ought to do about the flak?" Bob questioned.

"I've heard talk of nighttime bombing," Otto told him.

"Oh, like the Brits in the War? We could get a bunch of them over here and they could do it for us. Or show us how. I thought it wasn't very effective."

"It wasn't. It's hard enough to bomb by daylight. But I suppose it would be worth it to save some of our boys' lives."

"I think it would," Bob sighed, and the two friends walked back to their offices.

# Chapter 31
# Gathering In
# September 1950

Otto stood outside the terminal area, which was really just a room taken from part of a hangar set up for arriving and departing non-military passengers. He had received a telegram the day before that Betty and the girls would be on the first flight of the day.

Down the field he saw the big C-124 on final, moving down gradually and settling onto the runway. It rolled out and taxied toward where he stood. The aircraft stopped, and there was a delay while the stairs were rolled into place. The door opened, and Otto saw them immediately. They were the first ones off. One of the stewards was carrying Betty's flight bag, and she had the girls by the hand. They looked around and saw Otto immediately. Maria and Marion broke loose from Betty and ran down the stairs and across the tarmac, leaping into Otto's arms. "Daddy! Daddy!" they exclaimed. "We're so glad to see you!"

"And I'm so glad to see you!" Otto told them as he kissed one after the other. Betty had made her way down the stairs, and Otto embraced her, still holding the girls. "So happy you're here," he murmured to Betty as he kissed her.

She stepped back and brushed the hair from her face. "It's quite a trip, I'll tell you, but the girls were good and the other passengers and the stewards were so helpful. Now, where do we go from here?"

"Your luggage will be delivered to our housing, so all we have to worry about is your flight bag. I've already moved my stuff so we can move right in."

Betty surveyed the ramp. "So this is Okinawa. It surely is tropical."

"Yeah, and we have big snakes, too," Otto said, mostly for the girls' benefit.

"Don't like snakes," chanted Marion. "Ewwwww . . . snakes . . . "

Otto picked her up. "You have nothing to worry about, little miss. We're all together again."

They walked around to the back of the terminal where a line of cabs waited. Betty and the girls got in the back seat, and Otto climbed in front with the driver. "Four-four-one Armstrong Lane," he told him. The driver nodded, put the car in gear, and they were off.

"Look, Mommy," Marion said. "Funny-looking trees! What kind?"

"They're palm trees, Marion. They grow in the tropics."

Marion looked worried for a moment. "They have snakes?"

"No," Otto laughed. "They live far away from here. In fact, we'd have to go to the zoo to see some."

"No zoo with snakes. Not like snakes."

"Would you like to see some monkeys and tigers?" Otto asked.

"Oh, yes!" Both girls nodded their heads emphatically. "Yes, please!"

Otto looked at Betty quizzically. "How did they learn to talk like that?"

She laughed. "I've been reading a lot from *A Child's Garden of Verses* to them. They picked up the phrasing."

Otto thought for a moment, and then recited,

*At the Zoo*

*There are lions and roaring tigers,*
*and enormous camels and things,*
*There are biffalo-buffalo-bisons,*
*and a great big bear with wings.*
*There's a sort of a tiny potamus,*
*and a tiny nosserus too -*
*But I gave buns to the elephant*
*when I went down to the Zoo!*

The girls giggled. "Daddy, that's silly," Marion said. "Bears don't have wings, and elephants don't eat buns! They eat bananas!"

"Well," Otto told them, "We'll just have to go to the zoo and see." This is how it should be, he thought, as the taxi pulled up to their housing. "Here we are! Everybody out!" He paid the driver and they went up the short walk. "Welcome to your Far Eastern home, Mrs. Kerchner!" He opened the door with a flourish. Betty and the girls went in. Her hand flew to her mouth.

"Otto! It's lovely. How—who—what—" She looked at him with amazement. "Who decorated this?"

"Do you like it? I had it done by the wife of one of my pilots. She does a lot of interior decorating, so I had her come over and spiff up the place. I think she did a nice job."

Betty went around looking at the fabrics and drapes. "It's simply beautiful. We'll have to be careful with it, girls, so we don't ruin it. The colors and the designs are perfect. I love it." She embraced Otto. "Thank you so much for such a nice surprise!"

He kissed her. "You're welcome, Mrs. K.!" This is how it should be, he thought again.

*\*\**

A couple of days later, Otto was at his desk. There were no missions, so he was pleasantly surprised to look up and see Betty and the girls at his door. "The girls wanted to visit you," she said, and they ran over behind the desk and climbed on Otto's lap. They had settled in well. Betty had been to the PX and stocked the kitchen with groceries. She immediately started fixing incredible meals. Otto had never gotten used to OC food, no matter how gourmet it was advertised to be. Betty's food was a real taste of home, and Bob joined them for dinner the second day after they had arrived. The home front, if you could call it that, was proceeding well.

"Work, Daddy?" Marion asked.

"Yes, this is where I write things and sign papers and send the airplanes out."

"What airplanes do, Daddy?" Maria wanted to know.

"They try to fix things so bad people won't hurt our soldiers."

"And we hope that they get all the things fixed soon so the soldiers can go home to their families," Betty told her.

"How long we here, Daddy?" Marion asked.

"I think you'll be here for a while, and then we should be able to go home about next June."

"That a long time?"

"Yes, I know it seems like it. We'll have Halloween next month, and then Thanksgiving in November, and Christmas in December . . . "

"Yay! I love Christmas," shouted Maria.

Otto laughed. "I do, too! Then we'll have New Year's, Valentine's Day, St. Patrick's Day, Easter, and May Day, and then Flag Day we should be able to leave. We should be back in Wisconsin by the Fourth of July."

"Lots of special days."

"It will go faster than you think if you stay busy and do what your mama tells you to do."

Betty shot him a grateful look. The girls were basically well behaved, but they had their moments.

"OK, time to get down. Would you like to see some big airplanes?"

"Yes! Yes!" The twins jumped with excitement.

"Well, let's go. I just happen to know where some are."

Otto and his family walked out of the office. "Let's say hello to Major Donovan. He's right next door."

Bob was at his desk working on a report. The girls walked up to his desk. "Hello, Major Donovan," Marion said.

"Well, if it isn't Miss Kerchner! So nice to see you here!"

"My name is Marion. You working here?"

"Yes, I do. I work with your daddy. What brings you here today?"

"We came to see our daddy," Maria told him. "And he show us some big airplanes."

"He knows where some are, all right, and he can fly them, too!"

"He's a pilot." Marion looked serious.

"That's right. You're going to get to see one he's flown in a few minutes. I bet he'll show you around the inside."

"I hope. Good-bye Major Donovan."

Bob stood up and smiled. "I hope I'll see you later. Have a good visit."

They waved at him and he waved back. Otto led the little band down the hall and outside into the heat. Waves of heat shimmered off the asphalt, and he was careful to lead them down the shady side of the walkway. They turned a corner and soon came to the flight line. The silver polished Superfortresses stood in a row, gleaming in the sun.

"Wow!" exclaimed Marion. "Shiny!"

"That helps them fly faster," Otto told her. She nodded solemnly.

They walked up to the first aircraft. The guard on duty saluted Otto, and Otto saluted back. "My family would like to see one of the aircraft."

"Certainly, Major. Take your pick."

"Where is the *Mata Maria?*"

"It's about tenth down the line. That was your ship when you were flying, wasn't it, Major?"

"That's right, son."

Otto and his family walked down the line of Superforts. They came to the *Mata Maria* and stopped for a moment. "It's called the *Mata Maria*," he said to them.

"'Maria' like me?" asked Maria.

"No, that was your grandmother's name."

"Her name is Marion."

"*My* name is Marion."

"That's your other grandmother. This grandmother died before you were born."

"I see." Maria furrowed her brow in concentration.

Otto laughed. "That's right!"

"Why it's not my name?" Marion wanted to know.

"You didn't exist when I named it. Actually, this is the second airplane with that name. The first one I flew in the Second World War."

"Where is it?"

"I don't know what happened to the first *Mata Maria.*"

"'Mata' is for Aunt Mata," Maria chimed in.

"Right. I wanted to honor the two most important women in my life at the time."

"So now you could name it the *Betty Marion Maria.*" Betty added.

"You know, I could," Otto reflected. "Let me get right on that."

"That's good," Marion said.

"Yes, it is," Maria added.

Otto led them around the exterior of the bomber. They inspected all parts. The girls were most impressed with the landing gear.

"Wow! Big tires!" Marion exclaimed.

"Yes! Big airplane!" Maria added.

"It is that, although there is one bigger. It's called the B-36, but there are none here. They're used for very long-range flights, and they carry a very powerful bomb. Would you like to see the inside?"

"Yes, yes!" the girls chorused.

Otto helped them and Betty up into the fuselage. They went forward to the cockpit. "Here is where I fly the airplane," Otto explained.

"Golly, pretty! Lots of buttons!" Maria's curiosity was overflowing.

"Yes, I had to practice for a long time to learn which ones to push. After a while I just remember, like you remember your name and where you live."

"That's right." They looked around the cockpit for a while, and then Otto led them back to the front crew section. "Here is where the men sit who help us get where we're going and bring us back. Their jobs are very important. I couldn't do it by myself."

"Major Bob helps you?" Marion liked Donovan. Maria was shyer around people.

"Major Donovan has a bunch of airplanes he is responsible for, so we don't fly together. We did on the original *Mata Maria*. He's a great pilot."

"I like Major Bob," Marion said.

"And he likes you," Betty added.

"All right," Otto said. "We're going to the back part of the airplane. To do that, we have to go through a tunnel."

"I'm going to skip this part of the tour," Betty said. "My days of crawling through tunnels are over."

"I stay with you, Mommy," Marion said.

"I go with you," Maria told Otto. "I like tunnels."

Bob boosted her up to the crew tunnel and followed after. They came to the rear crew compartment. Maria was delighted by this part of the aircraft. "Look! Little beds! Like Goldilocks! I lie on one! Who gets to sleep here? Bears?"

Otto chuckled as her questions came one after another. "Yes, you may try one out. No bears sleep here, but some men do if they get tired."

Maria flopped on one of the cots. "This my bed!" she noted. She lay still for a while and then lifted her head and looked around with a perplexed look. "Don't like this. Too small. Not pretty."

"We don't live on the planes. Not yet, anyhow."

"What's this little pail?"

"It's where the crew goes to the bathroom," Otto told her.

"I use bathroom."

"I know. That's a very good thing to do."

"What this way?" Maria wanted to know, looking toward the tail gunner position.

"It's another little room. A small man sits back there and watches for things."

"Is he an elf?"

Otto laughed. "He could be. I'll ask him next time I see him."

"Elves help Santa."

"And we're glad they do."

"Oh, yes!"

"All right, speaking of helpers, we need to go back and see what Marion and Mommy are doing."

"All right, ready." She held up her arms for him to lift her to the tunnel. They crawled back from the rear crew compartment, where they found Betty and Marion lying on two of the cots, holding hands across the space between them and giggling.

"What are you laughing at?" Maria wanted to know.

"Just girl talk," Betty said.

"A joke?" Maria asked. "I like jokes. Tell me a joke."

"What has four doors and flies?" Betty said.

"A flying house?" Maria guessed.

"No—a garbage truck! Isn't that funny?" Marion and Betty dissolved into laughter again.

Maria smiled slightly. "It's kind of funny. "

"I have one for everyone: what's black and white and read all over?" Otto said.

"I don't know," the girls shrugged to each other.

"A zebra that someone has painted?" Betty offered.

The girls giggled.

"No—a newspaper!" Otto exclaimed.

"Oh, that kind of red." Betty rolled her eyes. "I like my joke better."

"I want to see a red zebra," Marion stated.

Maria shrugged. "I don't." The girls got along well in general, but they did see things differently. Otto thought how much he enjoyed being around them and how nice it was to have his family there.

"There's a silly poem about a different colored animal," Otto told them. It goes,

>*I've never seen a purple cow,*
>*I hope I never see one.*
>*But if I did I know for sure*
>*I'd rather see than be one."*

Marion looked at him. "Daddy, that's silly. There are no purple cows."

"Yeah," Maria said. "They brown or black and white."

"Don't give up your day job," Betty told him.

Otto sighed. "All right, tour's over," he called. "Who wants lunch?"

The girls jumped up and down. "Me! Me!" they both exclaimed.

"All right, let's go get something," Otto said and smiled at Betty. She smiled back.

# Chapter 32
# Air Power
# October 1950

A month later, Otto sat studying mission reports at his desk. The North Koreans had been turned back by United Nations forces out of the Pusan Perimeter. The invasion at Inchon, the port in Seoul, in mid-September had succeeded and Seoul was retaken by the 28th. A few days later, the North Korean People's Army had pulled back across the thirty-eighth parallel. United Nations forces continued to press on Pyongyang, the capital of the North, and it appeared the war was nearly over.

B-29s had carpet bombed enemy forces during September, helping take back the peninsula. The North Korean Air Force, such as it was, had largely been destroyed by then.

Otto hoped this meant they could all be home by Thanksgiving or certainly Christmas. It would certainly be great to be able to do that.

Bob stuck his head in the office. "Want to go to lunch?"

"Sure," Otto said. "I think everything's under control here." He joined Bob and they walked down the hall.

"You think this is going to be over soon?" Bob queried.

"Looks like it," Otto replied. "I'm hoping we'll be home by Thanksgiving or by Christmas at the latest."

"That's what I'm thinking as well."

"How is Frances' mother?"

"She's doing as well as expected. That's another reason I'd like for this to be over. Tending to her mom is a tremendous burden on Frances, although she doesn't complain. She could use my help, I know."

"Well, maybe you'll be home to give her some soon."

"I certainly hope so, my friend," murmured Bob as he opened the door to the OC. "Hope there's something good for lunch."

"Isn't there always?" Otto countered.

Bob made a face. "You know the answer to that, Major. Maybe we ought to start bringing sandwiches."

"Well, with the lessened action, we have time to eat out of the office, but I can ask Betty about making us some. What do you like on yours?"

"Almost anything but Spam. I got my fill of that during the war."

"Yeah, and powdered eggs." Otto made a face.

"You'll get no disagreement from me on that," Bob nodded as they sat down at a table.

A waiter came over to take their orders. The lunch special didn't look too bad, so they had that. Bob had water and Otto had a Coke to drink.

"Your kids still doing well?"

"Yes," Otto said. "They wanted to know if Uncle Bob will come with them to the zoo this Saturday."

Bob pretended to consult a mental calendar. "Why, yes, I believe I have that day free, unless General McArthur calls."

They both laughed. "Maybe he'll bring President Truman as well," Bob teased.

"I wouldn't count on it," Otto said. "I don't think the general and the commander-in-chief are part of a mutual admiration society."

"That's what I hear as well. They have very different personalities. And so do we, Major OK."

"Yes, but I was in charge of you for a long time," Otto reminded him.

"But no more, sir. I am free of your control."

"True, but you have others controlling you now."

"Yeah, but none of them is here at the present time."

They both laughed again and, as their blue-plate specials arrived, turned to attacking their roast beef and potatoes. Otto smiled at the prospect of a quick return home.

***

MacArthur met with Truman on Wake Island and predicted that China would not intervene in the war and it would be over by Christmas.

The bomber command temporarily quit flying combat missions for lack of B-29 targets, so Otto had more time to spend with his family. Together with Major Bob, they toured Okinawa and even talked about a trip to Tokyo. The Army of the Republic of Korea reached the Yalu River near Ch'osan, the border with China, October 26. The Chinese counterattacked and stopped their advance in that sector. Then the Chinese troops seemed to vanish.

Believing the Chinese would not reenter Korea in force, McArthur sought to ensure they would not by ordering a series of attacks on bridges across the Yalu.

Otto's squadron was one of those tasked with the bombing runs on the bridges. He was worried that MiG fighter jets were now in the fray when on November 1, eight MiG-15s intercepted about fifteen P-51s and shot one of them down. Even the US fighter jet, the F-80C, was not a match for the MiGs, with one shot down later that day. Otto knew that the B-29s, even with Mustang or twin Mustang or F-80 escorts, would be sitting ducks for the Soviet jets.

The squadron's mission went forward without a hitch, with no losses to the unit. Otto felt as if they had been lucky, although he admired the skill and courage of his crews. Props versus jets was just not a fair contest. On November 10, a MiG near the Yalu shot down a B-29 for the first time. The crew, assigned to the 307th BG, parachuted behind enemy lines and became POWs. On November 14, fifteen MiG-15s attacked eighteen B-29s bombing the bridges at Sinuiju and damaged two.

Thanksgiving at the air base was a somber affair, with the light and heavy bombers encountering increasing resistance from fighters, but with only damage to the United Nations aircraft and no losses. Otto and his family had Bob over and they had a traditional feast with turkey and all the rest. It was a welcome break from the pressures of conducting an air war.

On December 5, UN forces had to abandon Pyongyang, which they had held since October 19. The bomber command suspended attacks on bridges across the Yalu River since Chinese forces were crossing on the ice that had formed there.

The Chinese continued to press further down the peninsula, crossing the thirty-eighth parallel into the South on Christmas Day. Aircraft from the transport command evacuated troops and casualties. Otto began to understand that the conflict was going to go on a while longer with the Chinese involved. The Chinese launched an offensive against troops in the South on New Year's Eve. Otto and his friends didn't feel much like celebrating.

# Chapter 33
# Changes
# January–March 1951

Things went from bad to worse as Communist forces continued to push down the peninsula, retaking Seoul. Severe winter weather limited tactical and strategic bombing runs. MiGs reappeared toward the end of the month and tangled with F-80s and F-84s. The United Nations troop took the offensive and recaptured Inchon. Troops continued to press toward Seoul.

On March 1, Bomber Command B-29s launched the first mission of a new interdiction campaign. Twenty-two F-80s sent to escort eighteen B-29s over Kogunyong, North Korea, arrived ahead of the Superfortresses and returned to base because they were running low on fuel. MiGs attacked the unescorted B-29s, damaging ten, three of which had to land in South Korea. One B-29 gunner brought down a MiG.

The burden of all these missions began to weigh on Otto. One evening he sat in the living room listening to the radio. His coffee sat untouched on the table beside his chair. Betty put the girls to bed and sat on the sofa across from him.

"Why so down, my love?"

"All we seem to do is to chase the North Koreans and Chinese up and down the peninsula. We bomb the North Korean factories, and resupply comes from China. It's like trying to empty a water tank by drilling a few small holes in it while someone is pouring water in from a fire hose. It's so frustrating. And depressing."

"My dear Otto, this is so unlike you . . . what can I do to make things better?"

"What you're doing now, my sweet Betty. Listen to me and be my love."

She laughed and indicated that he should join her on the sofa. She snuggled up to him. "Do you remember the poem from senior English?"

"Which one? There were so many . . . "

"'The Passionate Shepherd to His Love.'"

"Don't recall it, but if you whistle a few notes, I might be able to sing it."

Betty laughed again. "That's more like my Otto. The poem goes:

*Come live with me and be my love,*
*And we will all the pleasures prove*
*That valleys, groves, hills, and fields,*
*Woods or steepy mountain yields.*

*And we will sit upon the rocks,*
*Seeing the shepherds feed their flocks,*
*By shallow rivers to whose falls*
*Melodious birds sing madrigals.*

*And I will make thee beds of roses*
*And a thousand fragrant posies,*
*A cap of flowers, and a kirtle*
*Embroidered all with leaves of myrtle;*

*A gown made of the finest wool*
*Which from our pretty lambs we pull;*
*Fair lined slippers for the cold,*
*With buckles of the purest gold;*

*A belt of straw and ivy buds,*
*With coral clasps and amber studs:*
*And if these pleasures may thee move,*
*Come live with me and be my love.*

*The shepherds' swains shall dance and sing*
*For thy delight each May morning:*
*If these delights thy mind may move,*
*Then live with me and be my love.*

And that's it."

Otto applauded. "I'm so impressed you remember it. Those things just seemed to pass through my head. We did have a navigator who recited poetry on missions."

"Was that Frank Detwiler?"

"Yes. He was an English major, so he had an excuse. He could come up with a line from poetry for almost any occasion. I didn't appreciate it so much on missions, but what he recited was appropriate, I'll admit that."

"So, what did you think of my poem?"

"I didn't know you were a shepherd."

"I'm not. I only play one in poems, kind of like Marie Antoinette."

"Didn't she lose her head?"

"Yes, but not because she played at being a shepherdess. Poor girl. She was so young and innocent in so many ways. She didn't understand politics at all, and that's what cost her and her husband their heads."

"I don't know much about politics, either. I'll leave all that to the politicians. As Detwiler was fond of reciting, 'Ours is not to reason why / Ours is but to do or die.' Seems to me that attitude works for any military man. Don't question orders."

"What if the orders are illegal, as in the Nuremberg Trials?"

"Well, in that case, a soldier has a duty to disobey the order. Not doing so is a war crime, as the remaining Nazis found out after the war. What have you been reading, Betty?"

"Oh, you know, a girl doesn't turn in her brain when she marries and has children."

"I've noticed, and I'm glad," Otto said and reached for her. Now there was a way to relax, he thought as their lips met.

# Chapter 34
# Things Fall Apart
# April 1951

Major changes had occurred in the command structure as MacArthur was relieved of his command by Truman on April 9 and was replaced by General Ridgeway. Nothing changed at the operational level, and on this day, Otto wasn't feeling well. His stomach was queasy and he had a mild headache as he waited for his bombers to return from their mission bombing bridges along the Yalu, which had thawed with warmer weather, forcing the Chinese to use the spans for resupply. They had put up forty-six bombers, with one hundred F-86 Sabres as escorts. The Sabres had come on line in the middle of December the previous year, and they were a match for the MiGs. Otto thought they would prove more than a match, from what they were being told about Chinese and North Korean pilot training and experience. As he sat at his desk and worried, the phone rang.

"Major Kerchner?"

"Speaking."

"Would you come to the ops office, sir? Something's up."

"I'll be right there." The knot in Otto's stomach grew tighter as he hustled over to the ops shack. "Something's up" was never good news and he wondered what the bad news could be. He would soon find out.

In the ops office, he was met by a captain, Ramos, he thought his name was. "Major, I'm afraid I have some possible bad news for you."

Otto felt a chill run down his back. "Give it to me, Captain."

"Sir, three of your B-29s have been shot down. The flight was jumped by between a hundred and a hundred twenty-five MiGs. They damaged seven others."

"Do you know which ones were shot down? Any parachutes?"

The captain shook his head. "No, sir, I'm afraid not. I'm sorry, sir. We're trying to find out more."

"Thank you, Captain."

Otto sank into a chair. He had gotten to know his crews, and the thought of losing any of them seemed unbearable. And yet it happened. How had

Rackham endured all those losses, all those young lives lost, all those letters that had to be written to relatives? And yet he did and kept going in his own energetic and profane way. Otto would have to do the same, minus the profanity. He was a rarity in that he hardly ever cussed. He just never got started, and that made him stand out in the army, where some soldiers couldn't utter a sentence without a stream of profanity. To use that much seemed to Otto to dilute the impact of the words. There were other ways to express anger or frustration or any other emotion without using expletives.

Bob Donovan walked into the center. "Word is there's bad news."

Otto gestured to a chair beside him. "Yeah, three of ours were shot down. Seven were damaged. We don't know which ones."

Donovan sat. "Whew," he said. "That's rough."

"I knew those MiGs were going to be trouble."

"Yeah, me too." Bob and Otto had spent a lot of time discussing the merits of fighters on both sides. Otto wondered if the Sabre pilots had gotten any of the MiGs. They would find out in good time, he supposed. They sat there for a few minutes and then joined the officers going to the tower to watch the bombers come in.

The group in the observation room was deadly quiet. The staff passed out binoculars, and everyone in the room searched the skies for the returning aircraft. One of the controllers spotted the first returning '29 and motioned in its direction. All the binoculars swung in that direction.

The damaged aircraft came in first, trailing smoke, followed by the rest of the flight. Otto tried to make out the tail numbers on the aircraft to see which were his, but he couldn't make them out. A controller tapped him on the shoulder. "Major, we just got word that one of the downed aircraft was part of your squadron. It's tail number three-three-four-six. The pilot was Lieutenant Erik Olson. I think they called the ship 'The OK Corral.'"

Otto took the report sheet from him. The knot in his stomach worsened. Dammit, he thought. Dammit, dammit, dammit. What did I not do that would have helped these fliers? Man, this is bad.

Donovan saw his expression and came over. Otto held the paper out to him. "Oh, no, not Olson!" he exclaimed. "Damn it to hell!"

"Yeah, it really stinks," Otto said. "He's only been married about a year. His wife's on base."

"Well, let's see if there's anyone else in our squadrons."

"God, I hope not."

The other two losses were from other squadrons, so Otto went down and talked to his pilots. They described the terror of being jumped by so many MiGs. The Sabres did the best they could, but obviously it was difficult to counter such a large force. The final report on the mission indicated that the gunners on the bombers shot down seven MiGs, while the F-86 pilots downed four more. That was small comfort to Otto and the other commanders who had lost crews.

"Who does notification of next-of-kin?" Otto asked Bob. "I'm drawing a blank right now."

"A casualty notification officer takes care of it with a chaplain," Bob remembered.

"All right, then," Otto muttered. "Let's visit his office. I want to do the notification of Olson's widow."

"You don't have to, you know."

"I know. This is something I have to do."

"I'll go with you."

"I think they only let one officer and a chaplain make the call."

"I meant I'll go with you to the house but won't go in."

"Thank you, Bob."

"You're in a rough spot. I'm here for you, buddy."

\*\*\*

Otto knocked on the door of the small government-issue house. The yard was carefully maintained and displayed a number of flowers that grew well in the tropical climate. The air force sedan idled at the curb, where Donovan sat behind the wheel. Chaplain Price stood beside Otto. They heard light steps coming toward them from behind the door, which opened slowly. A young brunette woman looked up at them with fear in her eyes. "Y-e-e-e-e-s?" she quavered.

"Mrs. Olson?"

"Yes, I'm Brenda Olson."

"May we come in?"

"Yes, of course. I know why you're here. Something's happened to Erik, hasn't it?"

"May we come in, ma'am? It'll be better if we sit down."

"Why, yes, of course. Please come in." She went in before them and indicated places on a small sofa that stood facing a couple of armchairs. "Please sit down."

Otto and Price sat. Otto took a deep breath. "Mrs. Olson, on behalf of the secretary of the air force, I regret to inform you that your husband, Second Lieutenant Erik Olson, has been shot down while on a bombing mission over North Korea. All the crew members on his aircraft are missing in action and presumed dead. I am truly sorry, ma'am."

Brenda Olson's face crumpled as she dissolved into tears. She quickly brought a crumpled-up handkerchief to her face, which had turned a bright red. "I was so afraid of this," she sobbed. "But he loved to fly. And he so admired you, Major Kerchner. He would have done anything you asked. And now he's gone." She completely broke down at this. The two men let her cry for a few minutes. She straightened up, wiped her eyes, and managed a half smile. "I've forgotten my manners. Can I get you anything to drink?"

"No, ma'am, we're here to offer any and all assistance to you that we can."

"I—I don't know what that would be."

"You have plenty of time to decide. I'll ask my wife Betty to come over in about half an hour to be with you. Is there anyone else you would like us to notify here on the base?"

"I can't think right now. I will be able to later."

"We'll sit here with you, then, until Mrs. Kerchner gets here."

"I've talked to her a few times at the PX. She is a very kind person. I can tell."

"Thank you. If I can use your phone, I'll call her and ask her to come over."

"Certainly. The phone's in the kitchen." She pointed to the back of the house.

Otto stood. "Thank you, ma'am." He walked a few steps into the kitchen, picked up the receiver, and dialed their home number. Betty answered on the third ring.

"Betty?" Otto began. He could hear Captain Price begin a passage of scripture.

*"Have ye not known? have ye not heard? hath it not been told you from the beginning? have ye not understood from the foundations of the earth?"*

"Otto! What's wrong?"

"*To whom then will ye liken me, or shall I be equal? saith the Holy One.*"

"Several of our bombers were shot down this morning. I need you to come stay with the widow of one of the pilots."

"*Lift up your eyes on high, and behold who hath created these things, that bringeth out their host by number: he calleth them all by names by the greatness of his might, for that he is strong in power; not one faileth.*"

"Oh, no, Otto! Who was it?"

"*Why sayest thou, O Jacob, and speakest, O Israel, My way is hid from the Lord, and my judgment is passed over from my God?*"

"Erik Olson. His wife's name is Brenda."

"*Hast thou not known? hast thou not heard, that the everlasting God, the Lord, the Creator of the ends of the earth, fainteth not, neither is weary? there is no searching of his understanding.*"

"I know her. I see her in the PX from time to time. Poor girl! I'll be right over. Give me the address."

"*He giveth power to the faint; and to them that have no might he increaseth strength.*"

"All right. I have it right here. The address is 331 Wake Street. We'll wait for you here. Thank you."

"*Even the youths shall faint and be weary, and the young men shall utterly fall . . .*"

"I'll be there as soon as I can. I'm sorry, Otto."

"Thanks Betty. See you soon." Otto hung up the phone and walked back into the living room. Price was finishing the passage.

"*But they that wait upon the Lord shall renew their strength; they shall mount up with wings as eagles; they shall run, and not be weary; and they shall walk, and not faint.*"

Otto sat down after he had finished the reading. Brenda held her handkerchief to her mouth. "Thank you, Chaplain. Those are comforting words." Her voice was stronger.

"God does comfort us in time of loss, Mrs. Olson, and I pray that you will feel that comfort."

"Not to be rude, Chaplain, but right now I just feel numb."

"That's to be expected," Otto offered. "You've had a tremendous shock to your system."

Brenda nodded sadly. "That scripture—I recognized it. It's from Isaiah forty, one of my favorites. It also has the text for 'Comfort Ye, My People,' which Handel used for a solo and chorus in the Christmas portion of *Messiah*. My father is a Baptist minister in Oklahoma, and I sang that solo in the choir."

Otto and Price nodded. "How long has your father been in the ministry, Mrs. Olson?"

"He's been a minister for forty-five years. He was a chaplain during World War Two and served in England, Germany, and France. He went ashore fairly soon after D-day. He doesn't say much about his service."

"We both served in World War Two," Price noted.

Brenda nodded. "And Major Kerchner is a war hero."

Otto waved his hand. "I had the misfortune to ruin a bomber. That little event is why I look the way I do."

Brenda's face softened with a memory. "Erik admired you so much. You were his hero." She dissolved into tears again.

Otto and Price sat quietly. A knock came on the door, and Price went to answer it. He came back with Betty. She went over to Brenda and engulfed her in a huge hug. Brenda began sobbing, and Betty held her and patted her on the back. They stood there for a moment, and then Brenda released Betty.

"Please sit down, Mrs. Kerchner. Thank you for coming. I just don't know what I'll do."

"Call me 'Betty,' please." She took Brenda's hand. "You and I are going to get through this together. I just know we will."

Brenda smiled through her tears. "Thank you . . . Betty."

Otto and Price stood up. "We'll be going now, Mrs. Olson. We both have paperwork to do. Someone from the casualty office will be in touch with you this afternoon. Betty will arrange for someone to stay with you tonight and for as long as you would like." Betty nodded at this. She smiled at Otto and Price and then took Brenda's hand again.

"Good-bye," Price said. "Please call on me if I can be of any help." He and Otto walked out of the small house to their waiting car. Donovan had shut off the engine and rolled down all the windows. Otto and Price climbed in.

"How'd it go?" Donovan asked.

"Rough," Otto said.

"It's never easy," Price added. "I never get used to notifications."

Donovan started the car and put it in gear, and they pulled off.

\*\*\*

Otto went back to the office and began processing the paperwork related to the loss of the bombers and their crews. He had to receive the official report for the mission, which would take a couple of days, but in the meantime he started composing letters that would go out to the next of kin. Each bomber had a crew of eleven, so that meant the commanders would write to a total of thirty-three families. Otto rubbed his eyes. He had a pounding headache. How in the world did Rackham write letters to all the families of all the casualties during the war? Sometimes their group lost twenty bombers. That would mean two hundred letters to grieving homes. My God, it's a wonder the man didn't crack in two. But here he was, nearly six years later, roaring along, not showing any sign of the agonies he had gone through.

The phrase in his mind caught Otto up short. He had gone through some agonies of his own, and what was he looking for from people in response to his experience and appearance? It would have to be compassion . . . and understanding . . . and acceptance . . . and even love, all of which Betty had showed him without hesitation. He teared up when he thought of her, of how she accepted and loved him in spite of everything. The thought made him think that he should call her at the Olson house and see how they were getting on. He looked up the number in the squadron roster and dialed the number. He heard the phone ringing. Someone picked it up on the fifth ring.

"Olson residence, Betty Kerchner speaking."

"Betty, it's Otto. I wanted to see how it was going."

"Oh, thanks for calling, Otto. She's doing about as well as can be expected. We had some tea and talked a bit and then she laid down for a nap. Poor girl is just in shock. Don't blame her. I can't imagine what I would do if something happened to you."

"I feel the same way, hon. Are you going to stay the night?"

"I'm thinking I should. The girls are with June next door and they adore her, so they'll be OK. I'll put together a simple meal here, although I don't think Brenda will be too hungry. Word will get out among people in the squadron and she'll probably have more company that she wants or needs, so I'll be here to screen her visitors. If you could get my nightclothes and toiletries and bring them by that would be helpful. And also something I can wear tomorrow."

"Will do," Otto said. "Anything else you can think of?"

"There are cold cuts in the refrigerator, so you can feed the girls and yourself with those. There are also some eggs and of course some bread, and you can fix those. June can stay with the girls tomorrow morning until I can get back. When Brenda's friends start coming in, I'll be able to leave."

"You're a good woman, Betty."

"And you're a good man, Otto. I'll talk to you later. Love you."

"Love you, too. See you in a bit."

"Bye for now."

"Bye."

Otto hung up the phone. What was the passage from scripture about a virtuous woman? He tried to recall. It was in Proverbs, he thought, something like,

> *Who can find a virtuous woman? For her price is far above rubies. The heart of her husband doth safely trust in her, so that he shall have no need of spoil. She will do him good and not evil all the days of her life.*

That could have been written about Betty. A good and virtuous woman. He shook his head. He was lucky to have her. He thought for a long moment, pulled a sheet of paper from his desk drawer, turned to the typewriter beside him, rolled the paper into it, and began typing.

*Dear Mrs. Olson:*

*On behalf of the president of the United States and the secretary of the air force, I wish to express my deepest condolences and regret at the recent passing of your husband, First Lieutenant Erik Olson, in action over North Korea on April 12, 1951. Lieutenant Olson was a credit to his service, to his unit, and to his country. Those who knew him spoke of his selfless dedication to his fellow airmen and to all he came in contact with. I was personally privileged to work with Lt. Olson during the training phase of his service, and I recall well his intelligence, compassion, and sense of humor.*

*My words cannot stem the grief and pain you are experiencing, but please know that they are offered with deepest sympathy and sincerity. If there is anything I or my office can do to assist you, please do not hesitate to call on us. We will be here for you.*

> *Your husband has gone on to join the ranks of those who gave their all in service to their country. He flies now without wings, and has, in the words of the poem "High Flight," "reached out and touched the face of God."*
>
> *I remain most respectfully and sincerely yours,*
>
> *Major Otto F. Kerchner*
>
> *United States Air Force*

Otto rolled the letter up in the roller and studied it. Yes, that would do. He sighed. Only ten more to go. Best to get to it.

# Chapter 35
# Night Riders
# May 1951

Otto yawned and studied the clock. Twenty-one hundred hours. Time to go to work. He staggered out of the bedroom to find Betty sitting in the living room leafing through a magazine. "Good evening," she smiled. "Would you like some breakfast?"

He went over and kissed her. "Good evening, my love. I'll just have some coffee. There'll be something to eat at the office." The recent shift for the '29 squadrons to nighttime bombing against enemy troops instead of earlier missions targeting their infrastructure meant he was on a different schedule. He arose about this time, followed the missions through the night, and then came home at 0900 hours to spend some time with Betty and the twins before he went to bed about 1300 hours.

Betty went into the kitchen, poured a cup of coffee, and brought it to him. "There you go," she said, "Strong, black, and hot, just like you like it."

"Thank you," murmured Otto, taking a sip. "I used to need it to keep me awake, but my schedule has shifted and nights are now days."

"Just like a baby when she's trying to learn when to sleep."

"Or babies," Otto reminded her.

Betty rolled her eyes. "Yes. Remember those days? Or those nights? They were wide awake and ready to play and I was so sleepy. Thank goodness I listened to my mother's advice and napped when they did."

Otto raised his cup. "Here's to you, my love, for all those lost sleepless hours raising our girls. And the sleep-filled ones. Or something like that."

Betty laughed. "Thank you, sir. My dad used to say 'The fleas come with the dog,' and I suppose that's true."

Otto looked at her archly. "Are you saying you've raised a couple of fleas, my dear?"

Betty giggled. "Sometimes they hop around like a couple of little fleas, but, no, our girls are a gift from heaven and I don't know what I would have done without them in our lives."

Otto nodded. "Nor I. I count myself the luckiest man on earth. Wow! I sound like Lou Gerhig. Remember that movie, *The Pride of the Yankees?* That echo of his speech in the stadium? 'Luckiest . . . est . . . est . . . est . . . man . . . man . . . man . . . man . . . '"

Betty nodded. "I remember that wonderful song that ran through the movie by Irving Berlin. 'Always.' Remember, Otto? We used to dance to it. You tried to sing along with it." She started singing in a light soprano:

> *I'll be loving you always.*
> 
> *With a love that's true, always.*
> 
> *When the things you've planned*
> 
> *Need a helping hand,*
> 
> *I will understand, always . . . always.*
> 
> *Days may not be fair always.*
> 
> *That's when I'll be there, always.*
> 
> *Not for just an hour.*
> 
> *Not for just a day.*
> 
> *Not for just a year,*
> 
> *But always.*

Otto smiled, finished his coffee, and stood up. "I'd ask you to dance, but I need to get to work."

Betty smiled back at him. "I'm always available for a dance with you anytime, airman."

Otto winked at her. "It's a date, lady." He kissed her and went out the door. "I'll be home at the usual time," he called.

"I'll be waiting," Betty said archly. Otto closed the door behind him, thinking how hot and humid it was at that time of the evening. Well, it was a tropical climate, he reflected. He walked over to his government-issue sedan, climbed in, and drove off toward the office. They'd need to update their cars when they got home, he thought. Betty was still driving her Packard, and Otto used the '36 Ford pickup Mata had gotten for them while he was away at war.

Time to come into the 1950s, he thought. Maybe a nice Ford sedan. He'd have to talk to Betty about it.

Otto drove the short distance to the office, walked in, and saw that Bob was already there, as he usually was. He stopped by.

"Hey there, sailor!" he exclaimed.

Donovan grimaced. "Arr! Do I be lookin' like some kinda swabbie sailor? Or a pirrrrate? Arrr!"

Otto laughed. "Actually, you look like Major Robert Bobolink, US Air Force."

Donovan threw him a mock salute. "At your service, Major Otto OK!"

Otto laughed. "Ready for another night of hours of boredom punctuated by moments of terror?"

Donovan responded, "As ready as I'll ever be." His tone was suddenly somber.

"I know what you mean," Otto returned. "Catch you at the flight line for takeoff."

Donovan waved at Otto as he left the office.

Otto studied the mission plan sheets at his desk. They were flying ninety-four aircraft tonight, close air support of the troops. Not what the Superfort was designed for, but what the hell. In for a dime, in for a dollar. He satisfied himself that he was familiar with the crews and aircraft for this mission, got up, and went down the hall. Donovan came out of his office about the same time, and they walked down the hall together.

"Ready to ride, Major Donovan?"

"Let's saddle up and git a-goin,' cowboy!"

"All right, podner! Let's do it!"

They both laughed. "I think we've seen one too many John Wayne movies, my friend," Donovan offered.

"What are you referrin' to, Pilgrim?" Otto came back with his best imitation. By this time they were outside and mixing with some of the other squadron commanders who were all business. Their banter faded.

They walked down the line of offices to the waiting rows of Superfortresses glistening under the night lights. No matter how many times Otto saw the lineup of bombers, he found the sight impressive. So much power and so much potential destruction contained in those silver bodies. These beautiful birds were indeed deadly.

The flight crews were loading into their bombers, and Otto walked past the '29s in his squadron. The pilots and co-pilots he could see through the clear nose of the bombers saluted or waved. Once down the line, Otto drew back to watch engine startup. One after another, the big propellers turned over on the powerful Wright Duplex Cyclone radials. The engines coughed, puffed white smoke, and then caught with a powerful roar. With all engines running on all the aircraft, Otto and Bob had to retreat into a hangar and put their fingers in their ears. The big aircraft pulled slowly away down the taxiways, moving to their takeoff positions on the runway. They could follow their navigation lights and flashing beacons. These, of course, would be turned off when they neared the target. One after another, the lights moved down the runway and lifted into the night sky.

"Godspeed," Otto murmured.

"Amen," Bob echoed.

They walked back to their offices. "Nothing to do but wait," Otto sighed. "Want to wait with me?"

"Can't think of anyone else I'd rather spend time with, other than Frances," Bob responded.

"Her mother still not doing well?"

Bob shook his head. "She's getting lower and lower. I don't expect she'll last another week."

"Well, sometimes these older folks surprise us. We'll keep praying for her and for you and Frances."

"Thanks, buddy. How does Betty like you on the night shift?"

"She's all right with it. I get to see her and the girls when I get home before I hit the sack. Say, we're going to take them to the Shikinaen Garden this Saturday. Would Uncle Bob like to go with us?"

"I'd love to! Tell you what—lunch is on me."

"You don't have to do that, Bob."

"I don't have to, but I want to. All of you have been so kind to this TDY bachelor, and you know I think the world of your girls."

"They're crazy about you, especially Marion."

"Yeah, Maria's a little slower to warm up."

"She's our thinker. Deliberate, likes to make sure of things before she commits."

"Maybe she'll decide she can be sure of me at some point," Bob laughed.

"In good time, Bobolink. In good time."

Otto put his feet up on his desk and his hands behind his head. Thank goodness they were flying ground-support missions for the present. They seemed to be a safer bet than the strategic bombing missions. The MiGs didn't seem to bother them as much on these nighttime missions. That was the idea, he supposed. Otto put his feet down and took out some paperwork, hoping it would pass the time. And so the night passed into the early dawn.

# Chapter 36
# Going Home
# July 1950

The bombing raids continued through the spring and into June. After the Soviet ambassador to the United Nations called for an armistice based on the separation of the two armies along the thirty-eighth parallel, truce negotiations began on July 1. By that time, Otto and Bob were out of the fray. They received their orders to pack up in mid-June and shipped out to the States a couple of weeks later. As it turned out, Otto and his family were on the same MATS flight with Bob. Betty had brought some toys and games to entertain the children with, but Uncle Bob played with them the entire flight. After a couple of hours, the twins went to sleep, as did Bob. Otto and Betty sat in adjoining seats, holding hands.

"Happy, Mrs. Kerchner?"

"Very happy, Major Kerchner. Happy to be with you and happy to be going home."

"It was quite an adventure."

"Yes, and one I wouldn't have traded for anything."

"Me either. But it will be nice to get back to the airline and the rest of the family."

"My parents have missed all of us tremendously. Holidays were the most difficult for them."

"Yeah, it never seemed like Christmas with temperatures in the 80s and no snow."

Betty smiled. "But we had nice holidays with the four of us and Uncle Bob."

"Do you mean Sleepy?" Bob was snoring away in the row of seats behind them. The girls were laid over on their seats as well.

"He would be the one. He's so good with the girls."

"He is that. It will be good to see Mata and Pete."

"It will be so good to see everyone."

"What do you want to do first when we get back?"

"Well, I don't have to worry about the house since Polly and Susan have been living there."

"They're such fine young women."

Betty nodded. "I know they've kept the place up, so I won't have to do any cleaning. Just wait for our things to arrive, I suppose." She looked at him seriously. "When do you suppose this 'police action' will be over?"

Bob sighed. "Wish I knew. Negotiations seem to be difficult with the North Koreans. I suppose things will continue until they see it's not to their advantage to be pounded into submission. It could go on for at least a couple more years, depending."

"Do you wish you could stay and continue the fight?"

"I consider that I've done my part for now. Guys are itching to get in there and have combat experience. They can have a turn now."

Betty put her head over on his shoulder. "So I have you all to myself again, Major Kerchner."

"I would say so, Mrs. K." He patted her hand. "Are you sleepy like our friends behind us?"

"I am. I'm going to take a nap."

"Me too." Betty closed her eyes, while Otto stared out the window at the clouds and the Pacific far below. Another twelve hours or so of this and they would be home. And that was what he had been fighting for all these years. Home, family, and God. Those were the main things, all right. He closed his eyes and slept a deep, dreamless sleep. The big transport bored on through the afternoon to Hawaii, while a thousand miles away bombs continued to rain from the shiny silver bombers.

# Chapter 37
# A Wisconsin Idyll
# August 1951

Otto came out of the M & M operations center and looked around the airport. It was bustling, with flights coming and going all day. In his absence, Polly and Mata had improved the lighting, remodeled a number of the buildings, and gotten the county to widen roads leading to the terminal. Representatives from Northwest were flying in on the 2:00 PM from Minneapolis today, bringing the paperwork that would make M & M a subsidiary. Otto was pleased with the work Mata had done while he was away, going to school and continuing to manage the airline, with Polly taking an increasing role. Jimmy had filled in for him as chief pilot during his absence and done a great job.

Otto stretched out his arms, basking in the Wisconsin sunshine. It was great to be home. They had been given quite a greeting when their flight landed a month ago, and the war in Korea seemed far away, although Otto knew it still raged day and night. There still existed the possibility that he could be recalled to duty again, but he hoped that the negotiators worked out a treaty before then. It would be best for everyone. A land war in Asia didn't seem to work out. The British found that out in Afghanistan. Well, time and history would tell.

Otto watched the M & M DC-3 on final as it came down the glide slope and touched down gently. Bob Rogers did a nice job. He rolled out on the runway and taxied over to the terminal. The ground crew rapidly moved the stairs into position. Otto spotted the representatives from Northwest as soon as they stepped onto the tarmac. There were three of them, two in dark business suits and one in a Northwest pilot's uniform. Otto walked toward them. The man in the uniform seemed to recognize him. As he came closer, Otto saw that he was Captain Harrison, the chief pilot who had turned him down for a job with Northwest years earlier. Harrison smiled as he came closer and extended his hand as Otto came up to him. Otto took his hand and shook it.

"Captain Harrison! Welcome to Pioneer Lake, the home of M & M Airlines!"

"Captain Kerchner! So very good to see you again. Thank you for such a warm welcome! May I introduce Mr. Dodge of our finance department and Mr. Borozinski of legal?"

Otto shook hands with the two men, murmuring greetings to them. That done, he addressed the three. "Allow me to show you to our conference room. Did you have a good flight?"

"Impeccable," Harrison observed. "A prompt departure, excellent cabin service, and a smooth takeoff and landing."

"I'll pass that along to the crew," Otto said. "Thank you. That means a great deal coming from the chief pilot of Northwest."

Harrison laughed. "Actually, since we last met, I've been promoted to vice president in charge of operations. They still let me wear my captain's uniform."

"My apologies," Otto told him. "I should have known better."

"I'm not sure anyone told your people about my title," Harrison reflected. "Your managers are quite impressive."

"Thank you," Otto said. "They're my sister and a young woman we moved up from a stewardess position."

"I like that," Harrison told him. "It shows that you recognize and encourage excellence."

"This is one busy airport for its size," Dodge interjected.

"It's small, but we like it," Otto smiled as he held open the door to the M & M operations office. The four of them went in. Mata and Polly were standing in the ready room as the men came through the door.

"Good afternoon, gentlemen," Mata greeted them as she extended her hand. A general round of greetings and introductions followed.

"Would you like some coffee?" Polly asked.

"No, thanks," Harrison said. The other two men nodded their assent. Polly went over to the coffee-service area and poured two cups and put them on a tray with cream and sugar.

"Let's go into the conference room where we can sit down," Mata smiled. She followed the four men into the room. Pete was already seated at the table, and stood when he heard them come in.

"Gentlemen, this is my husband, Pete Peterson. He coadministers the airline with me and Polly." Pete shook hands with each of the three representatives from Northwest, guided by the sound of their voices.

Pete, Polly, Mata, and Otto took seats on one side of the table; Harrison, Dodge, and Borozinski sat on the other. Dodge and Borozinski took some documents out of their briefcases and laid the papers on the table. Harrison cleared his throat.

"All right, we've been in talks about this consolidation for about a year now, mostly with Mrs. Peterson, who has been quite knowledgeable and very professional." Otto smiled at his sister. "We are ready to proceed with the signing of these documents by which M & M Airlines of Pioneer Lake will become a subsidiary of Northwest Airlines of Minneapolis. Major Kerchner, Mrs. Peterson, as co-owners of the airline, please take a few moments to look over the documents before signing them as indicated by the Xs." He passed the stack of papers to Otto and Mata. They leafed through them page by page, stacking them in a neat pile as they finished each one. When they had finished, Mata straightened the pile.

"We're ready to sign, Captain Harrison." At this, Dodge took out an expensive Parker pen and handed it to Mata. "Thank you," she smiled. She signed her name at the bottom of the last page and pushed it over to Otto. He quickly signed and slid the paper on top of the stack and handed it to Dodge. He signed the page and passed it over to Borozinski, who signed it and gave it to Harrison, who added his signature, capped the pen, and handed it back to Dodge.

"Very good," Harrison said. "We look forward to your being part of the Northwest family. I'm sure Mata has explained to you that your aircraft will continue to wear the M & M livery with lettering indicating your affiliation with Northwest. Your crews and staff will continue to wear M & M uniforms, but you will be able to take advantage of our maintenance facility at Minneapolis. Welcome to Northwest Airlines."

Both sides stood up and shook hands all around. Polly went out of the room and came back in with a tray of sandwiches. "We thought since it's close to lunchtime we'd have some sandwiches made, and we hope you'll join us."

"We'd be pleased," Harrison said, as everyone sat back down and passed the tray around.

"If you'll tell me what you'd like to drink, I'll be glad to get it for you," Polly announced. She took their drink orders, went into the combination supply room/kitchenette and soon came back with a tray of drinks. She served each person. "You do that so well, miss," Borozinski told her.

"I used to be a stewardess," she blushed. "All that training paid off."

"I'd say," Dodge added.

The group ate lunch quickly, talking about the airline business. Otto was exceptionally pleased with this turn of events. M & M had just about doubled its assets through this move, and he knew they would be able to add cities and flights to their routes. Northwest was a big draw, and their publicity would help spread the word about M & M to more people.

With lunch finished, the men from Northwest stood and thanked the M & M group for their hospitality. "We'd like to observe your operation if that's all right," Harrison indicated.

"Well," Otto mused, "Our airline is your airline now, so you're more than welcome. Let me show you around."

"Thank you so much, Major."

"My pleasure," Otto said with a bow, and he indicated that the three men from Northwest should go outside to begin their guided tour. He joined them in the bright sunlight.

Harrison turned to the two other men. "Would you give us a minute, gentlemen?" he asked Dodge and Borozinski. They nodded their assent, and he drew Otto aside.

"Major, I'm sure you remember the last time we saw each other and you recall that I had to turn down your application to be a pilot with us."

Otto nodded.

"I want to apologize for having to do that, and I assure you it was nothing personal. I was following company policy."

"I knew you were, Captain, and while I was disappointed, I understood your action."

"I'd say things have turned out well for you since then."

"They have indeed," Otto smiled. "Thank you for your concern. I'm doing well, as perhaps you can tell."

"I can see that. Thank you."

Otto turned to the other two men. "Shall we begin our tour? I'm Major Otto Kerchner, and I'll be your tour guide this afternoon."

The Northwest representatives laughed and followed him onto the tarmac.

# Chapter 38
# Fields of Gold
# August 1952

A year had gone by since M & M had become a subsidiary of Northwest, and, as Mata and Otto predicted, business had burgeoned, with four cities added to the combination airlines' routes. They hired four new pilots and six more cabin crew to take care of the demand. As the routes grew, so did the pressure on the airport, and about six months before, they had realized that the city would need a bigger airport. Mata put in the necessary paperwork, and now it had come down to a final hearing before the city council and the mayor. Mata knew all the members and the mayor from her work at the airport, so they didn't expect any trouble. The question was, would the voters agree to the bond issue to build the new airport? But first things had to come first.

Otto, Mata, Pete, and the same three representatives from Northwest filed into the council chambers. The council members and mayor sat at a long dais that stretched across the front of the room. A table sat before that, and the city clerk indicated they should sit in chairs at the table. They took their seats and saw they were a few minutes early. Only about three or four people were in the chamber as spectators. That was a good sign, Otto thought, that there weren't huge mobs protesting the establishment of a new airport.

Promptly at 7:30, the mayor struck his gavel on its pad. "This meeting of the Pioneer Lake Town Council is called to order. Will you all rise for the salute and pledge to the flag?"

After the pledge, the mayor looked through the papers in front of him. "First order of business is the question of a bond for establishment of an airport as voted on at our May meeting. Do I hear a motion on this question?"

One of the council members raised his hand. "I so move, your honor."

"And a second?"

Two council members seconded the motion.

"Very well. The question has been moved and seconded. The floor is now open for discussion."

The people in the room sat silently. "Major Kerchner, do you have anything you wish to say?"

Otto stood up. "No, your honor; I believe you know our position on the new airport."

"Yes, I am well aware of your position," the mayor smiled and others in the room chuckled. "And I want to thank you for establishing the present airport and making it such an asset to our city. And so, hearing no further discussion, I call for the question. Those in favor of the motion signify by saying 'Aye!'"

A chorus of "ayes" rang out in the chamber.

"Those opposed by saying 'No!'" There was dead silence.

"The ayes have it, and the question is so ordered. Thank you, Major Kerchner, Mr. and Mrs. Peterson, Captain Harrison, Mr. Dodge, and Mr. Borozinski. You have done yeoman's service on this issue, and we are grateful for all your work. We look forward to working with you as the project proceeds. Thank you for coming."

Otto spoke for all of them. "Thank you, Mr. Mayor, council members. We look forward to continuing to work with you." He and the rest stood up and filed out of the room. Once in the hall, they shook hands and congratulated each other all around.

"The evening's still young," Harrison said. "Where would you suggest that we go for a celebratory dinner?"

"There's the restaurant at the hotel that a lot of people around here use for special occasions," Mata said.

"What about a place for ordinary occasions where people like to go? Not that I don't think this is a special occasion. It's just that we've eaten at the hotel every meal since we got here yesterday."

"Well, there's Spencer's Diner," Otto noted. "The food's just everyday stuff, but they do a good job with it."

"Sounds ideal," Harrison responded. "If you'll lead, we'll follow."

"Let me call Betty and see if she can join us there. If you don't mind a couple of three-plus-year-olds for company."

"Not at all," Dodge answered. "I love kids. When I get married I want us to have a dozen."

Otto walked over to the pay phone in the lobby. He put in a nickel and dialed his home number. Betty answered.

"Betty, it's Otto. The airport proposal passed, so we thought we'd go to Spencer's to celebrate. Would you like to join us?"

"Oh, yes, provided I can bring the girls."

"Certainly. We'll meet you there in ten minutes."

"I'll be there. Bye."

"Bye."

Otto put the receiver back and walked over to the group. "It's all set. Let's go."

Mata and Pete piled into their blue '50 Ford. Otto and Betty had liked it so well they had bought a similar '52 model when they got back from Okinawa. Otto joined them, riding in the back seat. The men from Northwest got into their nondescript rental car, with Harrison driving. They followed Mata and Pete's Ford down Main Street to Spencer's, where it had been since Otto could remember. It hadn't changed much in that time, and that was probably part of its appeal. It was always crowded, and as the two cars pulled into the parking lot, the group saw that this night was no exception. They parked right as Betty drove in, parking next to them. There was a hubbub of greeting as she and the girls got out. Betty hugged Otto, Pete, and Mata and shook hands with the people from Northwest.

They pushed through the door into the diner. Rose, the waitress who had been there since day one, came up with menus. "Party of, let's see, I'm not sure I can count that high."

"There are nine of us," Mata told her.

"All right. Just a minute and I'll clear you a couple of tables." Rose turned and disappeared among the diners filling the tables.

"This is great," Borozinski exclaimed. "It reminds me of a place in my hometown. I go there when we're home for the holidays or whatever."

"It's the place a lot of people in town go, as you can see," Otto told them. "Betty and I came here before we were married."

"And when we broke up," Betty smiled.

The men from Northwest looked puzzled. "We sort of broke up before I went to the war," Otto remembered, "but we got back together when I returned. Thanks to Betty's doing."

"I see," said Harrison. "Sounds like a good story. You'll have to tell me the whole thing sometime."

"We'll have time as we're eating," Otto said. "And I want to hear your story."

"You got a deal," Harrison smiled.

# Chapter 39
# Progress
# November 1952

Otto walked across the gravel parking lot at the site of the new airport. Amazing progress had been made after the bond referendum had passed by a wide margin. The buildings were nearly done, the substrata for the runways had been laid, and the control tower was in place. It looked like they were on track to open on January 2, as projected.

Elections were held the week before, and Otto wasn't sure how he felt about a military man like Eisenhower being elected, although military veterans had certainly served well as president throughout the country's history—with some exceptions, like Grant. Let's see, Washington was of course the military man par excellence. Then there was Monroe, Jackson, Harrison, Tyler, Taylor, Pierce, Lincoln, Johnson, the aforesaid Grant, Hayes, Garfield, Arthur, different Harrison, McKinley, Teddy Roosevelt, and even Truman. Otto was surprised he remembered all the presidents he had to memorize as a junior in high school. Yep, old Mr. Stearns would be proud of him. Or maybe not. Well, some were great presidents, others not. We'll have to see, Otto thought. Eisenhower was certainly respected as the SHAEF leader in the war. Both parties had wanted him, and he went with the Republicans. And he promised to end the Korean War. It was about time. The negotiations to end the war were still going on. Maybe it would be over soon. Otto sighed.

He got back in his Ford and drove to the old Pioneer Lake Airport. It was still busy, but if one knew where to look, there were signs of change. The crews were slowly packing up tools and all the equipment necessary to run an airport. The plan was to keep Pioneer Lake open through the end of January and move the aircraft and other equipment to the new airport starting in December. It would take a lot of people and a lot of work to do so, but Mata and Polly had worked out a plan, and Northwest promised all the help they needed. That would be good to have.

Otto parked behind the operations building and walked into the waiting room. Mata was reading a report to Pete, who was taking it all in. He had an uncanny ability to remember what was read to him. It was a kind of compensation, Otto thought.

"Hi, troops!" Otto greeted them as he came through the door.

Mata looked up. "Hey, Bro!"

"Hi, Otto," Pete said.

"How are things coming for the big move?"

"We're getting there," Mata sighed, studying a chart.

"You don't sound convinced of that," Otto told her.

"Well, there are so many details. We're trying to run the airline operation and work on the move at the same time. I've never done anything like this before."

"Doesn't your coursework help with it?"

"Otto, I'm taking courses in industrial design, not project management. I'm making this up as I go along."

"Of course. It was dumb of me to say so."

"You're forgiven, dear Brother. Just keep on being chief pilot and Pete and Polly and I will work out the move. How are Betty and the kids?"

"Happy as clams since we got back from Japan. Although it was quite an adventure for all of us, it's one that I think none of us is willing to repeat any time soon."

"I bet. I wish they could negotiate a permanent cease-fire. The North Koreans are so unreasonable!"

"They're really a front for the Russians and the Chinese support. You know we had to take on MiGs flown by Russian and Chinese pilots."

"You would know that better than anyone, that's for sure. Do you all want to come over for dinner Thursday evening?"

"I'm sure Betty would love a break from cooking. About six? I'll have her give you a call to work out what she can bring."

"That sounds ideal. It'll be nice to see the girls. They've gotten so big!"

"They're about four and a half now, so they're doing a lot more. They're so entertaining! At least I find them so. Betty is around them more, so she's not as amused by them as I am."

"That seems to be a woman's lot, doesn't it?"

"So it seems. At least for now. I bet it will change in the future, and women like you are the ones to change it, Mata."

"Do you think so? Right now I'd like a magic wand to change this airport's location to the new one."

Otto laughed. "I need to do the check ride on the two o'clock to Eau Claire. I'll see you both later."

Otto walked out of the operations building with Mata and Pete's goodbyes in his ears. He knew Mata would get the job done on the move and do it well. He walked into the terminal and up to the gate where Flight 423 was boarding. They had gone to all DC-3 service when Northwest had taken them on as a subsidiary. The Beeches had been sold to some smaller regional airlines that were glad to have them. Otto thought it was great that companies in the airline industry helped each other out when technically they were commercial rivals. In this case, the companies they sold the Beeches to served other markets, so they were not in direct competition with Northwest or M & M.

Otto saw that the last of the passengers was boarding and that a new young hire, Angela Albemarle from Pioneer Lake, was the stewardess. Polly had interviewed and hired her about a month ago, and Angela had just completed her training a week earlier. She smiled when she saw Otto approaching. "Good afternoon, Major Kerchner! You must be here for the check ride."

"Hello, Angela," Otto answered. "You're right, but please treat me as you would any other passenger."

"Yessir," the young woman replied. "Except you're a passenger sitting in the jump seat today. Welcome aboard."

Otto climbed up the stairs to the cabin and made his way along the packed seats to the cockpit. The passengers were a mix of businessmen and young families with children. He thought that it would be interesting to know the destination and business of each person on the plane, but that was certainly their business and no one else's. He reached the cockpit and saw that the pilots were Scott Effler, a young fellow fresh out of the air force who had seen service in Korea and the SAC, and Tom Magee, who came to them from Kestrel Airlines, a feeder outfit out of Michigan. Effler was pilot in command today, and Magee was his co-pilot. They started to rise out of their seats when Otto came through the door. He motioned them down. "As you were, gentlemen. I'm Major Kerchner, here for your check ride. I want you to act as if I'm not here, which is a fairly tall order. I had these when I was in the air corps and air force, so I know what it's like. Just relax and you'll do fine."

"Good afternoon, Major," Effler said. "Welcome aboard. This is my co-pilot, Tom Magee, as perhaps you know."

Otto nodded. "Good afternoon, Major," Magee said as he reached back his hand for Otto to shake.

"If you'll strap in to the jump seat, Major, we're about ready for engine start. And may I say it is a pleasure to have a war hero riding with us this afternoon." Effler's face was serious as he became all business.

"Thank you, Captain. That 'war hero' business is overrated, I fear."

"What you did is well known in the piloting community. I salute you for it, sir."

"Well, I wrecked a perfectly good airplane. I'm lucky the government didn't bill me for it. I'd still be paying it off." Effler and Magee had the engines started by this time and, cleared by the ground crew and the tower, they started their taxi toward the takeoff point. Otto liked the way they worked together as the bird moved along the tarmac. They reached the runway and held there.

"M & M Flight four-two-three requesting permission to take off," Magee spoke into his mic.

Otto couldn't hear what the tower said but surmised that they were given the OK to proceed. Effler turned the ship onto the runway, stood on the brakes, and ran up the throttles. He and Magee looked over their instruments once more and then he released the brakes. The '3 accelerated down the runway, slowly at first, but then more and more rapidly. The tail came up and the aircraft lightened until they lifted from the ground, soaring into the chilly, cloudless November sky. This was living, Otto thought, as he watched from his vantage point through the windscreen. The silver, blue, and white airplane climbed for altitude as the earth faded beneath them like a distantly remembered dream.

# Chapter 40
# Generations
# November 1952

Otto pushed back his chair from the dining room table and wiped his mouth with his napkin. "What an excellent dinner!" he exclaimed. "My compliments to the chefs!"

"Why thank you, Brother, on behalf of Chef Betty and myself. Glad you enjoyed it."

"Why don't we have coffee and dessert in the living room?" Betty asked.

"Does dessert mean cake?" Maria wanted to know.

Mata patted her on the head. "You bet it does, Cupcake!"

"I didn't say 'cupcake'; I said 'cake'!" Maria insisted.

The grownups laughed. "You'll have cake," Otto assured her as the group got up from the table and moved to the living room. They seated themselves around the coffee table. Otto was still amazed at how well Pete navigated from room to room. Of course, it was his house.

Betty and Mata quickly served cake and coffee, with milk for the girls, and they ate in silence. When they had finished, Marion asked, "Mommy, can we go play with our dollies?" Mata kept some toys for the girls so they would have something to play with when they visited.

"Certainly you may. And no jumping on the bed," Betty warned them.

Once they were out of the room, Mata sat down next to Pete and took his hand. "We have an announcement," she started.

"Oh, I think I know what it is," Betty exclaimed. "Are you—"

Mata nodded with a broad smile on her face. "Yes! I'm pregnant. I'm due next July!"

"That's wonderful," Betty told her, as she rose to hug her and kiss her on the cheek. Otto stepped over and hugged Mata as well.

"Congratulations!" he told his sister. "And congratulations, Papa Pete," as he shook Pete's hand.

"Just a little project we've been working on together," Pete noted. Mata and Betty blushed.

209

"You should know that Mata and Betty are blushing," Otto said.

"She was a very important part of this project," Pete smiled.

Mata went over and hugged him. "Enough talk, Peter Peterson. You'll get us all in trouble."

The couples laughed. Otto raised his coffee cup. "To new life!" he called.

The others raised their cups, saying, "To new life!" and drank a toast.

"So, how do you think this will change your working at the airline?" Otto asked Mata.

"I don't know. We'll have to cross that bridge when we come to it, as Mama used to say."

"Yes, she did."

"I hope I can continue work if I can find someone to keep the baby."

"I'd be glad to do that," Betty chimed in. "I have plenty of experience."

"Thank you, Betty," Mata smiled. "That would be great. It wouldn't be long-term anyhow. I have a feeling Northwest is going to move to acquire M & M."

"Acquire? You mean buy?" Otto wanted to know.

"Yes, with the move to the new airport it would only make sense. We could get out of the airline business and I could open a design company."

"What will we do with the old airport?" This was Otto's question.

"Why not just convert it back to a general aviation field? We have enough people who lease hangar space from us, so that would work. In fact, most of them don't want to move to the new field where they'd have to continue to compete with larger aircraft."

"I like that idea," Otto exclaimed. He raised his cup again. "Here's to the renaissance of the old airport!"

"To the old airport!" the others echoed, and they drank the second toast of the evening.

As Otto looked around at smiling, familiar faces he thought, everything old is certainly new again.

"What will we call it? The new field is going to be Pioneer Lake Airport, so we can't continue to use that." Mata asked.

"How about Kerchner Field?" Betty proposed. "It would be named for the family and for our own war hero, like O'Hare in Chicago."

"I'm not a war hero," Otto said.

Betty looked at him. "A lot of people around here think you are."

"A lot of people are not renaming our airport."

"Children, no fighting!" Mata chided, smiling. "I'm sure we can come up with something."

"How about Barron County Airport?" Pete offered. "That would imply a wider reach than just Pioneer Lake." The group sat silently for a moment.

"I do like the idea of honoring someone," Otto said. "It just shouldn't be me."

"What was the name of that fellow who was killed in the raid in Korea under your command?" Mata asked.

"Erik Olson."

"How about Erik Olson Field?"

A moment of silence elapsed, and then nods and smiles around the room made it clear that Mata had come up with a winning suggestion.

"All right!" Otto exclaimed. "Erik Olson Field it is. I'll see if we can locate his widow and other members of his family and offer to fly them here for the renaming ceremony when we have it. How soon do you think that would be, Mata?"

"Let me consult my crystal ball, Major OK." Mata pretended to run her hands over an imaginary crystal ball. "I see . . . I see this ceremony as taking place . . . no earlier than . . . next March! The spirits have spoken!"

"The weather would be a little better then," Betty said. The group nodded.

"All right, let's shoot for then," Otto told them. "Forward to the past . . . and to the future!" Mata balled up her napkin and threw it at him.

# Chapter 41
# Things Present and Matters Past
# March 1953

Otto looked around at the crowd gathered in the cold March wind on the tarmac of the reconditioned airport. The airline logos and DC-3s were gone, operating out of the new Pioneer Lake Airport seven miles away. The small airplanes were in hangars or tied down off the taxiways. He held a piece of paper in his hand with a short speech he had written on it.

"Thank you all for coming today," he began. "We are reopening this airport today with a new name—Erik Olson Airport—in honor and memory of a young pilot who left us too soon." He looked up, right at Brenda Olson, who was standing with her parents and Erik's parents. "I was privileged to know Erik as a trainee on the B-29 bomber in Omaha and then again as a part of the bomber squadron I commanded in Korea. While on a mission during that war, Erik's aircraft was brought down by an overwhelming number of North Korean jet fighters in spite of a sizeable escort from our fighters." He paused for a moment and then continued, "Erik Olson was a representative of the finest this country has to offer: an excellent pilot, a good man, a faithful and loving husband, and a dutiful son. Those of us who knew him miss him, and we remember who he was to us and what he meant to all those whose lives he touched.

"And so, we dedicate this field to his memory and in honor of his excellence, commitment, and sacrifice. May all those who pass through here stop and remember him and all the others who have made the lives we lead possible.

"At this time, I will ask Erik's wife, Brenda, and his parents, Mark and Joanne, to come forward and reveal the memorial marker that has been erected at this spot."

Brenda and Erik's parents moved to the black cloth covering the granite block, pulled it back, and stood there looking at it. Those gathered around applauded briefly. Brenda smiled slightly and went back with Erik's parents to the place they had been standing.

"Thank you," Otto said, "and God bless you. This concludes our ceremony this morning, ladies and gentlemen. If you would care to join us in the terminal building, there are refreshments available."

A murmur arose from the people as they began to make their way to the terminal. Otto went over to Brenda. "I am so happy all of you could be here for this," he told her, her parents, and Erik's parents.

"Thank you for such an honor," Brenda murmured, wiping back tears. "We were so pleased when Mata called us and told us what you had done. Thank you."

Otto shook hands with the Olsons and Brenda's parents, thanking them for being there and for sharing in the ceremony. Betty joined them and murmured some comments to them. They then moved into the terminal building, where most of the other people had already gathered. No one had made a move for the food and drink; they were waiting out of respect for Brenda and her relatives. Betty guided them over to pick up some hors d'oeuvres and drinks and then walked over to seat them at one of the waiting tables. Once they were seated, she stayed with them. Otto, Mata, and Pete greeted people as they came through the line. Mata was showing. "Wouldn't you be more comfortable sitting down?" Pete asked her.

"I'm fine," Mata said. "If I get tired I'll sit down, but I'm all right for now."

About one hundred people passed through the line—employees of M & M and Northwest, townspeople, and Bob and Frances Donovan. When Donovan reached Otto, he shook his hand and embraced him.

"Major Donovan! How are you, my friend? And this must be Frances!"

"Indeed it is, Major Kerchner! And this must be Mata and Pete." He and Frances shook hands with them all. "So nice to meet you! Otto's told me so much about each of you."

"I hope it's all good, Major Donovan," smiled Mata.

"It is, ma'am. And call me Bob," Donovan returned, "or as your brother would call me, 'Bobolink.'"

Mata turned to Otto. "Bobolink?" she asked with a raised eyebrow.

"Well, he calls me Major OK!"

"What are you, ten years old? 'OK' is a positive term of affirmation. A bobolink is a small bird with a funny little call. There's a huge difference!"

"Mrs. Peterson, it's really all right. I take it as a term of endearment that shows Otto cares."

Otto snorted. "I'll care for you with my fist, Major Bob—" Mata shot him a look. "Just Major Bob," he said sheepishly.

"And while we're talking about names, please call me Mata."

"And call me Pete."

They all laughed. Otto turned to Frances. "What should we call you?" he wanted to know.

"Oh, call me Mrs. Donovan," Frances smiled. There was silence for a moment and then she broke into a huge laugh. "Gotcha!" she exclaimed. "You know you can call me Frances. From Bob's stories about Major OK, I feel as if they're brothers."

The group joined in laughing with her. "Frances has a really sly sense of humor," Donovan said. "I never quite know, even after all the years, when she's joking." Frances winked at Otto.

Frances saying he and Bob were like brothers was so true, Otto thought. They had indeed been through a lot together.

Mata announced, "Well, it's settled, then. First names for everybody! Sound good?"

There was a general murmur of assent.

"Is Betty here?" Frances asked, looking around.

"She's over with the Olson family," Otto said. "You can meet her when we get our food and go over and sit down."

By this time the last of the guests had passed by, so the group went past the refreshment tables and loaded their plates up. The Pioneer Lake crew had been up early preparing for the ceremony, and it had been quite a while since breakfast. They settled in at the table next to the one occupied by the Olsons. Betty excused herself from the table and came over. "You must be Major and Mrs. Donovan," she smiled.

The men at the table rose from their seats. "I'm so pleased to meet you, Mrs. Kerchner. And this is my wife Frances."

Frances held out her hand. "Please call me Frances."

"And please call me Bob." Mata shot a look at Otto. He grimaced.

"Well, then, I'm Betty."

"We just had this conversation," Frances smiled.

"Which conversation would that have been?" Betty asked.

"Forgive me; I didn't mean to be rude. We were over at the line deciding what to call each other. After some discussion, we settled on first names for everyone."

"That makes a lot of sense," Betty commented. "Titles and last names seem so formal among people who have known about each other for so long."

"There were other names mentioned as well," Frances winked.

"Oh? Names like what?"

"I'll tell you later," Otto murmured. "Mata might smack me if I told you now."

Betty looked puzzled. "Tell me now," she insisted.

"There were a couple of names Bob and I called each other in the service."

"Can you repeat them in polite company, Otto?"

"Yes, of course. Mine, as you know, is 'My Current Rank' plus 'OK,' or currently, 'Major OK,' and Bob's is 'His Current Rank' plus 'Bobolink,' or 'Major Bobolink.'"

"I see." Betty had a thoughtful look for a moment. "And who gave him this nickname?"

"I did," Otto admitted.

"What are you, ten years old?" Betty asked him.

The group roared with laughter. Betty looked puzzled again. "I'm sorry, but what's was so funny?"

"That's what Mata said," Frances chortled.

"Well, she and I know Major OK best."

"Second that motion," called Mata.

"Hey, what about a truce?" Otto declared.

"Truce." Mata and Betty spoke together. At that moment Brenda Olson came over. The men stood again. She was smiling, but her smile was a sad one, Otto thought.

"I want to thank all of you so much for this wonderful honor and the lovely reception. We'll need to be leaving in a few minutes, but I wanted to thank each one of you personally for all you've done for me and my family." She went around and hugged every member of the group, most of whom had to wipe their eyes. When she had finished, she looked at the group wistfully and said, "I know we'll meet again, just like the song says." She turned and walked back to her family. They stood and walked out of the terminal. Mata had made arrangements for Jimmy and Bob Owens to drive them to the new airport for their flight home to Spokane.

There was silence at the table for a few seconds. Mata and Betty got up and began circulating around the room bidding good-bye to the guests, who had begun to trickle out.

"Well, old man," Bob said to Otto, "I supposed we'd better be getting along as well. It was so good to see you, OK. I hope we can get together again real soon."

"I do, too, Bobolink. Don't be a stranger."

"If I got any stranger, Frances wouldn't let me out of the house."

Frances looked over. "You got that right, Bobolink."

Donovan made a wry face. "Looks like my name has spread."

Otto laughed. "I don't think Mata or Betty will be using it any time soon."

"They are two formidable ladies, OK."

"Don't I know it?"

Bob and Frances stood up, shook hands or exchanged hugs all around, and then walked quickly toward the doors. Otto and Pete sat down as the last few guests left the hall.

"Wheel stop," Otto called.

"Yep," Pete answered, taking the last sip from his drink. "This has been a good day."

"That it has," Otto smiled.

# Chapter 42
# Days Like These
# April 1954

Otto stood in the parking lot for Olson Field waving as Mata and little Hans, who had been born the previous July, drove away. The blond-haired boy looked a great deal like Otto at that age. Otto had been so pleased that Mata and Pete had decided to name him after the patriarch of the family. Children come and they do grow, he reflected. The girls would be six the next month and would start elementary school in September after a successful year in kindergarten. Such changes.

    He turned back to go into the office, thinking how well it had done in the year it had been open for business. They had seen an increase in charters, in pilots passing through en route, and in leases and tie-downs. Polly ran the business end, with Mata devoting much of her time to Hans. She and Pete still came in a couple of days a week to help with the business. Otto supervised any aspect of the operation that no one else covered, which meant he ended up doing a little of everything. His days were filled, but he kept thinking there was more he could be doing. The Korean War ended about the time Hans was born, so Otto doubted he would see any more military service. He hoped not, and he knew it would require major retraining for him to fly the jet bombers that were coming into service. The B-47 six-engine bomber had been in use since 1951, and word was an eight-engine model, the B-52, would be ready early the next year. The air force wouldn't waste time retraining an old sea dog like himself. Or an old air dog was more like it. Either way, he was done with the service. He was fairly sure of this.

    Otto turned over the possibilities in his mind. He should get Mata's ideas on additional uses for the airport. They were offering every other service that most general aviation fields did, so nothing seemed to be coming to him. Ah well, time for lunch. He could still walk home to their house, so that was nice. He came into the kitchen just as Betty was putting sandwiches and potato salad on the table. She gave him a kiss as he walked through the door. "Girls!" she called. "Daddy's home! Time for lunch!"

    The twins came running into the kitchen and grabbed Otto around the legs. He walked over to the table with them holding on, giggling loudly. "Arrgh!" he exclaimed. "What has a hold on my legs? Why are they holding on so tightly? Are they some sort of creatures from the lake in the back? Help me! Someone help me!"

"It's us, Daddy," exclaimed Marion. "Your daughters! We're not creechurs! Promise!"

"Yes, we're just little girls! I'm your daughter Maria! I'm not a monnsterr!" They continued to laugh as Otto reached the table.

"All right, girls, let your daddy go. You all can play Lady of the Lake later," Betty smiled as she came toward them. "Let's all sit down and eat."

"I'm starving," Otto said. "I could eat a horse!"

"Daddy, that's silly! We don't eat horses! Horses are for riding!"

"Yes! Will you get us a pony?"

Betty put out her hand. "We'll talk about ponies later. A pony has to be watered and fed and exercised. I think you'll need to be a little older to have a pony. When you're old enough, you can join the 4-H and raise a pony as a project."

"We're nearly six now. When can we join this 4-G club?"

"It's 4-H, honey, and you have to be eight. You have a couple more years to go, and then we'll see."

"That's a long time, Mommy! We want a pony now!"

"You'll just have to wait, Marion. There's nothing else to do for now. "

"Time passed so slowly when I was a child," Otto noted.

"Yes, it did. I remember when I thought Christmas and my birthday would never get here."

"It was hard to wait." They continued eating.

"Girls, you ought to ask your father about taking care of farm animals. He took care of milk cows when he was your age or younger."

"Is that right, Daddy?"

"Yes, it is, but I didn't like it very much."

"Why?" Maria wanted to know. "Cows are beautiful." She loved any kind of animal. So far they had resisted getting a dog or a cat on the grounds that the girls were too small to care for one. They had brought in a series of goldfish, which had not lived long. Betty had to explain what happened to the first fish, and they had a little goldfish funeral and buried it in a matchbox casket in the back yard. After that, the girls had their own funerals and burials. They had a lot of experience with it after the fifth Mr. Goldie died. Otto said maybe they could put their skills to work and become undertakers. It was a dying business, he said. Betty threw a dish towel at him by way of comment.

"They're a lot of work, and I didn't like farm work at all. I would have rather read."

"What kind of books did you read, Daddy? Were they like the ones you read to us?"

"No. My mother read children's books and nursery rhymes to me when I was a boy, but they were in German. I had to learn to speak better English when I went to school."

"Can you still speak German?"

"Well, I haven't used it for a while, so I'm rusty, but with a little practice, I think I could do well with it."

"So, what about the books you read?"

"I liked to read about pilots and flying. In fact, when I was just about a year older than you, I was reading a book about a pilot one day in the hayloft of the barn. My father called me to come help him and I jumped out of the hayloft and broke my leg. I was in a cast for six weeks."

"Did it hurt?" Marion asked somberly.

"At first it did, but then less and less. And my father was mad at me because he needed me to help on the farm. But my farming days are over. I'm a pilot now."

"And you love to fly," Maria observed.

"More than anything except you two and your mother. Come to think of it, I should take you up in the Cub."

"Take us up in a bear?" Marion looked puzzled.

Otto laughed. "No, it's an airplane called a Piper Cub. It does have a little picture of a bear cub on it. It was one of the first planes I learned to fly, and I taught your mother to fly on it."

"Can we all go up together?" Maria wanted to know.

"It only holds two adults," Otto told them, "But you and your sister would fit in one seat and either your mother or I would sit in the other and do the flying."

"I haven't flown much in recent years," Betty said. "I'll defer to you on this one."

"Hey, maybe we could get Mata and Pete to bring Hans and we could take turns going up."

"Oh, boy! Aunt Mata and Uncle Pete are going flying with us!" Marion exclaimed, clapping her hands.

"Yay! Aunt Mata and Uncle Pete!" Maria echoed.

"Well, I could do the flying and then also take your mother up so she can practice flying."

"Now that sounds like a plan," Betty mused.

"How about this Saturday?" Otto asked.

"Sounds good. I'll call Mata and set it up. About ten o'clock?"

"Works for me," Otto said.

"Yay!" the girls exclaimed, throwing their hands in the air. Otto and Betty smiled.

\*\*\*

Later that evening, after they had eaten and the girls were in bed, Otto came into the living room, where Betty sat looking through a magazine. "What are you doing, airman?" she smiled.

"Looking for a pretty girl," he told her.

"Will I do?" she asked, patting the couch beside her. He sat down and put his arms around her.

"I have something to discuss with you, Mrs. Kerchner."

"Oh yes?" She cocked her head to look at him. "Does it involve ponies?"

"No."

"Dairy cattle?"

"Ugh. Definitely not."

"The 4-H Club?"

"Nope."

"Let me think. What else is there?" She furrowed her brow in pretended concentration. "Oh, yes, I am seeing the answer now. It's becoming clearer and clearer. I see it now . . . does it involve . . . airplanes?"

"Ding! Ding! Ding! Ding!" exclaimed Otto. "You have won the prize!" He kissed her, and she responded eagerly. She broke away after a bit.

"Hold on there, sailor; do you want to talk about airplanes or do you want to do something else?"

"Honestly ma'am, I want to do both, but we'd better talk about airplanes first."

"All right, you have yourself a deal, mister. What's on your mind? Besides that, I mean."

Otto laughed. "I've been thinking lately that we need to do something else with the airport besides the general aviation business. I just can't think of what that would be, but I have a feeling there's something out there that we should be doing." He sat with his hands in his lap.

"I think I can help you, my darling."

He smiled at her and took her hand. "You always do, my love."

"I was reading an article in one of your aviation magazines—"

"I didn't know you read my aviation mags . . . "

She feigned shock. "I *am* a pilot, you know."

"Oh, yes ma'am. That slipped my mind in the presence of your considerable beauty."

Betty laughed. "Flattery will get you everywhere, my dear. But to the matter at hand—the article was about a kind of revival of flying circuses, you know, like they had after the First World War."

"Yes, I think Sparky was part of one. Seems I recall him telling Wilson about it during one of their drinking bouts, which were frequent."

"Poor old Sparky." Betty shook her head sympathetically. "Anyhow, we could set up a flying circus at the field."

"I love the idea!" Otto exclaimed. "I knew you'd come up with something!" He leaned over and kissed her. "We wouldn't be able to do it at the airport itself, though. It's too busy. But what we could do is acquire land next to the airport. The types of aircraft we'd be using, like the Cub, would be able to operate off grass."

"The article also said that there were traveling wing walkers and the like who fly from show to show. We could engage them."

"Right! We'll get Mata and Pete and Polly involved. I think they're feeling at loose ends since Northwest has taken over most of the operational side of M & M."

"Why don't we have them over for dinner Friday? The girls love playing with Hans, so we could talk while they keep him entertained."

"You have a deal, madame. And now to the other business on the agenda..."

"You're on, mister," Betty murmured as they embraced and rolled over on the couch.

# Chapter 43
# The Flying Circus
# July 1953

Otto scanned the sky around the field they had acquired for their flying circus. He heard the faint sound of a large rotary engine coming from the south and knew it was the Stearman they had hired as a wing-walking act for the first show of the M & M Flying Circus. Mata had joked that they should just go ahead and put everything under the umbrella of "M & M Enterprises" since everything they did seemed to have that name. Betty said that actually was a good idea and suggested Mata look into it. She said that Northwest would probably buy M & M outright in a year or so. They'd have to find something else to do or retire on the windfall from the sale of the airline. Otto thought that they'd deal with that when it happened. Right now they had a show to put on.

Mata's money management and the deal with Northwest gave them a nice cash reserve, which they used to buy some land at a good price right next to Olson Field. Mata arranged for bleachers to be put up, a hangar, a small building for a snack bar and restrooms, and a couple of parking lots. By the end of June, everything was in place and several acts had been hired, including the wing walker, a group which flew four AT-6s in formation, and a parachute team. Otto had worked with Betty to develop a comedy act with the Cub. Otto would dress as a farmer, come out of the crowd, jump into the Cub, and fly it around in various absurd attitudes while Jimmy chased him in a Ford Model T, shaking his fist. They hoped people would find it funny. The air show crew would find out, Otto thought.

The Stearman came into view, painted in red and white, and Otto could see the pilot with a passenger behind him. He knew it was a husband-and-wife team. He did the flying, she did the wing walking, and by all accounts, they put on quite a show. The throaty roar of the engine cut back to a deep rumble as the aircraft turned on final and kissed the ground in a perfect landing. The guy was some pilot, Otto thought. He had seen enough of them to know.

The biplane taxied up to where Otto stood. The pilot cut the engine and climbed out of the cockpit, stood on the lower wing, and helped his wife out. They jumped to the ground, pulled their helmets off, and walked over to Otto.

The man extended his hand. "Major Kerchner! I'm Dick Rockwell, and this is my wife Lois." Otto shook their hands.

"It's a pleasure to have you with us, Mr. and Mrs. Rockwell. Welcome to the Olson Field Annex. And please call me Otto."

"Thank you, Otto. Please call us Lois and Dick. Now, is there somewhere we can get something to drink and clean up a bit? These biplanes are great birds, but we do get dirty after a while."

Otto knew they had flown in from Champaign-Urbana, where they were headquartered. According to their promotional material, they flew all over the country during the warm months, doing shows and fairs all across the country. "Yes, if you'll come with me, we'll go over to the airport proper, where you'll be staying. You can clean up there and get something to eat."

"All right," said Rockwell. "Give us a few minutes to tie the aircraft down and we'll be ready to go."

"There are tie-down points right here," Otto told him, pointing to several small concrete pads with hardware protruding from them. "And I have the cables right here. I'll help you. I'm very familiar with the Stearman type from my air corps days."

"Thank you," Lois said with a smile. "That's very thoughtful."

"Takes a pilot to know a pilot," Dick observed. "Which theater were you in, Otto?"

"I was with the Eighth in England."

"I was in Italy with the Fifteenth. Flew B-24s and did thirty missions. How about you?"

"A '17. I completed twenty-three missions and pranged it on the twenty-fourth."

Rockwell's face grew somber. "Yes. We heard about what you did. You're to be commended for saving your crew."

"Thank you. That all seems such a long time ago."

They tied the airplane down quickly, got into Otto's car, and drove to the hangar at the airport. They had built a small suite of apartments for pilots who were passing through and didn't want to have to go into town for the night. Mata had done the decorating, and Otto thought they were nicer than most hotel rooms. Mata was waiting for them at the door to the suite.

"Hello, Mr. and Mrs. Rockwell," she said, holding out her hand. They exchanged names and handshakes, and Mata showed the two to their suite, explaining where everything was.

I'll leave you two to rest or do whatever you want. Our snack bar is down in the terminal. Just tell Judy behind the counter who you are and your meal is on us."

"Thank you," Lois said. "All of you have been quite gracious and kind. We're not always treated this well."

"We're looking forward to the show, and we're excited that you'll be a part of the first one."

"We are, too," Dick answered. "We'll see you later."

Mata went outside where Otto was waiting for her. "So we're good with the wing-walking act. And the precision flight team comes at . . . what is it?"

"They're scheduled to be here by four. I'll come get you when they show up," she replied.

"Oh, we'll all hear four AT-6s when they come in. No problem with that."

"You are such an airplane person, my brother."

"And happy to be one, Sister."

They both laughed.

*** 

The M & M Flying Circus was a huge success. About four hundred people came out on a beautiful Sunday afternoon and oohed and aahed at the precision flying of the Flying Texans Precision Aerobatic Team as they twisted and turned in the sky, seemingly only inches apart, sometimes running at each other in what looked to be a sure head-on collision. Bob and Lois did two shows to thunderous applause, and then Bob did an aerobatic display. The parachuting team of the Flying Devils from Oregon made a number of jumps, trailing smoke and creating colorful patterns in the clear blue sky. Otto, who was standing with his family and a group from M & M, commented that he didn't know why anyone would jump out of a perfectly good airplane. "You are truly a pilot," Pete laughed. Otto and Betty had not had enough time to perfect their Cub comedy act, but they promised themselves they would work on it for the next show.

The show lasted two hours and ended with a flyby of all the aircraft involved in the show, the big rotary engines creating a sound that was felt as much as it was heard. People filing out commented that they had never seen anything like it and that they hoped M & M would have a similar show very soon. Mata calculated from the attendance that they would do very well financially. After they had time to officially run all the totals, they would talk about how often they wanted to repeat the show.

One of the last people to leave was Bob Harrison. Otto and Mata had not known he was there.

"Greetings, Major and Mata," he smiled.

"Captain Harrison! We didn't know you were here! Can you stay and have something to eat with us?"

He shook his head. "I've got to get back to Minneapolis. But I want to set up an appointment for us to talk about Northwest buying M & M. Just between us, they're ready to move on that."

"All right," Mata replied. "Give me a call tomorrow and we'll set something up late next week."

"Have a good flight back," Otto told him as he shook his hand.

"It'll be good since I'm on M & M." Harrison smiled and then walked away.

Mata and Otto looked at each other. "That's a fortuitous development." Mata seemed awestruck.

"Sounds good to me."

"Well, as usual, we'll have to see what tomorrow brings."

# Chapter 44
# A New Day
# May 1954

Mata and Otto walked out of the administrative offices at Pioneer Lake Airport into a beautiful, cloudless spring day. The papers had been presented and signed, and M & M Airlines was now owned by Northwest Airlines. The brother and sister would have no more to do with the running of the airline, although Northwest had left all the employees in place and brought them in as Northwest workers. The airplanes would continue to carry the M & M livery.

"Well, how do you feel, Brother?"

"Like I need something else to do."

"How about running our little airfield?"

"I'm doing that already. I want to do something in addition to that."

"We'll think of something."

"You always do, Mata."

She slapped him lightly on the head. "You do flatter me so, good sir."

"I speak the truth," Otto returned, making a deep bow.

"We've come a long way in the past eight years. I just wonder what the future will hold for us."

"There's no way to tell. We've learned that."

***

Otto walked in to the airport office, where Mata and Pete were sitting at the table in the front room. Little Hans was asleep in a portable cradle. They brought him to work with them when they came in, and he did very well. "Good morning, fellow flying-circus operators! How are we this fine morning?"

"We're fine, brother of mine," Mata answered. "And so are Pete and Hans."

"I can speak for myself, my dear," Pete chided, smiling. "We have the plans and paperwork for the circus, Otto. We'd like to go over it with you."

"'O, 'tis a consummation devoutly to be wished,'" Otto recited.

"*Hamlet*, right?" Mata guessed.

"Yep."

"Are you sure you didn't major in English at some point?"

"Nope. Just had a navigator who did. When I would announce we were setting up for landing, that's what he would say. And he'd add which play it came from. It got to be a thing with the crew. If we hadn't heard from him, one of them would call on the intercom and ask if he was still with us. To which he would reply, 'I am too much o' this earth. *Hamlet.*' I wonder what happened to him."

"Maybe you ought to get your crew together."

"Other than Bob Donovan, I have no idea where they are or how to contact them. Maybe that'll be a project for another year. Right now we have a flying circus to attend to. Give me the lowdown."

"Well, it's all here," Mata started. "We start the first Saturday in June, although next year we'll start the first one in May, and run through the first Saturday in October. That will make for seventeen shows this year and twenty-one next year. If ticket sales hold up, we should make expenses and some profit, although we have plenty of backup assets."

"You don't think we'll wear out our welcome with too many shows in a limited amount of time?"

Pete answered Otto. "We're the only regularly scheduled air show in this neck of the woods, so if we have a quality product, which I think we do, we'll have no trouble attracting customers and repeat customers. This is the sort of thing that people go see, and if they like it, they take their friends and relatives and business associates. People keep coming back to see the Wagoneers play, and they have a miserable record every year." The Wagoneers were Pioneer Lake's Class A baseball team. They had stayed at the same rotten level of play for years, but people from the area still came out to support the home team. The Kerchners and Petersons had gone to a game the year before, and it was just embarrassing. Otto thought he could do better than most of the players, and he hadn't played in years.

Mata laid a sheet in front of him. "Here's a chart showing responsibilities and a timeline for each show. Your line is here"—Mata pointed to the second line on the chart.

"So basically I walk around and look like I know what I'm doing."

"If you can," Mata joshed.

"I'll practice," Otto came back. "I'll be ready in a couple of months."

All three of them shared a hearty laugh. Here we go on another adventure, Otto thought. Hope it works out well.

***

Otto was sitting at the desk in his office when he heard the door open and close. Mata stuck her head in. "I'm here by myself," she said. "The baby's colicky so I didn't want to bring him out. Pete's taking care of him." Otto had seen Pete tending to Hans, using touch and hearing to assess Hans's needs and taking care of them tenderly and quickly. It was remarkable.

"Always good to see you," Otto told her, looking over the fuel order for the next quarter.

Mata went to the incoming mailboxes and took out several days' mail. She stood over the trash can, discarding most of the envelopes without looking at them. She came to an envelope which, Otto could see from his seat, looked official. He had no idea what it could be, but Mata would take care of it. She sat down at the table in the front room, pulled a letter opener from a tray at her left hand, and started opening the envelopes. She opened the big envelope last, read what was written on the letter, and gasped. "Otto! Come here! Quickly!" Her tone was urgent.

Otto immediately got up from his desk. "Whatever is it?"

She held the letter out to him. "See for yourself."

The letter was from the lawyers who represented Northwest Airlines and ordered M & M Air shows and Exhibitions, Inc. to cease and desist from using the name "M & M" since under the conditions of the sale agreement signed by Otto and Mata, the name "M & M" was the exclusive property of Northwest Airlines and could not be used for profit by any other commercial entity.

Otto was stunned. This was the name they had thought up. The initials were those of his mother and sister. How could someone else claim exclusive use of it?

Mata went over to a file cabinet on the wall and pulled out a folder. She leafed rapidly through the pages and took one out. She read down the page and then brought it over to Otto.

"Here it is, in black and white. I don't see how I missed it."

Otto read rapidly down the page, and there it was in black and white. They no longer had legal use of the name. He stood silently, taking in the bad news.

Mata sat down in a chair and buried her face in her hands. "It's my fault," she whimpered. "I should have caught this. We could have negotiated something to retain use for certain specified uses."

"Maybe that could still be done," Otto assured her, coming over and putting his hand on her back.

"That would be up to the good graces of Northwest. Judging by this letter, those are in short supply with them."

"We'll see," Otto said. "Tomorrow is a new day. I've noticed that."

Mata wiped her eyes and patted Otto's hand. "Always looking on the sunny side. That's you, Brother."

"And I could very well say the same thing about you. As the song says, 'Keep on the sunny side.'"

Mata put her hands over her ears. "Please don't start singing. I have a feeling that's next."

Otto laughed. "Don't worry, you're safe—for now. But you never know when I might feel a song coming on."

Mata laughed, and Otto thought how good it was to hear that sound.

# Chapter 45
# The Show Goes On
# July 1954

Dressed in the most outlandish farmer's outfit imaginable, Otto stood at the back corner of the grandstand waiting for his cue. The Komedy Kub act of Sparky Duncan's Flying Circus and Exhibition was next to last, and judging from the murmur coming from the stands, the crowd was in a relaxed and happy mood.

Otto was burning up in the plaid flannel shirt and overalls Mata and Betty had costumed him in. He wore a big straw hat and what the fellows from the South in his outfit would call clodhoppers for shoes, and a red bandana hung from the rear pocket of the overalls. All my life I've tried to stay away from farming, he thought, and here I am playing a farmer. Well, at least it's only a role. And aren't we all poor players who strut and fret our hour on the stage and then are heard no more? There's a jolly thought, courtesy of Lt. Detwiler and Mr. Shakespeare. And so, once more into the breach, good friends. More Shakespeare.

Jimmy had taken the Cub up for a flyby, landed, and taxied to a stop. He jumped out, leaving it running, and raced for an outhouse that had been rolled to the edge of the field. Bob Owens was the announcer for the show.

"Uh oh, folks, it looks like Jimmy has heard the call of nature . . . and it's an urgent call. Let's cheer him on and hope he makes his goal in time!"

The crowd cheered, whistled, stomped, and applauded as Jimmy reached the wooden structure and slammed the door. The outhouse shook, eliciting laughter from the crowd. "He made it!" Bob shouted, which sent the onlookers into further gales of merriment. "All right! But Jimmy was in such a hurry he left the aircraft running. That's a hazardous situation, folks, so we're asking that no one go near the Cub until Jimmy finishes his business and comes back to shut it off. When you gotta go, you gotta go! But wait! What's this?"

Otto had come around the side of the bleachers and was weaving across the field toward the running Cub.

"Oh no! It's a distant cousin of the Kerchners here for a visit from Alabama. His name is Rufus and he farms cotton and comes up here every once in a while for a stay. Let's all say 'Hey!' to Rufus!"

The bleacherites responded with a hearty "Hey, Rufus!"

"Rufus" stopped, turned to the crowd, and gave them a big wave. Then he continued on his way toward the aircraft.

"Oh no," Bob intoned. "Rufus is crazy about airplanes, but he has no idea how to fly one. Rufus! Get away from that Cub!"

"Rufus" made a dismissive wave of his arms toward Bob, got to the Cub, climbed in, and shut the door. "Watch out folks! We don't know what he'll do! Take cover! Run for shelter! Hide the children!"

Most everyone in the crowd had seen the act or heard about it, so they stayed put, buzzing with anticipation. Otto gunned the engine, rolled down the field, and took off, immediately rolling so that one wing was just off the ground and perpendicular to the ground for a while. Then he rolled the other way onto the other wing. He straightened up, pulled an Immelman, and made a low pass over the field, porpoising the length of the runway. The crowd roared as if it was the funniest thing they'd ever seen. Otto climbed for altitude and once more turned the plane on its side. The door dropped open and Otto fell out of the cockpit, grabbing on to a strut to catch himself. He was secured by a strap since as he said he was not willing to jump out of a perfectly good airplane. Although the crowd knew he was in no danger, they still gasped. Otto awkwardly hauled himself back into the cockpit, leveled out, stalled, and started a spin toward the ground. He recovered just in time and buzzed the crowd, who clapped and cheered. He came around and acted as if he were going to land, but instead bounced the airplane down the runway. He wobbled around the sky for a while, did a couple more wingovers close to the ground. He pulled the Cub into a loop, did a series of rolls and a couple more stalls, and then came in and bounced to a stop. Jimmy ran out to the Cub and yanked "Rufus" out.

Otto fell on the ground and Jimmy pretended to pummel him. "Someone get help before Jimmy kills Rufus!" Bob exclaimed. Just then, Betty, dressed as a yokel, came running out. "Uh oh!" Bob called. "Here comes Sadie, also known as Mrs. Rufus. He's in a world of trouble now! Watch out!"

Betty was dressed in a flower-print dress, carried a huge purse, and wore a floppy straw hat. With great dignity, she marched up to Otto and Jimmy and began beating them both with her purse. She chased them back behind the stands and then marched to the still-running Cub, got in, shut the door, and took off. She buzzed the crowd and made a couple of low passes along the length of the field, waving a white handkerchief out the window the entire time. Then she disappeared over the horizon to join the other aircraft in the show for a flyby.

"Looks like Mrs. Rufus has taken off for Alabama," Bob announced. "Wonder if we'll ever see her again. And now, ladies and gentlemen, boys and girls, our final act—a grand parade of all the aircraft in our show. Annnnnd—here they come!"

A few seconds later, the Cub reappeared to great applause and cheers, leading the line of the aircraft in the show. They made several passes, waggling their wings, and then were rejoined by the Cub, trailing an American flag. The crowd rose to its feet, cheering and waving. Another successful show, thought Otto, watching from beside the grandstand. He went over to the gate and greeted people as they left, still dressed in his Rufus costume. Darn, the thing was hot, but it was nice to see everyone so relaxed and happy.

Betty came up, also still dressed in her rube costume. Jimmy joined them shortly after. "You might go easy on the purse next time," Jimmy told her.

"Actually, Mata suggested I put a brick in it."

"Uh huh," Otto said. "I'll deal with her later."

Mata walked up. "Good show, guys. We did well. I think part of the draw was people coming to see who Sparky Duncan was." They had initially changed the name of the show to "The Pioneer Lake Air Show and Exhibition" but decided to honor Otto's first flight instructor and called it "Sparky Duncan's Flying Circus and Exhibition." Jimmy dressed as an old-style aviator and made his appearance as the first act of the show by flying a Stearman in, doing a series of aerobatics, and then skimming the length of the runway before setting the big biplane down. He emerged trailing his long white silk scarf, waving to the crowd. He was introduced as "Sparky Duncan," World War I ace. Part of that title was true, Otto, thought, but no one knew any different. It was a great way to start the show.

The four agreed that the show had gone well and started walking toward the parking lot. Mata and Jimmy had seen that the ground crew at the airport was securing the aircraft used in the show, and they were hungry, dusty, and tired. Otto and Jimmy also had bruises from their comedy segment. When Otto showed one on his arm to Betty, she said, "That's what you'd call suffering for your art." Mata laughed as they climbed into their cars.

# Chapter 46
# What Is Past Is Prologue
# September 1954

Mondays were quiet at Olson Field after the air show on Saturday and the usual weekend activity. Late in the afternoon, Otto sat at the table in the meeting room looking over some publicity material Mata had designed for the show. The phone rang in the office, and he went in to answer it.

"Otto?" It was Betty, and her voice was oddly strained.

"Betty? What's wrong? Are you all right? Are the girls all right?"

"Yes, nothing like that. You need to come home." He heard the click of a hang-up.

Well, that was different, Otto thought, and uncharacteristic of Betty. He couldn't think of what might have happened, but he needed to get home fast and see what was going on.

"Polly," he said as he started for the door, "I need to go home. Something's up."

Polly looked up from her work. "I hope it's not too serious, Otto."

"I don't know what it is. I'll be back as soon as I can."

He raced the hundred yards to his house, flung open the door, and found Betty standing in the kitchen. She had an expression he couldn't read. He went over to her. She held him off with one arm. "You have a visitor. In the living room." she said flatly.

"Who is it?"

"See for yourself." She turned away.

Curiouser and curiouser, Otto thought, and he stepped into the living room.

Standing in silhouette against the window that looked out on the back yard was a slim figure of a woman. Otto couldn't see her face, but she spoke his name and he knew immediately who it was.

# Chapter 47
# Seems Like Old Times
# September 1954

"Alice," he murmured.

"Otto," she said, and stood there. "How are you?"

Otto couldn't speak for a few seconds. Then he found his voice. "Well, Alice, why would you want to know when you didn't care how I was after you saw my burns? Can you tell me that?"

"I had to come see you and find out how you were after you didn't answer my letter."

"I didn't want to answer your letter. I crumpled it up and threw it away, just like you threw us away, Alice. It's a little late to come asking 'How are you?'"

She began to cry. "I just wanted to see how you were."

"You keep saying that. How am I? *How am I?* That's a hell of a question to ask after the way you dropped me when I was really hurting. What would you like to know about? The pain? The series of operations? The feeling that my world had ended? You left me when I needed you most, Alice, and you have a lot of nerve showing up like this without warning."

"I had to see you."

"Why? Why now? Why here?"

"It just seemed like the right time . . . "

"There is no 'right time,' Alice. Our time is gone. It was over when you walked out on me."

"Forgive me, Otto; I was young and I didn't know what to do."

"I know what you can do. You can have to leave. Now."

Alice was silent for a few seconds, her eyes downcast. Then she looked directly at Otto. "I have our son with me."

Otto stopped. He felt as if he couldn't breathe. He gathered his wits and said, "Oh, even better."

"He looks like you. And I named him Otto."

My God, maybe this is a nightmare and I'll wake up soon. Please let me wake up. Please, Lord.

"Would you like to see him?"

"No. I would like for you to leave."

"We've come a long, long way. It wasn't easy."

"It wasn't easy dealing with what you did to me. Leave. Now."

Otto heard someone come up behind him.

"Otto, you're being very rude to our guest." Betty's voice was at his back. He swung around.

"You stay out of this. This has nothing to do with you."

"It has everything to do with me—with us. This is my house, and you will not be rude to a guest."

"She's not a guest, Betty. She's—she's—she's—an interloper!"

"She's part of your past, Otto, which means she's part of our past. And she will be treated with courtesy." Then to Alice, "You'll have to excuse Otto. Please have a seat. Would you like some tea? I know I don't make it in the proper British way, but I'll do the best I can."

A look of relief spread over Alice's face. "Yes, thank you. I would, and it has been such a long journey."

Otto was incredulous. "Betty! You are NOT—"

She turned to him. "I am not what, Otto?"

"You are *not* going to welcome this woman into our home."

"I'm doing just that, if you haven't noticed. And if you can't be civil, you can leave."

"I can *what?*"

"You heard me. Change your attitude or leave. Right now. And don't come back until you can act in a civil fashion."

Otto sputtered, unable to speak. He turned on his heel and slammed the door as he went out. He wasn't sure where he was going because he didn't have many places of refuge. There was home, and there was the airport. The airport it was, then. They kept the suite of rooms ready for transient pilots and if need be, he would stay there. Damn it all.

He went into the terminal building and made his way toward the back, behind the snack bar. He wasn't hungry, so he opened the door to the suite, which had a little living room, two bathrooms, and a small kitchenette. He sat down at the table and looked around. Now what? He could go back to the office and do some work, but he didn't feel like doing any work. He didn't feel like doing anything but disappearing for a while. Nah, that wouldn't work. What he really wanted was . . . was . . . to get drunk. That's it. He would get gloriously, totally drunk like so many of the crews between missions. He had imbibed a time or two in his lifetime, but he had never gotten drunk. Well, maybe today was the day. Time to start. Now all he needed was alcohol.

He knew they didn't keep anything like that in the overnight rooms, and he didn't want to go back to the house and get the car to drive into town to buy a bottle. Then something tugged at the corner of his memory. They had saved Wilson's old desk when they renovated the airport. In fact, he used it. He wondered . . .

He went back to the office and went to his desk. He had never bothered to explore all the recesses of the huge old rolltop, but he was sure there was a compartment big enough for the whiskey bottle Wilson and Sparky shared back in the old days. He also thought whiskey kept well, if there was any left. He was counting on there being some.

He opened one drawer after another and then got a flashlight and got down in the knee hole. There, at the side toward the back, was what looked like a panel that was a slightly different color. Some of the finish had been worn away at the top, apparently by fingers scraping along the joint for years. He pulled at it with his fingernails and a small door swung open. There, inside, was a half-full bottle of Jack Daniels, '39. He took it out and blessed the names of Herbert Wilson and Sparky Duncan. He went out into the conference room and put the bottle down in an air sickness bag. Then he walked back over to the transient pilot rooms.

He put the bottle on the table and went into the kitchenette to get one of the glasses they kept there. He poured the glass full of the rich amber liquid, hesitated, and said out loud, "Here's to nothing," and swallowed the whole glass. It burned like fire all the way down, but it made him feel strangely warm and light-headed almost immediately. He poured another, downed it, and then sat there for a moment. He didn't feel so good. And he felt very sleepy. Maybe he ought to go to . . .

He ran for the bathroom and upchucked violently. Whoopsie, he giggled. I barfed. He finished, took a washcloth from the cabinet below the sink, and washed his face. He threw the cloth down and staggered into one of the bedrooms, where he fell onto the bed and lost consciousness.

\*\*\*

Otto came to, but he wasn't lying on the bed in one of the pilots' rooms. He was standing inside a pure white room, one he recognized as the same one he found himself in after he lost consciousness in the B-17 crash. Maybe this is an alcohol dream, he thought. Kind of like the opium dreams Samuel Taylor Coleridge had. He went over to the door and stepped out into the garden he also remembered. There his father stood, as he had seen him before, standing in front of an unidentifiable bush at the other side of the small plot. He waited to hear his father's voice, but nothing came. Instead, his father looked at him with the deepest look of disappointment Otto had ever experienced. Then Hans slowly faded and Otto woke up in the bed he had fallen on.

\*\*\*

Morning was streaming through the window, and he had the worst headache of his life. So this is what a hangover is like, he thought, and sat up on the bed. Too quickly, he thought, as a wave of nausea engulfed him. He ran for the bathroom and made it just in time, sitting on the floor when he had finished. Slowly, he thought. Move slowly and avoid sudden loud noises. Just then someone cranked over an airplane on the other side of the wall, and he felt a stabbing pain shoot through his head. "Ow," he said aloud. "Ow ow ow ow ow!"

He sat there for a while until the throbbing subsided somewhat and then slowly stood up, washed his face and went and sat at the table in the kitchenette. He knew what he needed to do; he just needed to feel better to do it.

He sat there for about twenty minutes before pushing himself up from the table and starting for home. He was walking by the office when Polly came out. "There you are!" she exclaimed brightly. "I told Betty I thought you'd be here. She asked that you come home immediately."

"On m'way," Otto mumbled, holding one hand to his head. He could hear Polly chuckle once. Great. Now the whole town knows what's going on. He walked slowly to his house and gingerly opened the door.

No one was in the kitchen, but he could hear voices and laughter coming from the living room. He stepped through the door. Mata and Alice were seated together on the sofa, while Betty sat in the arm chair. They were all laughing but stopped when they saw him. Betty gave him an implacable look.

"Well, Otto, are you fit for polite company?"

He stood there for a long moment. "Yes. And I—I'm sorry the way I acted, Betty. . . and Alice. . . and even Mata, although you weren't here. I'm sure you've heard all about it. I was rude and inconsiderate and ask forgiveness from all of you."

"In that case, please have a seat. Alice has been telling us about their trip over here."

Alice nodded. "Yes. I had gotten as far as flying into New York. We took the train from there. Little Otto is so enthralled by trains, especially diesels. We mostly still have steam locos in England."

"Does he like airplanes?" Mata asked.

"Not as much as trains. He's frightened by large aircraft. It took some doing to get him on the BOAC flight over here."

"Maybe Otto could take him up in the Piper Cub. It seats two. Both Otto and Betty learned to fly on it."

"That would be delightful," Alice exclaimed.

Mata turned to Otto. "I'm sure you would like to take young Otto up." Her eyes told him what he had better say.

"Uh, yes, of course, I'd be delighted. I think I could do something this afternoon. I'm not feeling well just now and need to lie down for a while." Otto stared at the floor.

"Well, it's settled, then," Betty announced. "Airplane rides for everyone this afternoon."

"Well, if you'll excuse me . . . " Otto started to say.

"Don't you want to meet your son?" Alice wanted to know.

"Uh, well, yes, of course. Sure."

"The children are all in the girls' bedroom, playing. Actually, I think the twins are playing with dolls. Otto is more or less watching."

The four of them stood up and went down the short hall to the twins' room. Alice went in first. "Are you having fun?" she asked.

Otto heard a boy's voice reply, "Oh, yes, Mummy. I'm the father of the house and the girls are my nieces and we're going to have tea with their dollies."

"There's someone I want you to meet," Alice told him, stepping to one side so Otto could walk in. He saw a small, slim boy about nine years old with blonde hair. He caught his breath. Little Otto looked just like he did at that age.

"This is your Uncle Otto. He's married to Aunt Betty and is the brother of Aunt Mata."

So now we're aunts and uncles, Otto thought. Just one big happy family. He walked over to little Otto, who stood up, practically snapped to attention, and held out his hand. He looked at Otto with clear green eyes. God, this is like looking at myself.

Little Otto shook his hand. "Pleased to meet you, sir. My mother tells me you were a World War Two hero."

Otto didn't know what to say. "Well, young man, some people think so. I was just doing my job."

"Mummy says you're a pilot. I like trains better than I do airplanes, no offense to you, sir."

"None taken," Otto replied and thought, where did this kid learn to talk like this? He sounds like something out of *Wind in the Willows*.

By this time everyone was in the room, which made for a crowd, "Would you like to go flying in a little airplane this afternoon?" Mata asked.

Otto nodded his head. "Oh, yes, ma'am, I would. Will we all be going?"

"That's right," Betty answered. "We'll take turns going up. Uncle Otto can fly some, and I'll fly some. It's the same plane we both learned to fly on."

"That sounds jolly!" Otto exclaimed. "We'll be like Peter Pan, but with wings and without the pixie dust!"

Oh my God, I'm stuck in a British children's literature daydream, Otto thought. Or a nightmare. I can't tell which.

"Are we going too?" Marion asked.

"Most definitely," Mata reassured her. "I wouldn't leave my favorite nieces behind."

"We're your only nieces," Maria observed.

The adults in the room laughed heartily, all except Otto. Things were moving a little too fast with this little aviation day camp, he thought. But they'd have to see.

***

"Wizard!" Otto heard from the boy in the back seat as he brought the Cub over into a steep turn. He quickly turned it in the other direction. He'd have to be careful or he'd make the boy sick. This was the first ride on Sparky Duncan's Flying Circus and Exhibition, Junior Edition, and it was going well so far. Otto decided he liked the little fellow. He was polite, well spoken, and so very British. He also had characteristics of his mother which, Otto had to admit, made him easy to be around. Otto wasn't too sure how he would have handled being wrenched from his home at age nine and taken thousands of miles to meet some people who were supposed to be his long-lost relatives. He wouldn't be doing as well as Master Otto, he knew that.

He flew through some more gentle maneuvers and then called back, "Would you like to fly the aircraft?"

"May I? That would be keen!"

"All right, take the stick in your right hand and put your feet on the rudder pedals. You just need a light touch, so don't overdo it. When I say 'You have the aircraft,' it's yours. You're the pilot then. OK?"

"All rightie!"

Otto released the controls. "You have the aircraft!" he called.

The plane flew on straight and level. "You can move it around if you want."

"I'm rather afraid to," came the small voice.

"Don't worry, I've got it if you have a problem. I'll say, 'I have the aircraft' and that's your signal to release the controls. All right?"

"Yeeees . . ."

Otto felt the Cub move through a series of gentle turns. The boy had the touch for it. "That's it!" he said. "Now you're flying!"

They went on for about ten minutes and then Otto said, "Time to get back. I want you to hold the stick over all the way to the left and press on the left rudder pedal. The airplane will bank sharply to the left like I was doing a while ago, but that's normal. Let's have you make a big turn."

Master Otto hesitated and then made a beautifully coordinated turn to the left, coming around 180 degrees to put them on a path back to the airport. When they were lined up, Otto told him, "All right, center the controls and return the rudder pedals to neutral."

Little Otto did just that, and soon they were on final for the field. As they started down, Otto called, "I have the aircraft," and felt an immediate and almost imperceptible release of pressure on the controls. The boy had done well. They came in and taxied up to the hangar where the rest of the group was waiting. They climbed out to applause from the women and girls.

"Oh, Mummy, it was smashing!" Otto exclaimed. "I got to fly the airplane, and Uncle Otto said I did very well. I think I like airplanes better than trains now—at least the little ones!"

Alice hugged him and mouthed a "thank you" to Otto. He saluted her. "Who's next?" he said. "How about the ladies' turn? Betty? Mata? Girls?"

"I think I'll pass today," Mata allowed. "I'm feeling queasy." Betty shot her a look. Something's up, Otto thought.

"I'll take Alice and the girls up," Betty said. "We'll all fit."

"All right. Watch your landing speed. It's getting hotter and there's less lift."

Betty, Alice, and the girls crammed into the Cub and rolled to their takeoff point. Betty advanced the throttle and the small yellow plane accelerated down the runway and lifted into the clear blue sky. She steered toward the west, and soon the small aircraft was lost to sight.

Mata turned to Otto. "She's still in love with you, you know."

"I don't have a clue. It doesn't matter if she is."

"Maybe it doesn't, but I thought you should know."

"Did she say so?"

"Not in so many words, but a woman can tell."

"Humph. I'm feeling outnumbered here."

Mata laughed and they stood watching for the Piper to come back around. In a few minutes, it appeared, running the length of the field. "Alice is flying," Otto observed.

"How do you know?"

"The control movements are a little choppy. Betty is a very smooth flyer."

"Hmm."

The aircraft came around, made a few more passes, and then dropped in to land. It taxied up to them, and Betty chopped the throttle. The passengers and pilots climbed out.

"Daddy, Aunt Alice flew the airplane! Mommy said she did a good job!"

"I could tell from the ground," Otto returned. Alice gave him another grateful look.

"I was afraid I would ruin it," she said softly.

"It's hard to hurt one of these," Otto told her. "They're light and slow and don't have that much power."

"I can't imagine being at the controls of a big bomber."

"Yes, well, it's something else entirely. Shall we show you around our little airport?"

"I'd love that!"

"I'd like to see some more little airplanes!" shouted Otto.

Alice looked at him with surprise. "I don't think I've ever heard the boy shout. You've really made quite an impression on him."

"Well, good," Mata said. "A boy needs to do a little shouting now and then."

They went off to look through the offices and hangars, taking quite a while to examine all the light aircraft tied down along the flight line. When they finished, they stopped by the snack bar for some ice cream and sodas.

"We need to be getting back to pack," Alice told them. "We leave tomorrow morning, and we need to get ready."

"Can I do any laundry for you?" Betty asked.

"That would be wonderfully kind," Alice said.

"Let's go, then." Mata stood up. "I need to get back to Pete and Hans. I'll bring them both over after supper so you can meet them."

"That would be nice, Mata," Alice answered. "Thank you for all your kindness to us."

"It's been great meeting you after hearing so much about you." Mata stopped short when she saw the look in Betty's eyes. "I'll be back soon," she offered lamely.

"Good-bye, Aunt Mata," the children chorused.

They watched her walk to her car and drive off.

***

After dinner, Otto and Alice sat in the living room while Betty and Mata tended to the dishes. Pete stayed in the kitchen after Mata stopped him from going into the living room.

"So have you enjoyed your visit with us?" Otto wanted to know.

Alice laughed. "After the first bit, it was all very pleasant."

"I know. It was such a shock to see you. I just reacted."

"I suppose I don't know what I expected. I just wanted to see you and to know that you were all right. You're more than all right. That's very clear."

Otto sat silently for a moment. "What happened to you after I saw you last?"

"I've caught Mata and Betty up, so I'm sure they will fill you in, but basically after I saw you I didn't know what to do."

"Neither did I."

"My mother kept telling me I needed to go back, but, Otto, I was so young and so . . . I don't know . . . terrified . . ."

"Terrified? Of what?"

"I suppose that you would turn me away. That sounds odd, doesn't it, since I'm the one that put you off?"

"I suppose. I don't understand anything about it. I just had to put it—and you—behind me."

"I did very little. You were in the hospital, so I couldn't go there. I didn't want to go to work but my mum told me to get over myself and do it. I moped through the days. I cried a lot. You were the best thing that ever happened to me and I gave you up."

"And I suppose by the time you felt you could see me again I was gone?"

She shook her head. "I never reached that point. Only after Otto was born did I begin to come to terms with what had happened to you and what I had done. By that time I had married to give him a father and that was that."

"I see. And where is Otto's stepfather?"

"He had a terrible drinking problem. Had seen too much horror in the war. One day he was gone. I have no idea what happened to him. My mum and dad were terrific to help with Otto. I don't know what I would have done without them."

"How are your mom and dad?"

"They're about the same, getting older, but doing well. There's a certain sort of sadness about them. For that matter, there's a sadness about all of us."

"Wish them well for me, will you?"

"They are still so fond of you. They said you treated me right. With one exception." She smiled.

"Have you noticed how much Otto looks like me—looks like I did?"

"Yes, of course. It broke my heart every time I looked at him after a while. I wish I had been stronger."

"Well, as I say, water under the bridge."

She looked at him directly. "After all this time has passed, I can look at you and see that you are the same person you always were."

Exactly what Betty told me years ago, Otto thought. A knot formed in his stomach.

"Otto, I love you."

Otto sighed. "I'm sorry, Alice. It's a little late for that." He stood up. "So where is everyone else?"

Alice sat immobile on the couch for a few seconds and then quickly walked to the bathroom and closed the door.

Mata appeared at the door to the living room. "Anyone for dessert?"

"We can have some when Alice comes out of the bathroom. I'll fetch the kids."

As he walked to their bedroom, Otto thought, well, that's that. Little Otto was playing with a small metal airplane Otto had given him. The girls were reading. "Who wants dessert?" he asked.

Simultaneously they all cried, "Me! Me!" The twins ran out of the room. Young Otto stayed where he was and regarded Otto seriously.

"May I ask you something, Major Kerchner?"

What happened to Uncle Otto? he thought.

"Certainly. Ask away."

"Here it is. Please don't consider me rude or ill bred, but are you actually my uncle?"

Otto had to respond to such an honest question.

"No, I'm not."

"Are you my actual father, then?"

Otto couldn't think of what to say for a moment. Finally he said, "What makes you ask that?"

"I've been watching my mother lately. Obviously there is or was something between the two of you. She wouldn't make this trip unless there was a lot at stake . . . or something she wanted badly, and that was not to see how you were. She was hoping something would happen. Between the two of you."

Otto just stared.

"I know you think I'm just a little kid, but I notice things and I notice what people do and what they say—and what they don't say. The way you two are around each other says a lot to me. So does the way I resemble you."

Otto sat for a while in silence. Then he said slowly, "I think this is a question you'd best ask your mother, Otto. She should be the one to give you your answer."

Little Otto stood up. "I understand. Thank you, sir."

Otto stood as well. "Thank you, Master Otto."

# Chapter 48
# The Long Good-Bye
# September 1954

The next day, Otto and Mata drove back from the municipal airport, where they had dropped Alice and Otto for their flight to Minneapolis and then on to New York. Mata had arranged for passes for them to cut down their travel time. The silence as they had driven over was marked by the tension they all felt from the time Alice had come out of the bathroom the previous evening. Otto knew all the adults and young Otto had noticed it immediately. Something had changed. Alice was polite but distant. Probably embarrassed by what she had said, Otto thought. Ah well, he couldn't help that.

"So, what did Alice say to you last night?" Mata asked. "Or maybe more importantly, what did you say to her?"

Otto stared out the window. "I'd rather not talk about it, Mata, if you don't mind."

"Well, all right," she said, and they drove the rest of the way in silence. They pulled up to the airport office and went in. Polly was at work already.

"Mata, I have some papers for you to sign. Otto, there have been several calls from acts who want to perform with the circus. And Betty says she wants to talk to you."

I'll bet she does, Otto thought. He sighed. "All right. I'll be right back." He walked over to the house and found Betty sitting at the kitchen table with a cup of coffee.

"Would you like some coffee?" she asked him.

Otto sat at the table. "Yes, please." She poured a cup and then sat back down.

"It's been a remarkable few days."

"Yes, it has."

"I just have one question."

"All right."

"Did you invite Alice to come here?"

Otto sat for a moment. "That should have been obvious from my reaction to her being here. No. I did not."

"I just wanted to hear it from you."

"Any other questions?"

"No. Mata showed me the letter she wrote you."

"Mata kept the letter?"

"Yes. She said you crumpled it up and threw it away."

"Yes, I did. And that was the end of it."

Betty came over to him and wrapped him in a hug. "My dear, dear Otto. I love you so much."

"And I love you, Betty. With all my heart. There's something more you should know."

She stepped back. "And what is that?"

"Alice told me she loved me."

"I could see that. What did you say?"

"I told her it was a little late for that. And it is."

"Well played, Major OK. Well played." She kissed him and stood up. "Well, I have work to do and so do you. I'll see you at lunch."

"All right." Otto walked back to the office. Mata and Polly were conferring over some document. They looked at him quizzically. "What?" he said.

"Nothing," Mata said.

"Just so you know, 'God's in his heaven, and all's right with the world.'"

Mata and Polly smiled at each other and then bent to their work. Otto picked up the phone messages and went into his office. He had a business to run.

***

Otto pushed back from the table. What a delicious meal, he thought. "May we be excused to go play with Hans?" Marion asked.

"All right," Betty said, "but don't wake him if he's sleeping. He needs to finish his nap." The girls put their napkins at their places and went out of the room.

"So . . . " Mata began.

"So what?" Otto said.

"So I'm thinking that we need something special to finish up the air show this year."

"Like what?" Pete asked. "Have Otto jump out of the Cub while Betty is hidden inside and brings it down?"

Otto grimaced. "Pete, you know my rule about jumping out of perfectly good airplanes."

"Just checking."

"It's still in effect."

"Uh huh."

"I was thinking we need something different to finish off the season," Mata said.

"Like what? Fireworks?" Betty asked.

"I was thinking more like a baseball game."

"Who would play?"

"Otto, you're always talking about how bad the Wagoneers are…"

"Yes . . . "

"And they're not in the playoffs, right?"

"The Second Coming hasn't occurred either."

"So we can put together a team and play them. It would be a charity game to benefit the kids at Our Lady Orphanage." Mata had kept in touch with Sister Lucia and M & M collected toys and clothes for the orphanage every Christmas.

Otto sat back from the table. "We're not exactly knee-deep in baseball talent, and it's been years since I played."

"Coaches don't have to play," Mata informed him.

"So I'm coach now of this team. Have you named it?"

"I'm thinking of the Pioneer Lake Sparklers, you know after Sparky . . . "

"That would be more like the Pioneer Lake Inebriates," Pete observed.

"Quiet, Pete, or I'm making you umpire."

Otto chortled in spite of himself. "Excuse me," he said.

"It's all right," Pete answered. "I'm regularly the butt of blind jokes at home. Why, just yesterday, I picked up my hammer and saw."

"Hilarious," Betty said, but her expression said otherwise.

"Anyhow," Mata continued, "We can practice for a couple of weeks. I'll survey our people to see who's willing to play. It'll be coed."

"You could get up a team from the Little Sisters of Our Lady and still beat the Pioneer Lake nine," Otto told her.

"Actually, there's a new mechanic who pitched in Cuba. His name is Luis Vierra and he's quite good. He's too good for the Wagoneers, so there's a possibility he might catch on in the Braves' farm organization next year. He picked up his A&P certification when he was in Florida. He's a smart young fellow."

"Yeah, those Cubans are good players. So we got our pitcher. Any other ideas?"

"Well, you at short, Jimmy at second. I can play first."

"You can?"

"Did you not pay any attention at all to what I was doing when we were growing up?"

"No."

"I like an honest answer. Betty can catch."

"Betty can catch?"

"Yes, she played catcher on the girls' softball team. They called her 'Rifle Arm Ross' because of all the runners she threw out."

Otto turned to Betty. "'Rifle Arm Ross?' Any other nicknames I should know about, like Annie Oakley?"

Betty shrugged. "Can't think of any. I'll let you know if I do."

"Are we all agreed, then? I'll work up a roster and Otto, you and I can schedule practices. We'll shoot for the last Friday evening in September, right before our last show for the year. I think people will pay good money to see a group of ordinary people trample the local professional team."

"If you can call it a professional team," Otto remarked.

"Keep talking like that, Coach. I'll call the Wagoneers and set up the game. We can offer them part of the gate if they don't want to donate their time, but I'm sure I can shame them into it."

"Mata, you ought to run for president someday," Otto said, shaking his head.

"Don't think I haven't thought of it," she answered lightly.

I'm sure you have, Otto thought.

# Chapter 49
# Take Me Out to the Ball Game
# September 1954

It was the top of the sixth inning in the charity game on a temporary field set up on the air show field with snow fences for the outfield, and the Wagoneers were coming up to bat again, as if that would do them any good. Otto knew they were bad; he just didn't know how bad. Their basic skills were all right, but they lacked discipline and did dumb things in the field and on the bases. Otto's high school team was much better than they were. He looked over at the scoreboard. Yep, it was still 26–3 in favor of the Sparklers. His team was older but had some skill and good judgment, and that's what made the difference. That and a nearly Major League pitcher. Luis had a blazing fastball, a wicked curve, and some sort of Cuban special that dropped like a rock when it neared the vicinity of home plate. He basically struck out every batter, although about the fourth inning Otto told him to throw some soft ones so they could at least get a few hits. Even at that, they tried to stretch hits and were thrown out or overran each other on the bases. I couldn't script a more terrible team, he thought.

His team had acquitted itself well. Betty handled everything Luis threw at her with great skill, babbling encouragement to him all the way. Mata was a formidable first basewoman, stretching for throws and running down foul flies with alacrity. Otto didn't have much to do at short since most of the hit balls were weak pop-ups or anemic grounders that didn't go too far. His outfielders had complained that they were about to go to sleep at their posts. No one hit a ball to the outfield until the fifth inning. He found himself wishing there was a slaughter rule so the other team could be put out of its misery, but they hadn't counted on such a lopsided score so early. They just wanted everyone to enjoy a good time; they didn't intend to embarrass their hometown team.

The crowd was having a good time, at least, laughing and hooting at the Wagoneers, who gamely played on. The event had turned into a community occasion. They had even recruited the mayor as the umpire. He had called a good game, which wasn't hard behind the plate when the other team was pitching since most of the pitches were wild or hit by the Sparklers. Luis was so deadly accurate that he threw very few balls.

The last Wagoneer batter flailed weakly at another fastball, and it was the Sparklers' turn to bat. Time for a short team meeting, Otto decided. He went over to the mayor.

"You honor, we need a minute for a team meeting."

"Yeah, OK, but see if you can bring this to an end. I'm getting tired out here."

"I'll see what I can do," Otto told him. "Hey! Guys! Come here!" The players gathered around him. "We need to bring this thing to an end, so see what you can do to get out. We have more than enough runs, and there's no use creating bad feelings in a charity game." The players looked at him implacably. "And Luis—cut it back another notch."

Vierra nodded. "I will do so, Coach, but I don't think they can hit anything. If they were in Cuba, they would not be playing baseball; they would be cutting sugarcane in the hot sun." Some of the players giggled.

"Anyhow, let's ease up. We have to live in the same town as these young fellows."

Otto's team made a minimal effort from that point on but still scored ten more runs by the time the game ended. The other team threw the ball away or dropped it or just stood and looked at it as it went by. Otto wondered if they were on something that impaired their performance. Then he realized that at the end of a long losing season they had lost all hope. It wasn't that they were that bad (or maybe it was), but they had no spirit or life left in them. It was truly sad.

The game came to an end, the players shook hands, and the crowd gave them both a nice ovation. The First Annual Erik Olson Baseball Game was over. Mata had told Otto that the first time something was held it wasn't annual, because no one knew if it would happen again. The second game a year later would be the first annual one. Otto told her most people didn't know the difference and they would hear about it if they called it the first annual match the next year. "It's hard to be right about some things," Mata had insisted.

Betty was covered in dust from an evening behind the plate. Maria and Marion ran up to her from the stands where they had been sitting with Pete and Betty's parents. "Mommy, you played good!" enthused Marion. "We were cheering for you! And your team won!"

"Yes, we did," Betty allowed. "Now we need to go home and have some nice baths and something good to drink before bedtime. And I think there are some cookies I can find."

The girls jumped up and down. "Cookies!" they exclaimed. "Yay!"

"Let's go, Coach," Betty said to Otto.

"I'm ready," he answered. "I just hope the people on the other team are still speaking to us."

"I think you need to manage them," Betty offered.

"Hmmm," Otto said. "Not a bad idea. I'll have to think about that."

"Let's go home," she said.

"Yes, let's. Come on, girls!"

# Chapter 50
# You Belong to Me
# October 1954

The baseball game raised a respectable amount of money for Our Lady Orphanage. Otto, Mata, and Betty made a trip over to Minneapolis to deliver the check to the grateful sisters. Sister Lucia told them she had been praying for their success. "It worked well, sister. We won thirty-six to three."

She giggled. "Maybe I should have prayed for the other team."

"They could use it, Sister."

They flew back on the afternoon run, and Otto was pleased to see that Jimmy was the captain. He said that Northwest was treating him well, but he missed the family feel of M & M. He invited Otto to sit in the jump seat, but Otto declined, wanting to sit with Betty and Mata in the cabin. The aircraft still had the same livery that Mata had designed. The information card in the cabin read "M & M Airlines, operated by Northwest Airlines, Minneapolis, Minnesota." Otto felt a pang reading that.

Soon they were coming in for a landing at Pioneer Lake Airport, and then they made the short drive to Olson Field. Tomorrow was the last day of the season for the air show, and some of the acts were coming in already, so there was plenty to do. Mata had the idea to have a hangar dance in the evening to end the year's events. It would be similar to the one they had staged near the end of the war as a USO benefit, and once again, the proceeds would go to the USO. She had even managed to hire the same band that had played for that and for Otto and Betty's high school prom. Musicians tended to go on like that, she observed.

The three of them walked over to the hangar where the dance would be held. Workers were hanging a giant American flag from the back wall. "It looks great," Betty observed, and Mata and Otto agreed. She took Otto's hand. "This is going to be such fun, don't you think? We haven't danced for a long time."

"I hope I still remember how," Otto offered.

"I'm still available to teach you," Mata said.

"And I'm willing to practice," Betty added.

My cup runneth over, Otto thought, and he smiled.

# ON THE WINGS OF EAGLES

*** 

Couples filled almost every available inch of the hangar floor, jitterbugging to "Don't Sit under the Apple Tree with Anyone Else but Me." Mata, Pete, Otto, and Betty were sitting this one out at one of the tables that surrounded the dance floor. The turnout was excellent, and the consensus seemed to be that the air show had been a fitting end for the first year of weekly operation. It included a precision aerobatic team, parachutists, a mock dogfight, wing walking, and an appearance by Rufus the Flying Sharecropper. The four friends soaked in the ambience of people having a good time. Bob Harrison from Northwest had come, as had Bob Donovan. So had the Pioneer Lake crews and of course all the members of the flying circus team. Luis was there with a beautiful dark-haired woman he introduced as his cousin. Otto observed he was very close to his cousin. Ah well, those romantic Latins, he thought. He was wearing his air corps lieutenant's uniform, which had needed only a little letting out to fit.

The song came to an end, the couples applauded, and the female vocalist stepped up to the mic. "We're going to do something a little more modern now. Here's a relatively new song, 'You Belong to Me.'"

"I love that song," Betty exclaimed. "I've heard it on the radio!"

"In that case," Otto offered, "may I have this dance?" He stood and bowed to her.

"You certainly may, Lieutenant OK." He took her by the hand and led her to the dance floor.

Betty motioned to Mata to join them. "We'll sit this one out," Mata called. "You kids have a good time."

The music swelled and, after a short introduction, the vocalist sang,

> *See the pyramids along the Nile*
> *Watch the sunrise from a tropic isle*
> *Just remember darling all the while*
> *You belong to me*
>
> *See the market place in old Algiers*
> *Send me photographs and souvenirs*

> *Just remember when a dream appears*
> *You belong to me*
> *I'll be so alone without you*
> *Maybe you'd be lonesome too, and blue*

Otto held Betty close as they danced. "Wouldn't you like to visit those places?"

"That would be great. Maybe when the girls are older."

"No. I meant just you and me, mister."

"Your invitation is accepted, madame."

The vocalist continued,

> *Fly the ocean in a silver plane*
> *See the jungle when it's wet with rain*
> *Just remember till you're home again*
> *You belong to me*
>
> *I'll be so alone without you*
> *Maybe you'll be lonesome too, and blue*

Mata sat watching her brother and sister-in-law on the dance floor. So much had happened in the past few years, and yet it had turned out well. She smiled at them. They look like they're gliding, she thought, and then she corrected herself. No, Betty and Otto aren't gliding—they're flying.

> *Fly the ocean in a silver plane*
> *See the jungle when it's wet with rain*
> *Just remember till you're home again*
> *You belong to me*

# The End